"I find you very interesting, Dr. Katz."

Danica looked at Matteo and didn't look away when their eyes locked.

"I feel the same." Matteo's smile started at his lips and ended in his deep brown gold-flecked eyes. "I'd like to call you. You know, check on you."

She nodded and fished a business card out of her pants pocket. When she handed it to the handsome doctor, she asked with good humor, "Now, was this your subtle way of asking for my number?"

"Absolutely," he said. "Do you mind?"

"Not at all," she said. "I was just about to ask for yours."

He put her number into his contacts. A second later Danica's phone chimed and she slid it out of her pants pocket and saw that she had a new text message. She read the message and felt giddy, like a schoolgirl with her first crush.

Would you like to share our long stories over drinks and dinner this Friday? Six o'clock?

Still smiling, Danica typed her response.

Yes.

Dear Reader,

Thank you for choosing *Big Sky Bachelor*.

Danica "Danny" Brand is a fiercely independent real estate broker who has built an empire buying and selling houses for the very rich and very famous clients in the hot LA scene. As her fortieth birthday came and went, Danica was ready to marry Grant, her business partner and fiancé, so they could shift focus from building their empire to building their family. And then when she finds out that Grant had impregnated their office manager, Fallon, Danica retreats to Big Sky, Montana, her hometown, to recover and regroup. She isn't looking for love, but lightning strikes, and she finds herself deeply in love with the most eligible bachelor in Big Sky.

Dr. Matteo Katz is a family physician who is tired of being alone. After a difficult breakup, Matteo began to date the many lovely ladies in the Big Sky area. He found that all the women possessed their own individual wonderfulness, but none of them had felt like home. Then one day Matteo bumps into Danica Brand, a strikingly beautiful woman with intense blue eyes and a laugh that makes him smile. Matteo knows in his heart that Danica is the wife he's been waiting for. But can he convince big-city Danica to leave her fast-paced life in LA to become the wife of a small-town doctor?

You can connect with me via my website: joannasimsromance.love.

Happy reading!

JoAnna

BIG SKY BACHELOR

JoAnna Sims

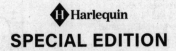

SPECIAL EDITION

Harlequin®
SPECIAL EDITION™

Recycling programs
for this product may
not exist in your area.

ISBN-13: 978-1-335-40216-5

Big Sky Bachelor

Copyright © 2025 by JoAnna Sims

For questions and comments about the quality of this book, please contact us at CustomerService@Harlequin.com.

TM and ® are trademarks of Harlequin Enterprises ULC.

 Harlequin Enterprises ULC
22 Adelaide St. West, 41st Floor
Toronto, Ontario M5H 4E3, Canada
www.Harlequin.com

Printed in Lithuania

MIX
Paper | Supporting
responsible forestry
FSC® C021394

JoAnna Sims is proud to pen contemporary romance for Harlequin Special Edition. JoAnna's series, The Brands of Montana, features hardworking characters with hometown values. You are cordially invited to join the Brands of Montana as they wrangle their own happily-ever-afters.

Visit the Author Profile page
at Harlequin.com for more titles.

Dedicated to Angela T.

Thank you for your kindness and support
as I hung up my therapist hat.

You are a truly talented, intelligent, strong woman
who shares my love for education and writing.

You are a blessing and I hope our paths never *un*cross.

JoAnna

Prologue

"Yes, of course, Prince Aziz," Danica Brand said. "Full price cash offers only. You have an exquisite property, it's still very much a seller's market, and I am certain that we will get a buyer in record-breaking time for a record-breaking price."

Danica, Los Angeles Realtor to the überwealthy and celebrities, was on the phone with one of her regular clients, a Saudi prince, when she heard the distracting sound of a woman weeping loudly. Danica tried to focus on the call but after a few minutes of the grating sound, she told Prince Aziz that she would call him back, hung up the phone and then walked purposefully toward the wailing.

Danica walked quickly past her fiancé and business partner's office but then stopped in her tracks. She spun on the heels of her four-inch stilettos, pushed the slightly ajar door open and saw Grant holding their distraught receptionist, Fallon, in his arms.

She stood in the doorway, while her brain jumped from annoyed to confused and then quickly landed on shock. "What's going on in here, Grant? I had to hang up with Prince Aziz."

Fallon, a Farrah Fawcett look-alike aspiring actress and model, had her head buried in Grant's chest.

The receptionist looked up at her with swollen, doe-like eyes and then her face crumpled as she got up, raced past her to the bathroom and then slammed that door behind her.

Danica stared at her fiancé of nearly twenty years while her stomach began to twist. She stepped into his office and closed the door behind her. Grant Fowler was a fastidious man; he was trim and fit, and his clothing was always neat as a pin, and there wasn't a strand of dyed brown hair out of place. So the large wet area on his shirt left by Fallon's tears drew her attention while her mind quickly sifted through the possibilities and finally landed on the most plausible.

"Please don't tell me that you've turned us into a cliché, Grant," Danica said in a cool, even tone. Her heart was racing but her poker face, something she was known for in her industry, remained in place.

Grant didn't respond right away but it didn't matter. She already knew, first in her gut and now in her mind.

With a sigh that almost sounded like he didn't want to be bothered with this conversation, Grant leaned back against his imported, heavily carved desk, ran his fingers through his hair and then gave a little shrug. "She's pregnant."

Danica felt her knees to begin to buckle and tears wanting to form. She locked her legs and *refused* to let those tears manifest. Wordlessly, she stared at this man whom she had built a life and a business with, but now she realized that she didn't know him at all. Grant squirmed, broke eye contact and then retreated to his ten-thousand-dollar executive chair and sat down. He leaned back casually, and that made Danica narrow her eyes. There was a very real part of Grant that appeared to be enjoying this.

"She's twenty, Grant."

"Twenty-one." Grant frowned at her while brushing something off his desk.

Grant was an undeniably handsome man; he had the even features and bone structure of a male model, still looked good without his shirt on at the beach, and with a little help from modern plastic surgery and a strict diet, those looks hadn't faded yet.

"What now?" he asked her.

"I'm sorry," Danica asked, "are you asking me?"

He tapped his finger on the desk while the sounds of Fallon gulping, coughing and then starting the crying all over again penetrated the door.

"Just hear me out," Grant said. "Fallon loves you…"

"Oh, please, Grant, do spare me," Danica snapped back. "Sleeping with my fiancé isn't exactly a love letter."

"Well," he seemed to concede, "she thinks the world of you. Respects you…"

"Quit trying to flatter me, Grant."

"She is going to have to give up a lot to keep this baby." He restarted, "She's very worried about her figure."

"Poor thing."

"That was sarcasm and I understand why."

"Thank you so much."

"You have always been a woman who thinks outside of the box." Grant made another thinly veiled attempt at flattery as he held up his arms and gestured around the room. "We've built an empire together."

And you and I both know that I own the majority stake.

"I love you, Danica," her soon-to-be ex said with a look in his eyes that had typically worked to earn her forgiveness when he needed to apologize for something. "I adore you."

Danica closed her eyes, took in a deep breath to keep her anger to a simmer before she picked up the nearest golf trophy and flung it at him. She had grown up in Montana and shooting guns, hunting, was just a part of the life; she was an excellent shot.

When she opened her eyes again, it did her some good to see that his smile had faltered; beads of sweat had formed a shiny mustache just above his now-quivering upper lip. He was nervous, as well he should be.

Grant leaned forward. "We've never found the right time to have a child."

She had frozen her eggs five years ago, but Grant had always pushed the timeline back. He always had reasons to *not* get married, to *not* have a child. Now that she was forty, she may have wasted years waiting for Grant and she only had herself to blame. There had been rumors and suspicions, but never any evidence. Now, a barely adult aspiring actress carrying Grant's child was undeniable proof. Two decades of her life, washed away like beach sand at high tide.

"If I recall, you had some doubts about carrying a child."

That's when the mask slipped. She took a step forward, and in a quiet, furious tone, Danica said, "Don't you dare, Grant. Don't. You. Dare."

Grant held up his hands in surrender. "Okay. Okay."

"How could you, Grant?" she asked him with a waver in her voice.

At the first sign of weakness, her ex stood up, rounded

his enormous desk, and then crossed to her and tried to take her into his arms.

Danica stepped back, held up her hand for him to stop. "You will never touch me again."

Now Grant looked as if he was going to cry. But she wasn't naive enough to believe that it was sorrow for his mistake or some deep abiding love he had for her. No, Grant was worried about the business, the money and the possessions they had accumulated, like his prize yacht that he had named *Got It Made*.

"I don't want to lose you, sweetheart," he said with a pleading tone. He reached out his arms and then put them back down. "Can't we come to some agreement?"

There was a very real part of her that, as if watching it unfold for someone else, wanted to hear Grant's proposal for a path forward.

"Which would be?"

He dipped his head down, looked at her with his hazel eyes. "You want a baby. Fallon wants a career…"

Danica could not move or think for a split second while she processed what she thought was Grant's *everyone wins* plan.

"You want me to adopt her baby?"

"Oh, no. *No*. She wants the baby."

"Okay. Let me take another stab at this then. Fallon wants a career, your baby and *you*. What do I get again?"

"Well—" more lip twitching "—we will have a home together…"

His name wasn't on the deed.

"We still have our love," he said, "and our business."

"Are you suggesting," she said with a small, disbelieving noise, "because I can't believe you would. But are you suggesting that I *share* you with Fallon?"

Grant took a handkerchief out of his pocket and dabbed his forehead. "Is it such a crazy idea?"

Now, that made her laugh, out loud, held tilted back, grateful for this moment of levity in what was turning out to be a no good, rotten day.

"Yes, Grant," she said, "it *is* a crazy idea."

She turned on her heel and Grant followed her, reached out to touch her arm as she swung open the door to his office. She put her Pilates to use, spun around and glared up at him, "If you don't back off, Grant, I am going to jam my heel so hard into your instep that you'll be limping for a week. Not to mention the damage it would cause to your precious loafers."

Grant backed away, his cajoling mask slipping. "Now there's that ice queen mean streak."

She stopped in the doorway, looked at him. The man standing before her now seemed to have shrunken from his six foot four height and his features were noticeably pinched.

"I get it, Grant, you need to demonize me to make you feel better. I guess that bump of self-esteem after getting Fallon into bed wasn't lasting."

Danica headed to her office and began to pack up quickly, putting her laptop in her designer case, putting files away in a locked drawer, shrugging on her cashmere coat, and then shutting off the light and locking her door behind her, taking the only key with her. Grant was standing in the doorway to his office watching her as she stopped by the bathroom to rap on the door.

"Fallon?"

"Yes?"

"Open the door, please."

Fallon shuffled toward the door, sniffling loudly. When she opened the door, her lovely face was blotchy and red, and it did touch Danica in an unexpected way.

"I'm so sorry, Ms. Brand."

"I know you are," Danica said in a kind tone that surprised her. "Unfortunately, most of us women have some version of this kind of mistake in our love lives. This one is yours."

Fallon blew her nose again loudly.

"Now, listen up, Fallon, because what I am going to say now is important." Danica felt Grant wanting to step in between them but he held back, watching her intently. "Grant has a very a huge golf memorabilia collection. It takes up two of my very large bedrooms, so I hope you have a good-sized home, because he will be taking those with him,"

"It's a studio, actually."

"Well," Danica said, "I suppose love will find a way.

"The Bentley is a lease," Danica continued. "Do you have reliable transportation?"

Now Fallon's eyes were wide as teacup saucers. "Well, actually, no."

Danica continued, "Now, Grant also has a very swollen prostate, it happens with men his age I'm afraid, and there have been many nights that I haven't gotten a wink of sleep because he's up and down and up and down all night. So my best advice is let him sleep on the bed closest to the bathroom so you can get your rest. After all, you are with child."

Fallon started to cry again while Grant appeared to be frozen in his spot.

Danica looked at Grant, threw her scarf over her shoulder with what she hoped was a dramatic flair, and then set off down the hall, chin up, head held high. Then she stopped, chuckled at herself with a small shake of the head, backed up a step, and then said with a sharp, decisive boss-lady tone, "And, Fallon, one last thing."

"Yes, Ms. Brand?"

"You're fired."

Chapter One

Big Sky, Montana
One month later

Danica Brand had arrived in her home state of Montana still stunned by Grant's betrayal. Instead of staying at their family's ranch, Hideaway, she had taken a rental in town, grateful that her Realtor connections allowed her to find a gem of a condo in the height of winter sports season in Big Sky. When she first arrived in Big Sky, she had given herself permission to grieve for one whole week; she drank wine, deleted pictures of Grant from her phone, changed her status on her social media and spent extra time in bed while she hugged a pillow and cried. After the week was up, Danica refocused her attention on her business and communicating with her attorney and financial advisers about how to untangle her life from Grant's.

One month post-breakup, Danica had established a routine that included taking power walks, which was her favorite form of exercising to reduce stress and to clear her mind. Big Sky Community Park fit that bill; they maintained their trails during snowy Montana winters. Now, weather permitting, she started her day with a brisk walk, exploring different trails for a change of scenery.

"How are you?" Leena, her junior Realtor, asked, concerned.

Earbud in her ear, her phone tucked into a pocket on her snugly fitting workout pants, Danica pumped her arms to propel forward with each long stride. "Right as rain."

"Fake it until you make it?"

"That's what I've told you. And that's what I'm doing. Don't *ever* let anyone see you sweat." Danica slowed down, feeling lightheaded. She still hadn't adjusted to the altitude and when she pushed herself, and she was *always* pushing herself, she felt dizzy and out of breath. This bout was different. This time, she had to stop, bend over, hands braced on her knees, eyes closed as she waited to catch her breath and let the dizziness subside.

Just as she was standing upright and while listening to Leena's litany of concerns about hosting an open house on her own for the first time, she heard a man's voice call out "Lu Lu" followed by a neon pink Frisbee flying over her head, and while her mind was occupied by that Frisbee for a nanosecond, a rotund pig, wearing a very chic pink-and-white polka-dot sweater with a matching toboggan covering her ears, dashed out in front of her, surprised her, bumped into her hard enough to get her off-balance, leaving her flailing her arms in an unsuccessful attempt to stop herself from falling. She twisted her body to take the brunt of the fall on her right side and her right hand, and she felt her ankle twist as she landed on the frozen rocky ground.

"Leena!" Danica interrupted her protégée's lengthy list

of worries about the open house. "I've got to go. We'll talk later."

"Are you all right?"

"For the love of peanuts, Leena! Please stop asking me that!" Danica exclaimed, assessing the damage. "I'm fine! I just got blindsided by a pig in polka dots!"

The last thing she heard Leena say before she hung up was, "And I thought LA was weird." As she rolled off her right hip, that quip made her laugh while she rubbed her ankle.

"Are you all right?" A tall man rounded the corner taking long strides.

"Yes," she said, laughing. "I'm okay."

The morning sun made a golden halo around the man's body, the features of his face in shadow. When he blocked out the sun with his broad shoulders, his handsome features came into view, and she discovered that she was looking at one of the most beautiful men she had ever seen. Strong nose, strong chin, square jaw, deep-set brown eyes framed by dark eyebrows. He had the bone structure of a Hollywood leading man and a hot bod to boot!

The man knelt beside her and smelled of saddle soap and pine needles. *Hello, handsome.* "How badly are you hurt?" he asked.

It took Danica a split second to respond because she had been quite distracted by his kissable lips. "Not too bad. A scrape, a bruise, twisted ankle. I'm not a doctor, but…"

"I am," he said matter-of-factly. "A doctor. If you'd let me, I'd like to take a look at your injuries."

Her mind immediately started a checklist on the man.

Handsome, check. Smells divine, check. Handsome doctor, check check.

"What happened?"

"A pig happened. Knocked right into me. I fell back, landed on my hip and my hand, with what I'm sure was catlike grace, and then I proceeded to twist my ankle."

"I am very sorry."

"It's not your fault."

"I'm afraid it is."

She studied him for a second as two plus two equaled four in her mind. "Oh. That was *your* pig in pink polka dots."

"I'm afraid so."

The man, still nameless, so in her mind, mysterious, helped her over to a nearby bench. When she was seated, she said, "Thank you. I don't even know your name."

"Matteo Katz," he said, before he whistled loudly, scanning the brush on either side of the rocky trail.

"Nice to meet you." She sent him a flirtatious smile that came out of nowhere, but she didn't regret it. After fifteen years, she was unexpectedly single, and she needed to dust off her "how to flirt" playbook and get some practice in. No time like the present. "Danica Brand."

"Hideaway Ranch?"

"Yes." She nodded. "Have you been?"

"No," he said, "but I've heard good things. And I've crossed paths with your sisters a time or two."

He helped her to a nearby bench and after she was seated, Matteo whistled the same whistle again and then soon after, Lu Lu the pig came out of the nearby brush carrying her pink Frisbee. She dropped the Frisbee at Matteo's feet, sat down with what Danica rated as a genuinely pleased smile and oinked loudly.

"Good girl, Lu Lu." He leaned down to give his pig a scratch beneath her ample chin.

Danica felt quite charmed by the man and his pig. She turned her body toward Lu Lu, leaned forward, and said in sweet voice, "Hello, Lu Lu. You are a very pretty pig. I'd go as far as to say that you are a fashionista. Your Frisbee matches your ensemble to perfection!"

"She picks the Frisbee that matches her outfit."

"Are you kidding me? I know plenty of people who can't do that," she said, her smile broadened as she looked up at Matteo.

"No, not kidding. She's very smart. She can be a real diva, I can tell you that right now. When she gets bored, and I try very hard to not *let* her get bored, she is two whole handfuls."

Danica leaned down and let the pig smell her hand with that large, round, wet nose. To Lu Lu she said, "It's okay to be a diva. I come from the land of divas. And I'll tell you a secret." She lowered her voice to a more private level. "Some people might even consider *me* to be a diva."

Lu Lu made some chuffing sounds in the back of her throat with her adorable curly tail wagging and hopped in a circle, which made Danica laugh more loudly and freely than she had in years.

"How does that ankle feel?" Matteo asked her, interrupting her good time with Lu Lu.

With a shake of her head and a self-effacing smile, Danica sat up and said, "I forgot all about it."

Now that it was back on her radar, her hip felt like she

would have a large bruise in a bit, and her hand was scraped at the wrist and had taken the brunt of the fall.

Matteo knelt and motioned for her to put her foot on his thigh, but she hesitated. "Now, before I let you examine me, what kind of doctor are you, exactly? I mean, you aren't a gynecologist or a large animal vet?"

He laughed with a broad perfectly white smile. "General practice. Humans only."

"So, ankle qualified."

"Yes," he said, then nodded toward her injured foot. "May I?"

"Not so fast, mister," she said, sliding her phone out of her pocket. "Full name, please."

"Dr. Matteo Katz-Cortez."

Danica searched his name and then said, "Hmm. Four-point-eight stars, two hundred and eighteen reviews. Nearly all women."

"To be fair—" he caught her gaze and held it "—I am a big fish in a tiny pond."

"A pond stocked with only female fish."

And, because he was still smiling at her, she found herself smiling back at him again. Three honest smiles in a thirty-minute window! Her one week of grieving Grant had been the exact right amount of time.

"So," he prompted when she just stared at him without any words forthcoming, "may I take a look at that ankle?"

"Yes, you may," she replied in her most controlled, professional, not *at all* thinking about your sexy lips, voice.

Given the go-ahead, he gently slipped off her tennis shoe, putting the shoe down by Lu Lu, who had been grunting, oinking and talking to them nonstop, and then he carefully lifted her foot to rest it on his rock-solid thigh. While he was examining her, she was most definitely examining him. And she was really enjoying this moment until he palpated her ankle and asked, "Does that hurt?"

"Yes." She frowned. "It does."

"How about this?" he asked.

"Still, yes!"

He sighed, pulled her sock back up and very much like the prince seeing if the glass slipper fit Cinderella, Dr. Katz placed her tennis shoe back onto her foot.

"Well, you've got some swelling."

"I do?"

He nodded. "You'll have a bruise most likely. You'll need to wrap it, ice it and elevate it."

"You really did me in, didn't you?" she asked, teasingly. She had just met him, but she felt comfortable with him. It was easy.

Matteo's lips turned up in a small smile, letting her know that he had taken her good-natured ribbing in stride. Still kneeling, he reached for her hand. "Minor abrasion. Clean it with alcohol and apply an antibiotic ointment."

"Okay."

He sat back on his heel. "You said you also landed on your hip? Are you experiencing any pain?"

She raised an eyebrow at him. "Now, Dr. Matteo, you will not be examining my gluteus maximus on a public trail. Just suffice it to say that it smarts."

He stood up with a smile and then said, "Stand up and let's see if you can put weight on it."

"Oh, please!" she said. "I'm sure I can put weight on it. I'm sure I could finish my hike on it. I've worn five-inch stilettos up a long drive in the West Hollywood Hills with a bad sprain before with not so much as a limp!"

"Humor me."

She shrugged and then she stood up and when she put weight on it, she said, "Ow!"

At the same time she was standing up, Lu Lu was foraging in the brush next to the trail and every time she leaned down and tried to get whatever delicious thing she had found into her mouth, her back legs lifted into the air, she would shift her weight back to get her hind legs on the ground, and that cycle repeated.

So Danica was cringing from the pain in her ankle while laughing at the antics of the rotund, stubby-legged pig.

"I'd like to help you back to your vehicle," the handsome doctor offered.

"Thank you," she said. It was an unusual feeling, this dependence on another person. She had built her business, and had thrived, in a man's world by being fiercely independent. That was why Grant lived in *her* house and had been made a partner in *her* company at a sixty-forty split with her holding the largest share.

"It's the least I could do," he said, bending down to put the leash on Lu Lu's harness.

And then she did something she rarely did; she hooked her arm with his and leaned on him, just a little bit.

Danica had to smile at the little pig jauntily walking next to Matteo, talking in her language the entire time.

"She certainly doesn't lack conversational skills," she noted.

That made Matteo laugh. "You are correct. She does not.

Not at all. Some of it's super-cute, but when she's mad? She goes from cute to bloodcurdling real quick."

She could feel his biceps flexing beneath her hand and it made her imagine what the gorgeous doctor might look like during the summer, in a clothing-optional situation.

"How long will you be in town?"

Still creating a rather racy image of Matteo in a shirt unbuttoned down to the waistband of snug-fit Wrangler jeans, her companion repeated the question and that time she heard it and responded.

"Maybe a month or two more."

"Business or pleasure?"

"Both," she said with a small sigh. "It's a long story."

"I like long stories."

She winced a bit; her right butt cheek hurt, her hand hurt, and her stupid ankle hurt, too! The best thing she knew to do was focus on her companions and push the rest aside.

"So, may I ask how you acquired your delightful pig?"

"That's a long story."

She glanced up at him. "I like long stories, too.

"Here's a question for you…does your wife, girlfriend, boyfriend or generally anyone who thinks they are currently in a relationship with you design Lu Lu's clothing?"

"Was that your not-so-subtle way of asking me if I'm in a relationship?"

"Yes," she said, "and just an FYI—that's as subtle as I get."

"I like direct."

"So do I," she said. "So many things in common."

"Seems like," he said with a rather sheepish smile, a

small spark of unexpected shyness. "I'm not spoken for. You?"

She shook her head. "Newly *un*engaged."

Even as slowly as they had walked, they reached the parking lot much too quickly. She pointed out her rented Cadillac luxury SUV. She opened the door, wishing that the walk wasn't over.

"Well, Lu Lu—" Danica bent down "—I hope we meet again."

She started to scratch the pig beneath her chin and the pig closed her eyes and extended out her neck.

"If you scratch her chin, she will be your friend for life."

"Is that true, Lu Lu? Will you be my friend for life?"

"But when you stop…"

"Uh-huh?" she asked, while still scratching.

"She will get mad," he said, with a warning undertone in his voice, "and then you'll be very sorry that you ever started in the first place."

"Oh, nonsense," she said, standing up, "She's an…"

Danica never got the word *angel* out of her mouth because the horrid, ear-stabbing, mind-blowingly shrill shriek that Lu Lu was making made her plug her ears.

Matteo distracted Lu Lu by tossing her Frisbee a few feet, still out of the range of any vehicles that may pass by.

"Now do you see why I'm still single?" he asked.

"Yes." She nodded, and then said to Lu Lu she when the pig brought the Frisbee back, "Good girl, Lu Lu. Scare all of them away."

Matteo helped her into the driver's seat. Danica climbed behind the wheel with a promise to Matteo that she could drive with her sprain.

He shut the door behind her while she cranked the engine; then she rolled down the window. "It was a pleasure to meet you, Dr. Katz."

"Thank you," he said. "I'm sorry for the circumstance. If you decide you want to sue me, I know a reputable lawyer."

She looked at him and didn't look away when their eyes locked. "I find you very interesting, Dr. Katz."

"I feel the same." His smile started at his lips and ended in his deep brown gold-flecked eyes. "I'd like to call you, check on you."

She nodded and fished a business card out of her pants pocket; she always kept a couple handy. She handed it to the handsome doctor and asked with good humor, "Now, was this your subtle way of asking for my number?"

"Absolutely," he said. "Do you mind?"

"Not at all," she said. "I was just about to ask for yours."

He threw the Frisbee for Lu Lu again while he put her number into his contacts. Danica's phone chimed and she slid it out of her pants pocket and saw that she had a new text message. She read the message and felt giddy like a schoolgirl with her first crush.

Would you like to share our long stories over drinks and dinner this Friday? Six o'clock?

Still smiling, Danica typed her response.

Yes.

Now Matteo was smiling again as he caught her gaze and held it. "Text me your address and I'll pick you up at six."

"I'll be ready."

* * *

"Wait, wait, wait!" her sister Charlotte exclaimed. "Are you telling us that you are going out on date with the most wanted bachelor within a one-hundred-mile radius?"

"And on a Friday? That's nearly a declaration of love!" Rayna's face was alight with happiness for her.

Danica was sitting in the living room of her family home with her ankle wrapped and elevated. When their mother, Rose, died, she, along with her sisters, had turned their family ranch into a corporate retreat. Even though she wasn't staying at the ranch, she spent much of her day at Hideaway Ranch with her sisters. Being with them always gave her a much-needed boost.

"I didn't know he was the most wanted bachelor." Danica took a small sip of the hot chamomile tea her identical twin sister, Ray, had prepared for her. "But I can certainly see why. He is the most beautiful man I've ever seen. And that's saying something—I live in the capital of beautiful men."

Charlotte, also known to friends and family as Charlie, leaned back against the butcher block island and said, "Now, Wayne is *the* most handsome man to me, but Dr. Katz? A very close, infinitesimal really, second."

Charlie, a cowgirl to her core, had been determined to keep Hideaway Ranch in the family by transforming it from a cattle ranch into a destination spot. Wayne Westbrook was a silver fox, jack-of-all-trades cowboy who had helped Charlotte reach that goal. Wayne was a perfect match for Charlie, on the ranch and in her heart, and they were the first romance to blossom at the ranch.

"Same." Rayna "Ray" was rocking in an old family rocking chair dated back three generations, under a quilt their mother had made just before her passing. "For me, Dean Legend is the most handsome man in any room. Tall, burly…"

Ray, a recently divorced empty nester, had moved back to Big Sky with a plan to figure out her next move. When she rekindled a love affair with Dean Legend, her first love and boyfriend all through high school, everyone knew what her next move would be.

"But if I *didn't* have Dean," Ray said with a sheepish smile, "I might've joined the hunt."

"He's smart, handsome, an animal lover," Danica said. "He's like a unicorn. Something *must* be wrong with him. Men like that aren't just roaming around like free-range chickens."

Charlie topped off her tea. "No one's without flaw obviously, but Dr. Katz is about as close as a human male can be to perfection. I've only heard good things."

Ray held up her own glass and said, "On these auspicious occasions, I propose a toast to our dear sister Danny, who managed to land the biggest fish in our Big Sky pond."

"And she doesn't even like to fish!" Charlie added with a smile.

Their conversation soon shifted from the hunky Dr. Katz to the changes to their website that highlighted the fact that "love blooms" at Hideaway Ranch. There was a number counter on the website now, one marriage, two engagements, one baby, and a long-distance romance that had inspired a cross-country move.

"I think it's perfect," Ray said. "I know when we started this venture we thought our bread and butter would be from corporate retreats."

"I did think that when I hatched the idea but looking at our bookings, these aren't corporate clients," Charlie agreed.

"No. They aren't. I believe our next guest is an author?" Danica asked Ray to confirm.

Ray nodded, "A *romance* writer, actually. We had a cancellation and Journey Lamar was the first name on our waiting list. I *love* that name."

"She might have seen our social media 'Love is always in season at Hideaway Ranch' advertisement campaign." The more Danica talked about it, the more excited she became about the ranch; she had handled the budget and the renovations of the main house remotely from LA. In person, where she could feel firsthand the energy of the place, now she understood that the intangible *something* happening on this land had to be *felt* to be understood. "I see us as a destination for weddings, anniversaries, honeymoons. The opportunities in the romance category are limitless! I can see people who are looking for love booking with us in hopes that some of our Hideaway Ranch love magic will align the stars for them. But we have to dig into the data regularly, analyze trend lines and shift our focus quickly, if need be, to reflect market demands," Danica explained to her sisters.

"I have no idea what you just said," Charlie laughed, "but I sure as heck agree with every single darn word."

"Me too," Ray joined in, "every darn word."

"Journey has us booked for two weeks. The beginning of the second week, her ten-year-old son, Oakley, will be joining with her."

Right as they were finishing up with a review of the website, their social media footprint and preparations for their guests, Wayne swung the front door open and slammed it shut in his haste.

"Is he here?" Charlie asked her fiancé.

"Heading down the drive as we speak," Wayne said before he tipped his hat to Ray and her. "Ladies."

Wayne noticed her ankle and asked, "What happened there?"

"I'll fill you in later." Charlie grabbed her cowgirl hat hastily before she looked at them. "We're done here, right?"

"Sure," Danica agreed. She was feeling unusually sleepy and could see herself curling up in one of the beds and taking a nap. Napping, generally, was not something she did.

"Who's coming?" Ray asked.

"Cody Ty Hawkins!" Charlie followed Wayne the short distance to the front door.

"I'm drawing a blank," Ray said.

"Me, too," Danica said. "Who is Cody Ty Hawkins?"

Before Charlie went outside, she turned and looked at them with a disappointed expression on her face when she asked, "Seriously? Who is *Cody Ty*?" She then shook her head. "How are we even related?"

Chapter Two

"What do you think?" Matteo held up two button-down shirts for Lu Lu. "Black or purple?"

"Would you like the other person in the room to share an opinion?" his sister, Estrella, chimed in. "I think both of those colors are a bad idea."

He had a close relationship with his younger sister by two years and even though she lived in Baltimore, they video-chatted at least one time a day. Lu Lu approached the options and made her choice.

"Lu Lu voted for purple," he told Estrella.

"But of course she did."

Lu Lu headed over to her oversize bed with her name embroidered on it and promptly went to sleep.

"I guess that decision really tuckered poor Lu Lu out." Matteo turned the phone so his sister could see his swine companion.

"She may have sleep apnea," Estrella noted. "That's quite a snore."

Now with his outfit for tonight's date picked out, it was time to go to the kitchen for a quick protein shake and then off to work. Estrella kept him company while he gathered ingredients.

"Why are you so nervous?" his sister asked him. "You have nothing *but* gorgeous, googly-eyed women dropping at your feet on the daily! All of these women fanatical over my dorky brother."

"First of all, I'm not a dork."

"Uh, yes you are."

"And, second, this is different." He began to cut up his fresh fruit. "*Danica* is different."

"How? She's blonde with a stunning face. She looks like a fitness model, she's obviously accomplished, age-appropriate, which is more than I can say for some of your past dates. So I guess *that's* a plus."

"She's witty, intelligent. I love her laugh. There was a spark between us and I know she felt it, too," he told her, and then added, "I knew you'd look her up."

"Of course you did. And of course *I* did," Estrella said. "I actually like her for you, in theory. But her life seems to be very well-established in California, Matteo. Are you willing to break your ban on long-distance relationships?"

"*Hermanita*, let me get through the first date and I'll get back to you on that." Matteo finished cutting the fruit, put it into the blender and then added unsweetened oat milk to the mix.

"Okay, okay," his sister said, laughing, "at least you got the pig thing out of the way."

"Danica loved Lu Lu and the feeling was mutual."

"Maybe she is the one for you," Estrella said. "She met you while playing Frisbee with your pet pig? And she didn't sprint back to the Hollywood Hills?"

Estrella shrugged. "Maybe your crazy jibes with her crazy."

"Thank you, I think?"

"Call me after!"

"I will."

"No matter how late."

"I *will*."

"Okay." His sister blew him a kiss that he used his hand to catch and put on his cheek. "I've gotta go. *Te amo*."

After his sister signed off Matteo turned on the blender, which awakened Lu Lu, and soon her annoyed squeal overtook the sound of the machine. He shut it off, drank the shake right from the blender jar, rinsed it out and then stopped by Lu Lu to say he was sorry, and then he headed to the main bedroom. As he was getting ready for work, Matteo couldn't stop thinking about Danica. In fact, ever since they had met, she was a frequent visitor to his thoughts. It was the chemistry between them that had caught him completely off guard. It was undeniable, electric, that intangible connection that could not be planned, only experienced. And he had that with Danica, and he believed, to his core, that she had felt it, too.

He couldn't deny that he was apprehensive about his sudden-onset feelings for Danica. Ever since his last relationship ended, he had become a serial casual dater who preferred to spend his time with women who were in town for winter sports. They would have a wonderful time and then he would see them off at the end of their vacation, and the relationship would just naturally fade away. This lifestyle had suited him; was he lonely at times? Sure. But he loved his career, he loved his life in Big Sky, he had good friends and plenty of outdoor activities that kept his life full, and, of course, he had Lu Lu. His life was rolling along, and he didn't see any real reason to change it. Then Danica happened. He had a gut feeling, an intangible instinct, that no matter how much time he had with Danica, it would *never* be enough.

"What do you think?" Danica twirled for her sister Ray.

"Oh, Danny," Ray said, "it's simply gorgeous on you."

Catrin, Dean's ex-wife and mother of his two daughters, was a clothing designer whose business, Poem, had a global reach. The dress she was wearing for her first date in nearly fifteen years had been a gift from Catrin to Ray.

Danica looked at her reflection in the mirror; the figure-flattering sheath dress had a scoop neck and an hourglass fit. The sleeves were quarter-length; the skirt of the dress hit below the knees, giving the dress both a sexy and classic look. The entire dress was decorated with a hand-painted scene of the skyline of Paris. Each dress was a one-of-a-kind and Dean's ex-wife had been kind enough to give a work-of-art dress to Ray.

"She's a genius," Danica said.

"Yes, she is."

Danica met her sister's gaze in the mirror. "Are you sure you want me to wear this, Ray?"

There was no hesitation when Ray said, "Yes."

She sat down on the velvet bench at the makeup station in the large, ornate bathroom while Ray fixed her hair. The two of them fell into a familiar pattern even though their lives had taken them in wildly different directions.

When she was done, Ray had slicked back her icy-blond hair into a classic chignon and then her sister began to work on her makeup.

"I was blessed with two awesome boys, so I'm a little rusty in the makeup department," Ray said. Ray worked quickly and when she was done, Danica studied her reflection; the makeup was subtle and clean, and brought out her cheekbones and her eyes to perfection.

"You're a genius, too, Ray."

Ray shook her head. "No."

Danica stood up and hugged her twin sister, feeling nostalgic about all of the years they had lived their lives apart from each other.

"Thank you."

"Of course, Danny. Your happiness is my happiness."

They had picked out a strappy pair of heels that were a perfect match for the dress and then found a small clutch that she could use to carry her wallet, phone and a tube of matte lipstick.

Danica was walking around the bedroom and could only detect the tiniest twinge of pain from her nearly healed sprained ankle. She circled back to Ray for one final opportunity to edit the outfit when her sister received a call from Dean.

"Oh no," Ray said. "I'm leaving now."

Ray's face had just drained all of its color and she stood stock still, seemingly stunned by the phone call.

Forgetting about her outfit, Danica put her hand on her sister's arm and asked, "What's wrong?"

"It's Buck," Ray said in a monotone. "They're transferring him from the hospital to the ranch. He wants to die in his own house."

Buck Legend was a dear friend of the family, a neighbor, and Danica's soon-to-be father-in-law.

Danica knew that words could not help, so she simply put her arms around her sister and hugged her tightly.

Buck had always been as strong as a Cottonwood tree as long as she could remember. It was difficult to accept that the strongest of men would eventually slip away from them. Buck had been ill with lung cancer for several years and he hadn't been doing anything to prevent it from killing him, bit by bit, day by day. He had become a shell of a man after his beloved wife, Nettie, had died, and he wanted to be free of his body so he could be with Nettie in heaven.

"I have to go," Ray said, wiping the tears from her face.

"Of course," she said. "What can I do?"

"Pray for him," her sister said. "Pray for him."

"I don't have to go on this date, Ray. Actually, it feels really callous to go have a good time in light of…what's happening."

Ray gathered her things. "No! Please don't cancel. You need this, Danny, and there isn't one thing that you can do right now other than go have a much-deserved good time. It's what I want." Ray hugged her one last time, and said of Dean's daughters, Paisley and Luna, "Thank goodness the girls are in Europe visiting their mother."

"If you need me, call me," Danica told Ray. "Promise."

"I will."

Danica closed the door behind her sister, turned around and then leaned back against the door. She had spent the morning fighting with Grant via their attorneys about the business and the home they had shared. Now her sister was in crisis. It didn't feel *right* to be going out on a date. She sighed, picked up her phone off the coffee table and was just about to call Matteo to cancel their date when the phone rang.

"Hi, Matteo," she answered the phone.

"Hi, Danica," Dr. Gorgeous said in his silky baritone voice that should be banned as a secret weapon. It made her heart race accompanied by goose bumps on her arms, a shiver up her spine and a tingle in places on her body that hadn't had a *tingle* in quite a long while.

"I'm just calling to confirm our date."

She had full intention to cancel on him, but now that she was talking to him, she waffled and wavered.

"Danica? Are you still there?"

"Yes. I'm still here. Sorry. My sister just had some difficult news."

There was a brief silence from the other end of the line, and then Matteo asked, "Do we need to reschedule?"

"Yes," she said, and then, "I don't know. I mean, no, we don't. But I might have to cut things short if Ray needs me."

"I understand," he said. "So, I'll pick you up in an hour?"

"Yes. One hour. I'll look forward to seeing you then."

"Likewise."

Matteo sat in his metallic gray Audi R8 sports car. He didn't often bring it out during the winter, but Danica was a luxury kind of woman and he wanted to show her that, even though he was a small-town doctor, he could do luxury just the same as any LA man.

Matteo pulled into a parking spot, turned off the engine and sat in the silence for several minutes. He was nervous. Really nervous. And he couldn't remember feeling this way *ever* in his life. Women naturally gravitated toward him, so he never had to put too much energy or effort into woo-ing a woman. And yet, even with her straightforward self-confidence and her willingness to ask for *his* number, he felt out of his depth. He wanted to impress her; he wanted to win her heart. He had just figured out *that* fun fact on his way over to pick her up.

Matteo took one last look in the rearview mirror before he stepped out of his Audi. He wore a long cashmere over-coat, black slacks, polished shoes and the purple shirt that Lu Lu had picked out.

"Why would you let a pig pick out your shirt?" Matteo asked himself under his breath as he walked to the front door.

Too late to change now.

After he rang the bell, Danica opened the door rather quickly wearing a slim-fit dress that hugged her modest curves in the best way. His eyes quickly followed the pat-tern of the dress before he said, "You are stunning."

"Thank you."

That compliment drew a small, pleased smile from Dan-ica, whose full lips were perfectly colored a deep shade of matte rose red. And those lips looked incredibly kissable. His reaction to her, and the swiftness of his *body's* reaction to her, confirmed to him that Danica Brand was somebody special to him.

Danica slipped into a long black coat, stepped outside and locked the door behind her. Matteo offered her his arm and she took it. He puffed out his chest and felt like a very lucky man to have a woman like Danica by his side.

"I'm glad to see you," he said.

She looked at him, her lovely face, with its pert nose,

high cheekbones and wide cornflower-blue eyes, turned upward. "Isn't that funny? I'm happy to see you, too."

"Well, good," Matteo said as he opened the passenger door for her. "I'm glad that I'm not the only one in this boat."

Once she was settled, he walked swiftly around to the driver's door. When he joined her, she said, "Audi R8. Very nice."

He cranked the engine, pleased that she appreciated his second "baby," only surpassed by Lu Lu. "I rarely take it out during winter, but I wanted your carriage to be worthy of you."

Danica had been rather subdued since he had arrived; she laughed her lovely, tinkling laugh and said, "I think you have a rather inflated opinion of me. I'm just a woman from LA."

"Who has built a multimillion-dollar business…"

"Yes." She gave a small smile. "There is that."

She glanced over to him. "Someone's been doing some research online."

He didn't try to deny it. "You can learn a lot."

"Yes, you can."

"What did you learn about me?"

"Who said I did any searching?"

Their eyes met and she confessed, "I did a little snooping. And so did Ray. And so did Charlie."

"The Brand sisters stick together. I wouldn't have expected anything less," he said, driving them toward one of his favorite places to eat. It did strike him that he never took other women he had dated to this spot. He'd eaten there with friends or alone. "Did you find anything useful to assess my character?"

"Well," she said slowly, keeping him in suspense, "seeing that all of us have a digital footprint dating back to our birth…"

"Oh, no."

"Oh, yes," she said with a sassy flair, "I was quite surprised and pleased to see that you were second runner-up in your elementary school talent show…"

"I will *never* live that down," he groaned. "My sister, Estrella, brings that up whenever she thinks I'm getting too big for my britches."

"Why do you have to live that down?" Danica said in teasing tone. "Ventriloquism is a very impressive talent. A little girl won *America's Got Talent* a couple of years ago. What was her name?"

"Darci Lynne," he said automatically. When he felt Danica looking at him, he glanced her way with a half smile. "I like to keep up with my other ventriloquist peeps.

"I was a big fan of Edgar Bergen. And my mom bought me a replica of his doll, Charlie McCarthy," he admitted. "Most people don't even know who he is."

"Do you mean the very popular entertainer from the 1920s who asked a wood-carver to make him a doll whom he later named Charlie McCarthy? They starred in fourteen motion pictures together, toured with the USO overseas during World War II, and had a career that spanned fifty years."

After a quick second, he said, "You looked it up."

"I looked it up."

They laughed together and he was happy that he chose the Audi; they were together in semi-tight quarters, and he could smell the fresh lilac scent of her skin. He pulled into a parking spot outside of the Block 3 Kitchen and Bar and shut off the engine before he came to his date's side of the vehicle.

"This looks nice," Danica said, popping the collar of her coat up.

"It's my favorite." He offered his arm again. "Shall we?"

"Yes." His date had a pleased expression on her face. "Let's."

It did not escape her notice that when they walked in the door, nearly every head in the restaurant turned.

"You know how to make an entrance," she said.

Her date leaned his head down toward hers and whispered, "Ten percent me, ninety percent you."

The hostess, who couldn't seem to stop blushing when she was talking to Matteo, showed them to their table and then glanced back several times to look at him before returning to her lectern. But she couldn't fault the women and the men who were struck by Matteo's handsomeness. He was simply too handsome to *not* look at him.

Matteo removed his long gentleman's coat, took hers and draped them carefully over the empty chair at their table.

"I love that purple shirt on you," Danica said. "You get high marks for that."

"This is all Lu Lu," he said.

"Lord, do I love that pig." She laughed. "She's got great taste in fashion and in men."

He sat down at their table and the expression on his face, and the way he looked at her with a spark of energy in his deep brown eyes, she could easily read his appreciation of her. It was there for anyone to see. "Thank you. Most women can't see what I see in Lu Lu."

"She's a good companion."

"Yes," he agreed, "she is that. Now, may I recommend the barrel-aged Manhattan?"

"Are you trying to get me tipsy, sir?"

"Maybe just a little bit." He winked at her. "And I'm driving, so…"

"Why not?"

"Exactly. Why not?"

They feasted on cheese fondue, grilled asparagus with oven-roasted tomato pesto, and chilled seafood platter. Matteo also ordered roasted chicken and sipped on water while she had a second barrel-aged Manhattan as they transitioned from the dining room to some comfy seating in front of a toasty fire.

"Did you enjoy your food?" he asked.

"Oh! It was positively delicious. Thank you so much." Danica felt her stomach pooching out a bit in the body-hugging dress but felt that the hand-painted scene provided some camouflage. "I hate to say this, but I wasn't expecting much. When I was growing up, Big Sky wasn't exactly known for its cuisine."

A waitress came by, and he ordered them both hot coffees before he said, "We do have some hidden gems.

"So." Matteo focused his attention on her, something he had done all evening. And his actions certainly made her feel special in that his eyes never once followed the several beautiful women who had walked by, looking at his face, perhaps hoping to steal his attention away. "Should we just get our long stories out of the way? That way, we won't have to deal with it on our second date. I would like to see you again."

She couldn't stop herself from smiling at him; he seemed to know exactly what she needed to hear, and his actions matched his words. "I would like that."

"Now that I've locked you down for a second date, would you like to go first? Or shall I?"

"You should go first. I've been dying to know the backstory of how Lu Lu came into your life. I have a feeling it has something to do with a woman. An ex-wife perhaps?"

"Not an ex-wife, but as close as I've ever been."

Danica finished her cocktail, feeling loose and languid and warm all over. She took her coffee in both hands and listened.

"I was engaged," he told her, "to a single mother."

"Oh. There was a child."

"There was." He nodded, and she saw the fleeting sadness in his eyes and the first frown she had seen on this man's handsome face.

Instinctively, she put her coffee mug down, turned her body to face him and put her hand on his arm. "You don't have to tell me that story. I'll go."

He put his hand over hers with a slight shake of his head. "I want to tell you."

"Okay. I'm listening."

"I met Lindsey at the hospital where I had my residency. She was a nurse on the graveyard shift, and we took our breaks together. I don't think either one of us thought that we would end up together. She was just coming off a divorce and I was a very sleep-deprived doctor. But one thing led to another, and we fell in love, or at least we thought we did."

He continued, "When I met Emerson, her daughter, I was a goner. Those big blue eyes, that sweet little face. She was just a joy. A light in my rather dark world."

"She must have loved you."

Matteo swallowed several times, and she felt the emotion rising up in his throat, but he stopped it from expressing as tears. She could feel his pain nonetheless.

He cleared his throat and then he continued, "I had a buddy who said that this region of Montana was desperate for doctors. After my residency, I came out here and fell in love with it. I asked Lindsey to marry me. I often wonder if we both were doing it for Emerson and not for us."

"So they moved here."

"Yes. They did." He nodded. "And my sweet Emy wanted a pig."

Danica let out a sigh she hadn't known she was holding. "Lu Lu."

Again, he nodded, pain naked in his eyes that he hadn't tried to hide from her. "Neither of us was planning the wedding, neither one of us had even talked about setting a date. And then one day, it was just over. Lindsey moved back to Baltimore, and I tried my best to stay in touch with Emy. But Lindsey got married…"

"Oh."

"And her husband officially adopted Emy."

Danica's heart sank for him, and she reached out for his hand. "I'm so sorry, Matteo."

"Me too," he said, and then tried to smile. "I'm sorry I've turned our first date into a bummer."

"I'm not. And it isn't," she said quickly to reassure him. "A bummer, I mean. It helps me understand you better—Lu Lu symbolizes your relationship with Emy."

"Yes. Thank you," he said, still holding on to her hand, "for understanding."

Danica was about to take her turn with her own long story, but a phone call from Ray stopped her.

"Danny! Call Charlie, tell her to come quick. Bring Wayne, and you come, too! Please come quick!"

"I'm leaving now!" Danica said in a rush before speed-dialing Charlie. "I'm sorry, Matteo. I have to go."

He helped her into her coat and paid the tab and they left the restaurant together. When she was in his car, it occurred to her that she had two strong drinks.

"I can't drive!" Danica said loudly. "I can't drive!"

"I'll take you," Matteo said without hesitation. "I'll take you."

Chapter Three

Danica did not speak during their ride to the Legend ranch and Matteo didn't expect her to. Their connection was strong in a way that was inexplicable and yet very real and very tangible; when he reached over and put his hand on her arm occasionally to offer some comfort in this troubling time, she accepted that comfort, and even covered his hand with hers to signal to him that she appreciated it. The roads were slick with ice, and he had pondered switching out vehicles, but time was of the essence, and he didn't want to risk Danica arriving late and missing her chance to pay her respects to Buck Legend.

"It's been years," Danica said as he pulled off the freeway onto the winding lane leading up to the grand brick house with columns on the front porch and four chimney stacks.

"So much has changed," she said in a soft, melancholy voice.

Matteo parked his car while Danica quickly texted her sisters that she had arrived. Then Matteo met her at the passenger-side door, opening it and holding out his hand for her to take. Danica was wearing very sexy shoes, but they weren't designed for ice and snow.

"Thank you, Matteo," Danica said, taking his hand.

"I'm glad to be of service."

Danica hooked her arm with his and he ensured that she reached the front door safely. The front steps leading up the grand porch designed in an antebellum style had been recently salted; even so, he didn't let go of her until she was standing firmly on the welcome mat. Before Danica had a chance to ring the doorbell, the front door opened and Charlie was standing in the doorway, her eyes red from crying. Wordlessly, Charlie hugged Danica, and his date, who hadn't shed any tears on the ride over, began to cry.

"Tonight?" Danica asked.

Charlie nodded. "We think so."

Dean appeared behind Charlie and said, "Dr. Katz, please come in. Dad would want you here. You were the only doctor he respected, and he never forgot the way you took care of Mom in her last days."

Matteo entered the house, shook hands with Dean, and knowing that the look Danica was giving him had a question mark in it, he said, "I was Buck and Nettie's primary care for many years. It wasn't my place to divulge that."

He helped Danica out of her coat and hung it on a nearby coatrack. And together, they followed Charlie and Dean to the large library with floor-to-ceiling windows looking over hundreds of prime cattle pastures. Nettie had collected books, rare and beautiful, from nearly every genre from fiction to history and everything in between. When Buck became ill enough to need a hospital bed and round-the-clock nurses, Dean's dad insisted that he be moved from the first-floor primary bedroom to the library, Nettie's favorite room in the house. Matteo was there for that move but then he had to turn Buck's case over to an oncologist.

Ray saw her twin and she waved her over to where she was seated, holding on to Buck's hand. Buck appeared to be unconscious. Ray let go of Buck's hand, stood up and hugged Danica tightly. "He's leaving."

"I know he is," Danica said. "He's going home to Nettie."

Ray nodded, new tears following old, and said to Matteo, "Thank you for bringing her."

"My pleasure."

Matteo said his last goodbye to Buck, a man he had met soon after moving to Big Sky and had grown to respect—the man who had prioritized his wife and children and had built a legacy that could be sustained for generations.

He shook Dean's hand and excused himself. He was grateful to say farewell to Buck, but he wasn't family and didn't want to intrude. Danica saw him preparing to leave, left Ray for a moment to see him to the door. After he put on his coat, he took Danica's hands into his.

"I had a wonderful time," Danica said. "Thank you—for being so kind."

"You're welcome," he replied. "Thank you for letting me."

"I remember Buck the way he was when I was in high school," Danica said with a far-off look in her eyes. "When I see him…like that, I wonder why I stayed away so long."

"He is a great man. I have always admired him," he said with an emotional catch in his voice. Seeing Buck in his last moments on Earth had struck a chord; even incredibly strong, bigger-than-life men faced their own mortality at some point. And when he saw Buck listless in that hospital bed, and when he looked around at Danica's sisters and their men, it made him begin to reflect on his own life. What was he waiting for? Buck, he was sure, would remind him, as he had in every doctor's appointment, that nothing ventured, nothing gained.

"I want to see you again, Danica," he said, quite taken with her lovely face, and the depth and honesty he saw in her wide, blue eyes encouraged him to ask but then he said, "But I know family is first."

And, because Danica was a no-nonsense, no-drama, straightforward woman, she didn't play coy. "I want to see you too, but—"

"Your family needs you," he filled in the blanks.

"Yes—" Danica nodded "—they do."

Matteo took her into his arms, held her tightly, and then took her slight hand in his and kissed it. "I'm here, Danica. If you need me, please call."

"I will."

After one last hug, Matteo said goodbye to his date and on the way back to his car, he felt a bit stunned. He hadn't ever fallen in love at first sight before, so he hadn't ever really believed that it was an actual thing. But meeting Danica Brand, blond bombshell, had made him rethink his long-held belief. Perhaps there was such a thing as love at first sight.

Danica sat by Buck Legend's bedside, supporting her sisters and Dean in the wee hours of the morning. Their cat, Magic, a robust black-and-white cat with striking green eyes, had jumped up onto the bed, placed his paw over Buck's heart and purred nonstop for hours. Though Buck was not much of a cat person, Magic and his persistence had turned him into a cat lover, and it seemed fitting that Magic be a part of his final hours.

Wayne had joined them but had to leave at dawn to see to the animals and, just after Wayne's departure and as the sun began to rise, flooding the library with the beautiful morning light, Buck's eyes fluttered open, and they all stood up, surprised, and called out his name. But the look in his eyes was otherworldly, staring through them, not at them, and they read his lips as he whispered, *Nettie*, and then took one more breath; that one breath was his last. He slipped away on a long exhale, leaving behind a hole in their lives that could not be filled by another.

Danica sat down in her chair, stunned at the unexpected loss of a man who was an integral part of her most formative years. He had always treated the Brand triplets as his extended family, and she felt honored to be a part of his last moments. Charlie came to her side, and they held on to each other while Ray and Dean consoled each other. Danica leaned down to kiss Buck on the forehead. And the emotional and physical toll of sitting at his bedside caught up at once. She slumped down into a nearby overstuffed chairs that she had sat in many times before in her teenage years.

"Yes, Catrin," Dean said to his ex-wife, "he passed. I'd like to tell the girls myself." Dean paused then said, "Thank you, Catrin. Give me a couple of hours and I'll call back."

"They will be crushed," Ray said, refusing to leave Buck's side.

Dean was a burly lumberjack of a man, but in this moment, after he had held it together when he talked to his ex-wife, bent down to hug his father, his tears soaked his father's pillow.

"He loved you so much," Dean said to Ray. "I'm so glad he got to see us together."

Ray nodded. "Me, too."

"Our union inspired him to hang on just a little bit longer."

"He's with Nettie now," Ray said. "May he rest in peace."

Danica dozed off curled up in the chair; she awakened just in time for the funeral home to arrive and take Buck's body away to prepare for the burial. He would be laid to rest by his beloved Nettie. And then the machines were turned off and his morning nurse arrived to discover that the job was done. She gave her condolences to Dean and Ray before she began to wrap up cords and move machines to the side, out of the way. It was strange; these mundane tasks had to be done even as a giant of a man had left the world. Life did keep going.

"Let's head back home." Charlie helped her up.

They checked on Ray, who was keeping herself busy with the regular chores that kept a large ranch going.

"Will you be okay?"

Ray nodded. "Eventually."

The three sisters put their arms around one another's shoulders, heads touching in the middle; it was something they had done for as long as they could remember and even longer according to their dearly departed mother, Rose.

"Whatever you need. Whatever Dean needs, we are here," Danica emphasized.

"Thank you. I'll be over later," Ray said. "We have to make some final preparations for our guest. She arrives in one week."

"You let us handle that, Ray. You focus on Dean and his girls."

Ray, who appeared dazed and robotic, did seem relieved that she could step back from Hideaway Ranch while they handled the details. After another triplet hug, Danica and Charlie got into a truck and drove the short distance to their ranch. The Legends and Brands had shared more than just a property line; they had shared the good times, bad times, happy and sad times. Their families were irrevocably intertwined.

With a promise to touch base later, Charlie dropped her off at the main house while she headed to the restored 1900s cabin that had been built by their ancestors. That was the home she now shared with Wayne. Exhausted, Danica stripped out of her clothes, drew a very hot bath, and then, after she dried off, climbed in a bed that she had chosen and purchased from LA.

"This is very comfy," Danica said, as she snuggled down into the feathery mattress and the silky bamboo sheets. "Not too shabby, Danny. Not too shabby."

Journey Lamar turned onto the gravel road that would lead her to Hideaway Ranch. She was a Michigan gal, so ice and snow didn't scare her. But horses *did* and she was pushing through this lifelong phobia in order to do important research for her next book. She had always dreamed of writing romance novels and that dream had come true and her first book, *How to Wrangle a Cowboy*, had been published the previous year. It was wonderful and great and terrifying and deeply disappointing. Reader reviews had ripped apart her book, complaining about the characters, the dialogue, the realism. After the twentieth one-star re-view, written by a blogger with the handle Romance4Life, *and* who wanted to give her minus one star for the most annoying heroine in the history of her blog, Journey had turned her social media private and made a solemn vow not to look at *any* reviews so she could focus on her next book.

She refused to be a one-book writer, and this meant she needed to head west to Montana. She'd always loved a sexy cowboy, but Michigan wasn't part of the romantic West and other than some saloons and Little Leagues, her only way to research was online. She was the type of writer who needed the scents, the language, the grit of cowboy life in order to authentically tell a story the way she wanted to tell it.

"Hello?" She answered the call as she crept along the driveway wanting to absorb this first introduction to Hide-away Ranch.

"How do, little lady," Riggs, her best friend from ele-mentary school to the present, greeted her in a manner not typical.

"Well, giddy-up, cowboy!"

They laughed together and then Riggs said, "Give me all the deets! Have you seen any sweaty shirtless cowboys yet?"

"It's January. In Montana. No one is topless."

"Ugh," Riggs said with a dramatic flair. "I hope the rest of your trip isn't a total snooze-fest. Why couldn't you set your book in someplace tropical?"

"Cowboys sell books," she told him.

"How am I supposed to argue with you when you're al-ways right?"

"Bye, Riggs."

"Bye, gorg."

Riggs was perpetually single because he always wanted to mingle; he had inherited an obscene amount of money from his grandfather so didn't have to work. It seemed like an impossible friendship with her being a single mother to a ten-year-old boy and helping her mother take care of both grandparents. Somehow, it just worked, and they just were friends. And even though many people thought he was juvenile and careless, Riggs was the only person other than her mother who was always there; no matter what time of day or where he was in the world, Riggs was there. It was rare to find a friend like that.

After she hung up with her best friend as she drove through a gate with a rustic wood-and-metal archway embossed with *Hideaway Ranch* that led to the main house where she would be staying, Journey had to turn off the engine and just absorb the scenery. The log cabin was lovely and raw and made her feel as if she had just driven into a past that had long since gone away.

"This is absolutely perfect." Journey opened the car door, swung her long legs around and then stepped into a slushy puddle. The midafternoon sun felt warm on her cheeks just as it had warmed the brisk air and melted the snow from the night before. She walked behind the rental and saw a man working with a horse in a circular area that was called a round pen, a place to exercise horses. The cowboy in the center of the pen was wearing a well-loved brown cowboy hat and black jeans that were faded almost to a light gray, and he looked exactly like the type of man she had been hoping to study.

She snapped a picture discreetly and then posted on her

social media, "*The Horse Whisperer*, circa 1998, Robert Redford," and then added several heart-eyes emojis. She was spinning around in a circle, trying to, all at once, process and file away every amazing detail in her mind.

"Journey?" asked a pretty woman wearing a mustard-colored coat with a sheepskin collar, jeans and tall brown boots, with a pair of the brightest blue eyes she had ever seen in her life.

"That's me!" She waved with a smile.

"Welcome to Hideaway Ranch! I'm Charlie. We spoke on the phone."

"Yes. Hello!"

Charlie waved her up to the porch. "Just leave your bags. I'll have my fiancé grab them in bit."

"Are you sure?" Journey asked. "I'm actually stronger than I look."

Charlie waved again, and Journey thought, *Well, why not?* She climbed the steps up to the wide front porch with the rocking chairs covered in layers of melting snow.

"Nice to meet you." Charlie had a strong handshake. "We're happy to have you."

"I'm happy to be had!" Journey said with a bright smile, and she couldn't seem to stop glancing over to the man and his horse.

Charlie noticed and said, "That's Cody Ty Hawkins. One of the greatest rodeo champions in the world."

Journey didn't know the name, but she intended to research him later on. Two strokes of luck! First on the cancellation list *and* a rodeo champion on-site?

"He's fascinating," Journey said, and there was a flicker

of understanding in Charlie's eyes made her a smidge self-conscious.

"Yes, he is," Charlie said, opening the door. "He's the real deal."

Journey stepped into the cozy atmosphere of the main cabin. There was a fire burning in the fireplace, a faint scent of pine, and the minute she walked into the cabin, she felt at ease and at home as if she had been there many lifetimes ago.

"Make yourself comfortable." Charlie shrugged out of her jacket and hung it and her hat on the horseshoe hooks next to the door.

"Thank you." Journey hung up her coat as well and then sat down at the butcher block-style island.

"Coffee, hot cocoa, hot buttered rum?"

"Where have you been all my life?" Journey asked. "It's five o'clock somewhere. Hot buttered rum? Yes, please."

Her son wouldn't be arriving for a week, and she fully intended to delve into some self-care and let her proverbial hair down. Oakley was her heart and her world, but mothers needed a break, too.

Charlie joined her and together they enjoyed the warm drink and then had a second.

"So, you write romance?"

Journey put her mug down and held it to keep her hands warm. "Yes. I do. Well, really just the one."

"One's better than none."

"True." Journey loved Charlie's energy; it was such a good vibe.

"I love your hair," Journey said about Charlie's thick

long silver-and-brown natural hair that was plaited into a long braid down her back.

"Thank you," her host said. "I just couldn't be bothered with it. I look way older than my sisters, but the horses don't care."

Charlie's sense of humor plus the buttered rum served to relax Journey and she could see herself feeling right at home in Montana.

"Let me show you to your room. Wayne just texted, he's on his way over to help with your bags."

Journey followed Charlie; she was interested in the photographs lining the hallway and stopped to ask questions about the people featured in them.

"So much history here," she said, awestruck. "Didn't the website say that this property has been in your family for generations?"

"Five." Charlie led her to a spacious room with a king-size bed and windows that overlooked expansive, snow-white pastureland.

"That is truly amazing. I feel honored to be here."

"We're honored to have you with us."

Journey took the tour and discovered a luxury en suite bathroom that had been completely updated and featured a soaker tub that had her name on it.

"This is all for me?"

"We only book one group at a time. When they arrive, your son and mother will have the rooms across the hall." Charlie smiled at her. "Wayne's here. Let's go meet him at your car."

"Oh! Wait a sec. I'd like my mom to have this room. I'll share the bathroom with my son."

"Okay by me." Charlie gave her a thumbs-up.

Wayne was her very first *real* cowboy experience. Button-down shirt, silver goatee, intense deep-set eyes; he wasn't much of a talker, but he tipped his hat to her several times and greeted her with a "how do?" That was also a first. She kind of liked it and was definitely taking mental notes to add some color to her cowboy characters.

"Ma'am." Wayne tipped his hat to her again after he brought her bags into her room that shared a Jack-and-Jill bathroom.

"Thank you, Wayne. Nice to meet you."

"Likewise." The cowboy headed out of the door, but then he stopped, turned and caught her gaze. "We'll be sitting around the campfire this evening. We'd be pleased if you'd join."

And there it was, cowboy magic! Anyone with just one eye could see that Wayne was a goner for Charlie. But when he gave her that direct look plus the set of his chin, the roughness of his hands, all wrapped up in cowboy boots, a silver buckle and that button-down shirt with some chest hair showing—she didn't have to wonder a moment longer. She was hooked on cowboys now. And in record time.

"Thank you." She gave him a nod. "It would be my pleasure."

A wake was held at the Legend home a week after Buck's death. Between her own issues in California, which seemed to be heading in the wrong direction, and supporting Dean and Ray, Danica only had time to text with Matteo. They had several short conversations, but he had a busy medical practice, and the planets didn't align for them. As it turned out, the next time they saw each other in person was at the wake.

"How are you?" Matteo asked her. "How are Dean and Ray holding up?"

Danica breathed in and let it out on a sigh. "Devastated. And the girls, Paisley and Luna, they are heartbroken. And Dean and his ex-wife Catrin don't agree on how things should be handled."

Danica lowered her voice and Matteo leaned his head down. "Catrin does not want them to attend the funeral. She follows her Buddhist tradition. The body should not be embalmed but should be cremated."

"I see."

"Well, that makes one of us," Danica said in a sharp tone. She was tired of fighting with Grant, she was tired of the tug-of-war happening with Dean's daughters. She felt angry that Dean's ex had refused to cut the girls' visit short to allow them to attend the funeral.

"I'm sorry," she said almost immediately, "I haven't had much sleep."

"I understand. Hard, emotional times," Matteo said, kindly, and that made her feel seen, heard and supported.

"Thank you." She put her hand on his arm. "I like you very much."

The smile he gave her made her spirit lighten for the first time since the night they lost Buck. "I like you very much, too."

The wake was an emotional roller coaster for Danica; so many people had traveled from around the state to pay their respects. The long driveway to the main house was used for parking on both sides with some parking on the berm of the highway and then walking the rest of the way in.

The wake, per Buck's last wishes, was not a downtrodden affair. Buck loved everything classic country music, so the house was alive with the sounds of Loretta Lynn, Johnny Cash, Garth Brooks, Dolly Parton and the Judds. All of Buck's favorite foods were prepared by Ray and Miss Minnie, a woman as round as she was tall, who had worked for the Legends so long that she was a valued family member.

"I miss that ol' curmudgeon," Miss Minnie said. "I truly do and I truly will."

Danica walked in just in time for a taste test after she hugged Ray. "Mmm. The taste of our childhood."

"It is," Ray agreed. Buck's all-time favorite was cowboy mashed potatoes with baby carrots, garlic, white corn, butter, chives and some shredded cheddar cheese. "It never tastes this good when I make it, though."

"If you don't mind, take this batch out for me." Miss Minnie had a sheen of sweat on her round face, standing with her hands on her broad hips. "My dogs are really barking today. Bad feet, bad hips, bad back."

Ray walked over, gave Minnie a hug. "Beautiful heart."

Miss Minnie smiled, pleased, and it seemed to give her a much-needed boost to keep her going. "All right now, we don't need to be sitting around blathering and blubbering with all of this work to do."

Ray and Danica took the mashed potatoes to the buffet-style setup. The main entrance and the library were filled with people laughing, crying and telling stories about Buck, a true man among men.

Charlie broke free of a conversation and joined them at the buffet.

"Buck sure did mean a lot to so many people," she said, then asked Ray, "What's the news on Dean's girls?"

Ray sighed. "Most of the time, Dean and Catrin can negotiate a middle ground, but both of them are in their corners just waiting for the bell to be rung."

After a few minutes watching the guests quietly, lost in their own thoughts, Charlie said, "What were you and Dr. Drop-Dead Gorgeous talking about?"

"Oh," Danica said, "he'd like us to get together this week, but…"

"But nothing," Charlie and Ray said in unison.

In a lowered voice, Danica answered, "It seems, I don't know…"

"Disrespectful to Buck?"

Danica nodded. "I suppose so."

"Look around, Danny," Ray said. "Does Buck want any of us to hold back on living because he died? No. He wouldn't. So go out with your handsome doctor. And think of Buck sitting on a cloud, happy as a clam, with Nettie by his side."

Chapter Four

"If you love me, please don't stand Dad up for Shabbat dinner again," his sister said. "I'm running out of excuses."

Their mother was from the island of Puerto Rico and their father's family had fled from Austria in order to escape persecution for being Jewish. The family practiced Judaism and still got together on Friday night via video chat for prayers and to eat challah—braided bread—and drink wine together. For their parents, it eased the pain of distance from their adult children, while ensuring that the family, and grandchildren if they should come, continue the Jewish traditions. This was, above all else, their father's wish.

"I'll be there," Matteo said. "It's been a tough week."

Matteo had learned how to bake challah from their grandmother, and it was one of his favorite things to make. He put the loaf of bread in the oven and then sat down at his dining room table. Lu Lu was snoring on her bed nearby.

"So, what's the news?"

Matteo leaned back against the kitchen counter, arms crossed casually. "I lost someone I admired. I attended the wake and I plan on going to the funeral."

His sister's expression changed from frustrated and annoyed to empathetic and concerned. "I'm so sorry. I didn't know. And here I'm bugging you about Shabbat dinner."

"You have every right to bug me. It's not fair for me to lean on you to play interference."

"Well," Estrella said, "I'm still sorry."

"Thank you."

"Changing the subject…" His sister had a glint in her eye when she asked, "How's it going with Danica?"

"Actually, I have to call and cancel our date tonight. You aren't the only one on my case about Friday evenings." Matteo worked half days on Friday so he could prep for the Friday night Sabbath.

"Mom?"

"Bingo. *And*, she was speaking in Spanish."

"No bueno."

"Exactamente," he agreed. "When Mom breaks out the Spanish, we know someone's in trouble."

"But why ask her out on a Friday? You know that's a conflict."

"Because," Matteo said, going to the fridge to pull out some vegetable snacks for Lu Lu, "Friday night is for serious dates, and I am serious about Danica."

"Saturday nights are the same as Friday night dates."

"I usually hang out with my friends most Saturday nights, but sacrifices will have to be made."

"Well," Estrella said, frowning, "you're rearranging your life for her. I hope she's as serious as you are."

"You let me handle my love life," Matteo said, before waving goodbye and ending the video chat. Lu Lu hoisted herself out of bed and did her waddle-walk, curly tail wagging, and talking in oinks and grunts all the way to her bowl. Matteo sat down on the floor with her. When she was done, she went outside to soak up some of the afternoon sun and he picked up the phone to reschedule the date. Eventually, he would like to invite Danica to their family Friday night dinner. For now, he would put a temporary hold on Saturday night hanging out with his buddies in Bozeman. He loved his tight group of friends; on the other hand, he had no idea how long he had Danica in Montana so he could successfully lock that down. He didn't want another long-distance relationship, but he had to make an exception for the beautiful Realtor.

Lu Lu finished her snack and then used her nose to flip his phone out of his hand, which was her way of saying *pay attention to me, not your phone.*

"Okay," he said affectionately, "let me make this call first and then you will have my undivided attention."

"How's Dean holding up?" Danica asked Ray, who had made a habit of coming over to her condo rental. It was nice for Danica to have their twin bond strengthened.

"Not good," Ray said, drinking down a green smoothie. "I've never seen him like this. He's lost his appetite. He's trying to solve everything through work. And, unfortunately, he's still going back and forth with Catrin."

"Did they at least find a compromise?"

Ray nodded while she made another green smoothie for her. "Catrin is borrowing her fiancé's private jet. The girls will be home in time for the funeral."

"Good. That will help."

Ray put the smoothie in front of her and she drank it down quickly.

"Are you still connecting with Matteo?"

She nodded. She had just spoken to Matteo, who asked to change their dinner to Saturday night and, not only did she agree, but she was also grateful. She had been fighting with Grant through their lawyers *every* day. And to make matters worse, many of the people she had counted as friends were trashing her on social media, taking Grant's side and wondering how he had managed to put up with a "cold fish" like her for as long as he did. She had blocked and unfriended so many people over the course of the week that it had taken an emotional toll.

"He's fantastic. But I'm not sure I can really be anything more than friends. The constant fighting with Grant is exhausting and maddening. He acts as if *I'm* the one who cheated. He's threatening to sue me for *emotional distress*."

"Oh, you're kidding, right?"

"No. I'm not. I don't think it will go anywhere. I have no idea who this man is. Is *this* who he's been this whole time?"

Ray walked over and hugged her tightly. "I'm sorry, Danny, I really am."

Grateful for the hug, Danica said, "He's dragging my name through the mud, Ray. It took me over a decade of work to build my reputation and my good name. How can he begin to dismantle the entire structure with a couple of nasty tweets and putting our dirty laundry out at every party he attends? And I can easily see that some of my so-called friends were my enemies because they are inviting him and Fallon to their parties and plastering their images all over their social media."

"You might just have to sue him for slander or defamation of character," Ray said, then added, "You need a break."

"Yes. I really do. I think I'm still in shock. No one expects their lives to blow up the next day," she said with a shake of her head. "Maybe I should schedule a massage. Or a facial. Or a lobotomy so I can forget Grant ever existed."

"Or—" Ray had raised eyebrows and an overly excited and happy expression on her face that made Danica laugh "—you could join my goat yoga class. It's so much fun! I *promise* you—" Ray had her hands together in a plea and a prayer "—you will be saying *Grant who?* five minutes in."

And that was how she wound up being lovingly coerced into her first goat yoga class.

Journey had quickly developed a routine at Hideaway Ranch. In the morning, she made herself some avocado toast on whole-wheat bread with a cup of black coffee. The Brand sisters had stocked the fridge and pantry with all of her favorite foods. She made the bed, cleaned up the kitchen and then put on her hiking gear and set out on foot to explore the wild land surrounding the inhabited area of the ranch. At night, she heard many nocturnal animal sounds, and she had already gone through Charlie's *How to Handle Wildlife Encounters* tutorial and had bear spray and air horns to scare off bears if they should charge. She also was taught how to handle bison, elk and wolves. Most people might have thought that her fear of encountering a bear was much less than the fear she had of horses. But then again, she hadn't had any bad experiences with a bear or an elk or a wolf; when she was a young child, she had a very bad experience with a horse and had feared them ever since.

When she returned from her walk, she saw Ray pull up to the main house and get out with a striking blond woman who Journey assumed was Danica Brand, the only one of the Brand triplets she had yet to meet.

"Journey!" Ray called out to her with a welcoming smile. "Come meet Danny!"

Journey waved at them and headed back to the house.

Danica Brand greeted her with the same friendliness Charlie and Ray had exhibited.

"Wow!" Danica exclaimed, "you are *gorgeous*. And so statuesque! Do you model?"

Journey smiled. "I did when I was younger. When I became a mother, traveling for photo shoots wasn't practical anymore."

"During the pandemic, I decided to give writing a chance. I was addicted to Harlequin books. I devoured them. Harlequin is the reason why I don't understand fractions."

"Did any of us really need to know fractions?" Charlie interjected.

Journey smiled and rolled her eyes. "So unnecessary. But at least it wasn't 'new' math that my son is being taught. It's a bunch of boxes."

"Tragic," Charlie said.

Danica had been listening but not really participating in the conversation; she examined her like a woman admiring a sports car she was interested in buying before she asked, "Would you consider modeling for our website and social media? You are so striking, I think everyone, men, women, and everything in between, would gravitate to you."

"I'd consider it," she said. "Absolutely."

Ray checked the time on her Apple watch. "I've got to get the goats ready for class. Are you joining us, Journey?"

"That would be a big fat yes."

Feeling accepted by the Brand sisters, Journey rushed to her room, changed out of her hiking gear to her yoga clothing. She swept her waist-length honey-blond hair up into a long pony and checked herself out in the bathroom mirror and then hurried out the front door. From the porch, she saw Ray leading five goats that were braying and hopping around. Ray promised, with a money-back guarantee, to work the zygomaticus major and minor, aka the smile muscles of the face.

One extra curious goat with black and white spots on its body and a lightning-bolt shape in white down its dark gray head made funny hopping motions on its way over to a persistent weed pushing through the melting snow.

"Hickory!" Ray called after the baby goat, who ignored her and kept on exploring.

"I can get him!" Journey said, wanting to get her hands on that sweet little goat.

"Are you sure?"

"Sure, sure," she said, taking the porch steps quickly and walking with her long-legged stride to scoop up the goat.

"I got you!" Journey picked up the baby goat and held him safely in her arms. "You are a handsome doll baby, aren't you?"

The goat went soft in her arms as he licked the tip of her nose and that moment meant so much to her that she felt a swell of emotion rising to the surface. "How can you be this cute?"

She took Hickory over to Ray and then followed the

other goats into a walkout basement with floor-to-ceiling windows that let in the warm sunlight while giving the goat yoga participants an incredible view of the Montana mountains.

"Thank you," Ray said with a small laugh. "Hickory, Dickory and Dock are new yoga instructors."

Danica arrived with two more young goats by the names of Tick and Tock. While Journey helped the sisters to set up the mats for the class, and as guests began to arrive, the baby goats were running, headbutting, hopping and braying and as promised in the advertisement, her smile muscles had already gotten a workout and the class hadn't yet begun!

Once the mats were set up, and exactly at 1:00 p.m., Ray opened the doors and let in the excited group of women who were gathered at the entrance. The minute new people arrived, the goats ran up to them, stubby tails upright, all vying for attention.

"Come on in! Find a mat and let's get our yoga on!" Ray said, and Journey loved her upbeat, positive vibe.

"I'm going to stick with you." Danica took the mat next to her.

"I'm already having a great time."

"Me, too. Surprisingly."

"How so?"

"I'm not typically a person who exercises in a group, but I love this already. When Ray first came up with the idea, I was all for it. I had no idea that it would become one of the most lucrative ventures for this ranch."

Ray began to take them through basic yoga poses while the goats ran around, chasing each other, jumping on the patrons' backs while they were holding the table pose. The room was filled with laughter at the antics of the young goats.

"I invite you to keep your tabletop pose if you have a goat standing on your back!"

Dock kept right on circling back to her and she took every moment she could with him, loving the softness of his fur and the sweet, trusting blue eyes.

"I need to pack you away in my suitcase," Journey said when Dock walked beneath her while in the downward dog pose. "Take you home with me."

At the end of the class, Journey picked up Dock and cuddled with him.

"I didn't expect this," Danica said, snuggling with Hickory. "We didn't have goats when I was a kid. It makes me wonder how I managed to live forty-plus years on this planet without them!"

They helped Ray clean up the basement and then took the goats back to the warm barn. Two males had caught Journey's attention: Cody Ty and Dock. After she put Dock down in the clean, refreshed hay, Journey asked Ray, as casually as she could, about Cody Ty.

"I don't know much about him, really," Ray said. "Charlie is a better person to ask."

As if on schedule, Charlie walked into the barn, covered in mud and dirt, with patches of water stains on her coat and her jeans.

"Hey!" Ray called Charlie over while Journey tried to shrink down and wished she had never asked the question in the first place. "Journey has some questions about Cody!"

And just when she thought things couldn't get more embarrassing, Cody Ty appeared in the barn just as Ray was yelling that to her sister.

She was six feet even in her bare feet, so she had no way to hide. She held herself very still and hoped that he wouldn't zero in on her. But he did zero in on her and their eyes met, and when they did, her body felt like it had just turned into wobbly Jell-O, and she took an involuntary step back, as if the sheer force of that electricity between them had knocked her for a loop.

"Well, he's right here." Charlie turned around to gesture toward him, but he was gone.

Right before he took his leave, he tipped his hat to Journey, and that nearly made her hyperventilate. For the first time, she was experiencing that cowboy romanticism, the draw of women, regardless of the age or geography. That cowboy *thing* had just smacked her in the face, and she couldn't imagine writing a book without a cowboy as the hero.

"Well, he *was* there," Charlie said, laughing. "That man is always on the move. So, what's going on?"

"Journey was interested in him."

"For research," Journey was quick to add. "A secondary character."

Charlie looked at her like she had grown a flipper. "Cody Ty, as a character, has to be the leading man. Yes, he's clocked some miles, but he wears them well. I actually think he's more handsome now. He's rodeo royalty—if he was entered into a competition, everyone knew that he couldn't be beat, so they fought each other for second and third."

Charlie continued, "He's handsome, strong and kind-hearted."

The three sisters and Journey walked back toward the main house.

"How's the book coming?" Ray asked.

Journey sighed and let it out on a long breath. "I was so inspired on day one that I thought I'd be several chapters in by now, but I have writer's block. I can't seem to get words on the page. So instead of writing, I hike, or organize my suitcase, or make some coffee. You guys get the idea."

When they reached the main house, Journey continued to the front door. She thought it might be rude to *not* invite the triplets for coffee and conversation, but she just couldn't do it. She needed to be alone with her thoughts; she needed to call Riggs because she had just been hit with a lightning bolt with Cody Ty's name on it.

Buck Legend's Wake and funeral were held one week after his death. The Wake was held at the Legend ranch while the funeral was held at the Soldiers Chapel in Gallatin Gateway, a town that was a short distance from Big Sky. The church looked like a perfect fit for Buck; it was a rugged chapel, with a masculine flair of stone and wood, and had a circular window of stained glass just above the large orangish-brown entry doors. The chapel was sitting alone in a sea of white snow with a snowy roof and glorious snowcapped mountains in the background. They waited a week after his death to allow the many people in Buck's vast network of ranchers and farmers across the state of Montana to make travel plans to arrive in time for the burial. There would be overflow in the church parking lot and the service would stream live for those who couldn't make it. Danica was amazed at the sheer volume of mourners and relieved when she saw Matteo standing tall and cutting a fine figure in his somber black suit with a black shirt and a tie that had a matte and shiny black geometric pattern design—so much so that she naturally changed course and walked over to him.

Matteo saw her and he walked to meet her halfway. At the point where they met, Matteo hugged her. It was exactly what she needed. And it was just as natural for Matteo to reach for her hand, as she reached for his. Was this a declaration? She wasn't really sure, and she didn't really care about optics. She'd lost Buck, a man who had always treated her as one of his own, and the fact that she hadn't made a concerted effort to return home and visit her parents and the Legends cut deep. In her late twenties and early thirties, she had been focused on her career, to the detriment of most everything else, and now, looking back as they buried Buck Legend, it dawned on her that she had been misguided. No matter what her career demands, she should have made time for her family. She knew that her family noticed that she was holding hands with Matteo, but after an exchange of curious looks, her sisters returned their attention to the priest, who had been the Legend and Brand families' go-to for baptisms, weddings and, yes, funerals as well.

The Legend family members occupied the first three rows and then the next two rows were reserved for the Brand family. Ray was sitting in the first row with Dean, his daughters, and his ex-wife Catrin; Catrin had had a change of heart and flown with the girls from London to attend the funeral to support her daughters. Matteo quietly asked Danica if he should sit on the guest side of the church, but Danica held his hand firmly, so she sat next to Charlie and Wayne, and he sat sandwiched in between her and Wayne; his broad shoulders and height made him a tight squeeze for the rest of them. And she worried that he might block the view of the folks sitting directly behind them. She forgot about that concern and focused her attention on the priest.

After opening remarks, Dean walked up to the lectern. He looked somber and heartbroken as he began to give his eulogy. After several minutes, Paisley and Luna had begun to cry. Luna held on to Ray for comfort while Paisley had folded over with her head pressed against Catrin's chest. After Dean's remarks, several of Buck's best friends spoke about their friend; sometimes there was laughter and sometimes there were tears. Danica found herself solidly in the latter category; Dean's eulogy had gotten her crying and she couldn't seem to stop. Matteo offered her a handkerchief and she took it gratefully.

After the service was over, everyone piled into their vehicles and drove to the cemetery where he would be laid to rest next to his beloved Nettie. At the last minute, Danica decided to ride with Matteo. Yes, her sisters would have questions about the connection between the most eligible bachelor and her. And she would answer questions if she actually had an answer. From the very beginning, not very long ago, the electricity between them hadn't been planned for either of them. It just *was*. And ever since they had met, she was following her gut, her intuition, not her head.

"It was a beautiful ceremony," Danica said, riding in Matteo's GMC Sierra 3500 HD Denali.

Matteo nodded his agreement.

"I was happy to see you," she added.

"I was happy to see you, too." He looked at her with a smile before refocusing on the still-icy roads.

They both rode in quiet remembrance of the man they had just lost. There were profound shifts in her priorities, and she wondered how it would ultimately impact her life. Matteo followed the slow-moving procession following the hearse. Parking was easier with fewer people attending the burial. Snow was about to hit, and folks needed to get home while the roads were passable.

They huddled together in tents as they lowered the casket into the ground. Catrin had taken Paisley and Luna to the Legends' ranch; this was their compromise. The girls would attend the funeral service but not the burial. When the casket reached its destination, Dean placed his hands on the casket, telling his father how he loved him and how much he would miss him. Then this big, tough, burly man, rarely showing his emotions as his upbringing demanded, dropped to his knees and wept. And Ray, ever Dean's ally, knelt beside him and put her arm around him, her own tears streaming down her face.

Danica was triggered by Dean's sorrow, and she found it impossible to keep her fresh tears at bay. She spun around and left the tent, ignoring the fat, fluffy flakes of snow falling. Matteo followed her but this time she wasn't so sure she wanted him to. Her strength had come from being independent and self-sufficient, and leaning on others rarely. The heels of her shoes dug into the mushy grass as she headed down another row of headstones. At one point, the right heel of her shoe snagged on something, and that tweaked the ankle that she had twisted the day she met the handsome doctor and his adorable pig Lu Lu.

"Ow!" she exclaimed. "Gosh darn it!"

Matteo was at her side, offering his arm, and she accepted the help even as her brain was short-circuiting because she had already leaned on the doctor too many times already. For the love of peanuts, she had held his hand for over an hour! What was wrong with her?

"Getting soft," she muttered.

"What was that?" he asked.

"Nothing," she grumbled. "I seem to fall around you."

"Well," Matteo said, "I'd rather see you fall *for* me. But I'll take what I can get. Now where are we going?"

"Just up this row."

Together they walked toward a large headstone at the end of the row. Danica let go of his arm, bent down and brushed the snow from the headstone. Once the snow was gone, the names on the headstone were Butch and Rose Brand.

"My parents."

Matteo gave a small nod of understanding.

Danica was all out of tears, but her heart ached for her lost parents. If she hadn't been betrayed by Grant, how often would she have traveled to Big Sky to spend time with her sisters? Not a whole heck of a lot. She preferred to keep her involvement with the ranch while continuing her life in LA.

"They must have been lovely," Matteo said.

"Yes, they were," she agreed.

"Time goes by too fast."

She nodded, never taking her eyes off of her parents' graves. When she looked up, she saw Charlie and Ray heading their way. Matteo stepped to the side to make room for her sisters. Silently, and using their telepathic connection that had only grown stronger since they had reconnected after Rose's death, they found themselves in the same place. They put their arms around each other and touched their foreheads together as they acknowledged the parents, Brand and Legend, they had lost.

"May you rest in peace," Charlie said.

"Amen," Danica and Ray said.

And then, arms linked together in union, the triplet women walked back toward the burial site with Matteo following behind them.

"May I give you a ride home?" Matteo asked her once she had finished giving condolences for the Legend extended family.

"Yes, you may," Danica said simply. There was no sense trying to fight this connection between them. She didn't have a crystal ball, so she didn't know how this was all going to pan out. But for now, they were here together, and the future would just have to be handled when it became the present.

Chapter Five

The Saturday after Buck's funeral, Danica went to Matteo's house for an early dinner. His home was small and rustic with some acreage necessary to keep Lu Lu occupied with enough land for rooting, which was her nature. As a Realtor, she always believed that she could learn almost everything she needed to know about a client just by looking at the inside and the outside of the house. Matteo's house was decorated in an eclectic style and the majority of the odds and ends were from his travels. It was a masculine house with a masculine color palette of dark browns and blacks; wood was the dominant material with stained wood shiplap and high-end leather furniture. The kitchen was just as moody as the rest of the house; it was a chef's kitchen with professional-grade gas stove and double-wide refrigerator. The accent color, a sunburst orange, gave the eye somewhere to land. It was a sophisticated look that made her think that the handsome, much-sought-after bachelor had a deeper, richer side to him that in their short time together had not been tapped.

There were two walls of bookshelves, overflowing with books on art, horticulture, cooking, travel, martial arts and anatomy. Three shelves were dedicated entirely to how to raise a pig.

"Is this Emy?" Danica stopped to look at a picture on a bookshelf. "And is that Lu Lu as a piglet?!"

Matteo was cutting vegetables for the stir-fry dish he was making for them; he looked up and smiled. "Yes and yes."

"Emy is adorable. And so too is Lu Lu." Danica walked back to the large quartz island, picked up the bottle of wine she had brought for them and asked, "Do you need a top-off?"

"Sure," he said before he threw the freshly cut vegetables into the hot wok.

Danica poured another glass for herself, and then watched Matteo's mastery in the kitchen. She hated to tell him that she had used a personal chef for the last eight years and could not cook an egg. This was the one area where she was not as independent, but she had many restaurants on speed dial, so she wasn't in any danger of starving.

"You are accomplished," she said.

Matteo soaked in the compliment, giving her a wink and smile. "I considered becoming a chef, but my dad expected me to be an attorney or a doctor."

"You seem happy with your choice. Fulfilled."

"I am. Medicine wasn't my first choice, though."

She raised her eyebrows at him to let him know that she was listening and wanted him to continue.

Matteo drank some of the wine in his glass before he said, "I went to law school first."

Danica leaned forward, eyes wide open, and asked, "Are you an attorney, too?"

He laughed. "Yes. I went to school, passed the bar, had

an internship with a big firm in Baltimore and found out real quick that I wasn't cut out for that."

"Well," she said, "I'm impressed."

"Good. I'm glad."

After a moment, she asked, "So when you said you knew a good lawyer, were you speaking of yourself?"

He laughed. "Yep."

They talked while Matteo cooked and while she set the table for them. He didn't have to tell her where everything was kept because she had a similar setup in her LA house.

"We are definitely a match when it comes to how to set up a kitchen. And a living room, actually."

"Lucky for me."

They sat down at his modern metal-and-glass dining table; the juxtaposition of the traditional, masculine dark wood with select ultramodern pieces such as the table and some of the light fixtures drew a picture of a man who was traditional, decidedly male, but forward-thinking, an out-of-the-box man. And she loved what she saw—in his decor and in the man himself.

"Well—" Danica put down her fork and looked at her empty plate "—that was the most delicious meal I've had in a very long time."

"Better than Block 3?"

She nodded.

"Better than anything in LA?"

"Let's call it a solid tie." She laughed. "I do love a man who can cook. Would you like to get married?"

She had said this in jest, but he sounded rather serious when he said, "Yes, I would."

They cleared the table, he put the dishes in the sink to soak, and they took their wine to his living room.

"I wish I had gotten to see Lu Lu," she said, feeling very comfortable in Matteo's house.

"I know," he said, "but it was better this way, trust me. If Lu Lu is in the room, she commands attention. And if she doesn't get it…"

"Ear-curdling squeal?"

"Exactly. So I fed her an early dinner and she is happily sleeping in her house."

He took his phone out of his shirt pocket and then showed her a video of Lu Lu happily sleeping in a giant, squishy pillow bed. And of course, she was snoring loudly with a content smile on her face.

"Oh!" Danica exclaimed. "She has pajamas!"

Matteo smiled.

"I love her," she told him. "I just adore her."

"Do you know, you're the very first woman outside of my ex who has taken to her?"

Danica shook her head. "Is that why the most eligible bachelor is still single?"

"Yes," he said bluntly, "and I'm not saying that she is as important as, or equal to, a child, but she is the closest thing to a child that I have. She's part of my family and I made a promise to Emy that I would take care of her always. And I intend to keep that promise."

Danica reached over to put her hand on his and said, "You are a kind, honorable man, Matteo."

"And you are an incredibly kind and beautiful woman, Danica," he echoed.

He reached for her hand and threaded their fingers together. The look of admiration in his eyes, the expression of pure acceptance and raw, unmistakable attraction from him to her, made Danica duck her head, blushing. She had forgotten what it was like to have this kind of interest from a man; the spark had gone out of the relationship with Grant years ago. But they had been comfortable and shared the same goals. Or at least she had believed that.

"Do you feel this *thing* between us?" he asked her.

She was too old to play coy. "Yes, I do."

"I'm glad you didn't say no," he said. "That question could've gone one of two ways for me," and then he asked, "It's magnetic, right?"

"Yes, it is."

Matteo dragged his fingers through his hair with a small shake of his head before he looked back at her with a steady, unwavering, gaze. "I've never felt *this* before."

"It's oddly comfortable."

"It *is* oddly comfortable. This is a first."

"For me, too." Danica tucked one leg under the other. "I feel like I've known you for years instead of weeks. It's *familiar.*"

"Exactly." He nodded. "Exactly," then quickly added, "but not like brother-and-sister vibes."

"Oh, God! Why would you even *say* such a thing?" She hit him playfully on the arm. "Don't put that image in my head! What's wrong with you?"

"Platonic!" He laughed with that deep baritone laugh that made her smile. "I was going for platonic!"

"Okay. But in *that* case, you could have said that you don't want to be friend-zoned."

"I don't want to be friend-zoned."

"Well, neither do I," she said and then, as if to emphasize the silliness of his concern, she did something she hadn't done since she was in high school. She crossed her eyes at him.

That made Matteo laugh and because he was laughing, so did she. It was the comic relief that they both needed.

"You're beautiful, funny, intelligent," he said. "You're a triple threat."

"Was that a triplet joke?"

"I wish I had been that clever," he said. "I guess you're a triplet who's a triple threat."

Danica ducked her head, feeling self-conscious in that she wasn't used to being looked at the way Matteo looked at her every time they were together: appreciated, admired, attractive, and he always focused on her no matter how many wealthy knockout women were milling about in Big Sky. And there were plenty; this pond was fully stocked. The few times they were out together, his focus on her never wavered, and she had a gut feeling that he never would disrespect her that way. And it was something new, something rare and precious, because she had never experienced that with Grant; that man had an eye for the ladies and the older he got, the younger the women that caught his interest were. Fallon, case in point.

"I can't say where this might take us, though," Danica said, prepared to share her *long* story with him. He needed to know, particularly now that she knew he shared her feelings of undeniable attraction and chemistry that was also deeply quiet and relaxed. She had never been a romantic like Ray; she didn't believe in soulmates. Until now.

Matteo took a last sip of wine, put his glass down on

the coffee table, and then took hers and put it next to his. He unthreaded their hands and then he closed the short distance between them, put his large, warm hands on her face, and said in a voice that sent shock waves of anticipation leaving a wake of goose bumps across her body, "I want to kiss you, Danica. Any objections?"

"Yes," she said in a sultry voice that was brand-new. Forty years and then suddenly she had a sultry voice in her repertoire! "I mean, no."

"No, I can't?" Matteo needed that confirmation, and she didn't blame him. "Or yes, I can?"

"Yes, you should." She melted into his strong arms, head tilted back, being enveloped by the woodsy scent of his skin, and then his firm lips were on hers, gentle, questioning and so sweet.

Matteo cradled her head in his free hand while he kissed her again, lovingly more than passionate, but these kisses held promise of steamier kisses further down the line. At this moment, these lovely kisses were exactly what she needed.

Matteo leaned back and Danica put her head on his chest and loved the feel of his strong arms holding on to her, and the feather kisses he was dusting across the top of her head. She didn't want this moment to end, but she also didn't feel right not sharing her long story. Grant was currently making her life miserable with no sign that he would stop, just to be spiteful. Many of the women she had considered friends had taken Grant's side. She wasn't emotionally ready to jump into another committed relationship when she was very much tangled up in the last one.

Danica pushed herself upright and looked at Matteo. "Can I tell you my long story?"

Cody Ty Hawkins had lived most of his life in the spotlight. He had been a top junior rodeo competitor with only a few rare losses on his score card. Then, when he aged out of the junior circuit, he went straight to adult rodeo and cleaned up there as well. That was his life for the majority of his adulthood, living on the road, staying in seedy hotels, too much drinking, too much fighting and too little time at home. He'd had a pretty young wife, Jessa, his high school sweetheart, whom he married the day they graduated, and instead of a honeymoon night, he headed off to the next rodeo. On one trip home, they made themselves a baby, and he was tickled about it. But he wasn't there for the birth, and he had missed nearly every birthday his daughter, Abilene, had.

When Jessa got pregnant with another man's baby, he had only himself to blame. They divorced while he rode the wave of his success and celebrity as the reigning rodeo champion in the world. For a good long while, he was undefeated. Other cowboys vied for the second and third slot when he was at the event. Everywhere he went, someone recognized him, wanted to take a picture with him and get an autograph. Booze and women were in a seemingly endless supply, and he had been a greedy man. When the free booze and willing women began to taper off to a trickle and there weren't crowds of fans waiting to cheer him on, or grab those pictures and autographs, Cody had slipped into a deep depression that fueled the self-destructive drunken phase that had landed him in jail time and again.

The landslide from adored to scorned had been much quicker than the climb to reach the pinnacle. And then, when he'd thought he'd reached rock bottom, he found a new low. He was living out of his truck, doing odds and ends for local folks, making enough to fill up his tank, buy some cheap whiskey and maybe eat if there was money left over. At his very worst, he ran into an old friend by the name of Wayne Westbrook and that colliding of two lives changed his life for the positive and he hadn't let a drop of liquor or beer pass through his lips for a decade. He'd gotten back to his passion of gentling young horses and getting them under saddle, and he made a fine living, even put some money aside for his retirement. Perhaps he hadn't always made the best choices, but he'd always been loyal. He hadn't forgotten, and never would, how Wayne helped to dry him out, get him back on his feet and give him work on his crew in Wyoming.

So when Wayne called him to help train some young horses on a ranch in Montana, he hitched up his travel trailer and headed toward Hideaway Ranch.

"She's got a fine conformation." Wayne stopped by the round pen where Cody had been working with a red roan filly with a reddish-brown face, speckles of red and white down her back, and a black mane and tail.

"She's a good-looker and willing," Cody said, moving back a couple of the steps, removing his pressure on her hind end, signaling to her that she could stop trotting down to walking. The filly, ears perked forward, eyes on Cody, halted and turned her body toward him and when he invited her into the circle, she walked over to him and put her head down for a scratch.

"Damn, Cody," Wayne said with appreciation. "Not one word was said, and she knew exactly what you wanted her to do."

"They read energy," Cody said, "and I thank you for the compliment."

"You're welcome," Wayne said, "and thank you. This is going to be another revenue stream for this ranch."

Cody walked forward and the filly followed him, accepting him as her herd boss. "You say you get these horses from Bozeman?"

"One of Charlie's kin, Jock Brand. Sugar Creek Ranch. They have one of the best quarter horse breeding programs I've ever seen."

"So he gets a cut," Cody said, "and you get a cut."

"The ranch really," Wayne said, "and you get a cut. Three-way split."

"Well, I appreciate it," he said, putting the halter on the red roan's head. "It's a fair deal. Maybe *too* fair of a deal."

"No—" his friend shook his head "—it's more than fair. No one else is better at this than you."

Cody Ty had learned over the last few years to smile. "Is it too late to renegotiate my fee?"

That made Wayne laugh. "I'm afraid so, my friend."

Wayne set off to his ranch chores; in this life, there was always more work to do than anyone had the time, or the energy, to do. It was an ever-updating list of "must-dos." Cody led the pretty red roan filly to the barn when he saw a tall woman, looked to be in her late thirties, come out of the main house to the snowy porch. Her loveliness slapped him in right in the face because he had lived his life out of a suitcase and he had *never* encountered a more beauti-

ful woman in all of his travels; she resembled a palomino
mare with her thick honey-blond hair that cascaded down
her back to her waist; her skin was as golden as wheat
growing in a field.

Not wanting to get caught staring at her, he made a
quick turn to the barn with the rambunctious filly dancing around him.

"Now, that," Cody said to the filly after putting her in a
vacant stall, "is a bona fide gorgeous woman."

Cody led a colt, a young male horse, out to the round
pen and was both relieved and disappointed that the woman
was gone.

"We don't have time for distractions, do we?" Cody said
to the frisky black colt, with a white star on his face with
matching white socks up to his knees. "We've got work
to do."

"Why would anyone avoid you? You're the nicest person ever and if that cowboy doesn't get that, tell him to go
kick rocks," Riggs said, while he used hair product to mold
spikes all over his head. "Which do you prefer? Green or
hot pink?"

"Neither."

"Spoilsport," Riggs said, painting one spike neon green.

"I don't know," she said about Cody, pulling her hair over
her shoulder and twisting it while she thought, "maybe it's
my imagination."

But even as she said it, she didn't think that was true.
When their eyes met in the barn, he *noticed* her in the same
way she had noticed him during her first couple of days at
Hideaway Ranch. She had hoped to see him at the regular

evening campfire singing and storytelling when weather permitted; her hope was dashed because he never came. All work, no play.

"Well, I do." Riggs took a short break from his hair and looked at her directly. "You either ignore him like a bad habit, *or* track him down and *make him* pay attention to you."

"I don't like either of those choices."

"I call it like I see it," Riggs said. "Wish me luck. I'm going to an art gallery and I hope I can find a buyer for my boat."

"You are very weird."

Riggs grinned at her, and that grin always took her back to the first time they had met as kids. Riggs was being bullied and her father, a man who had desperately wanted a boy, decided to make lemonade, and taught her how to box. She punched that bully square in the nose and then finished him off with an uppercut. She got sent to the principal's office and her father acted really disappointed in her. Once they were out of sight, he got her an ice cream cone. It was one of the best memories she had of her dad.

After she ended the video chat with Riggs, Journey sat for a minute to think about what her bestie had said. Maybe she should take the forward approach. Yes, there were other cowboys milling around on the ranch who could be her muse. But none of them drew her attention like Cody Ty. She had, of course, researched him and burned the midnight oil until she seemed to have found everything online that she could find. Now that she knew at least part of the backstory, she needed to meet the man *behind* those articles and old newspaper stories. Who was Cody Ty, really? She only had a one-dimensional, shallow view of him. She wanted to know the flesh-and-blood man behind the fame and, ultimately, the fall from grace.

"So, Riggs is right, *again*." Journey stood up, gathered her hair into a ponytail and put on her cowgirl boots, which were dusty and dirty; she was proud that her boots now looked like Charlie's and Ray's boots. "If I want him, I'm gonna have to put on my big-girl drawers and go get that cowboy."

Cody was brushing down a blue-eyed, white-faced colt whose body markings looked like a black-and-white Rorschach test. He was a good one, this colt. Cody could already tell that this little guy was a hard worker and wanted to please.

"I might just ask Wayne if I can have you instead of my cut. You're a good boy."

"Hello."

Cody heard the voice, a light, melodic sound, and knew at the core of his being that it was his palomino. His hand kept on brushing the colt while his knees tried not to buckle. He caught her eye for the briefest of moments, registered that she was even more beautiful up close, before he said, "Howdy."

That made his palomino laugh. "Howdy. I wasn't at all sure if this was a myth or made up by Hollywood writers, but people around these parts, at least the locals, actually *do* say howdy."

She was so tickled by this minute detail that he found himself smiling. Just for a bit.

"Folks do, I suppose."

She got tickled again, rocked forward on her feet, and then said, "Folks. I love that."

"Can I help you, miss?"

"Funny you should ask," Journey said. "You *can* help me. I'm Journey, by the way."

"Pleased to meet'cha," Cody said and tipped his hat to her. "I'm Cody."

Journey clasped her hands. "And the tip of the hat. I love it. I wish more men in the city would wear a hat just so they could tip it at me."

Cody did his best to keep his focus on the colt, but the colt's eyes were wide, he was nervous, and he kept trying to see behind him.

"Miss," Cody said, unhooking the colt's halter from the crossties, "you're spooking my youngsters."

"I'm sorry." Journey's brow drew together. "How am I doing that?"

Cody let the colt face Journey so he could get a good look at her. "Horses read energy just better than about any creature on this green earth. If you're nervous, they're pro-grammed to assume that you are dangerous. A predator."

Journey's blue-green eyes widened. "I'm not a preda-tor. I'm petrified."

That unexpected confession made him chuckle as he put up the colt and it seemed to change the tension in the air for all of them.

"Now, why are you petrified of horses? They don't mean to hurt nobody."

Journey had her hands in her pockets and her feet were firmly planted in the middle of the aisle. This was the barn where the young horses were housed. She loved the goats and totally wanted to pack Dock into her suitcase, but horses? No, no, no, no, no. *No!*

"I don't want to bore you with my childhood trauma."

"When it comes down to horses, I don't bore easy."

"Well, that makes one of us," she said with a nervous laugh, hands out of pockets and her arms twisted together like a pretzel.

And because Journey was out of her depth in his environment, some of Cody's initial shyness with the lovely palomino had given way to his confidence when it came to horses.

"Can't hurt to tell me," he said, "and it might just help."

"When I was four or five, we went to visit my mom's sister on their farm. I loved horses, and really, I still do, they are one of nature's most amazing creations."

"Amen."

"My cousin John put me on one of their horses and he hit that horse on the butt with a crop and that horse took off with me, spooked at my other cousin waving a plastic bag, and then it bucked me off. I broke the fence with my body, broke my arm, and I had to get stiches under my chin." Journey lifted her head and pointed to her scar, then shrugged. "I wasn't afraid of horses before, but this *fear* of horses is so ingrained in my body now that I can't imagine ever overcoming it."

She was shaking, reliving the trauma, and she hugged her arms tightly to her body and finished by saying, "I'll just continue to love and admire them from afar."

Cody stared at her for a moment, and then he said, "I'm real sorry that happened to you. I truly am. If you give me two weeks of your time, I guarantee that you'll conquer your fear."

Chapter Six

The night of their first kiss had turned into morning and Danica awakened in Matteo's bed. After a whole bottle of wine, and talking into the early hours of the morning, Matteo had given her the king bed in the main bedroom while he bunked in the guest room. Danica looked at her phone for the time, then checked in with LA and her sisters. It had felt good to share her "long" story with Matteo; he took it in stride and understood that she was mired in the recent split. His thoughts? Enjoy each other's company now and let the future take care of itself. She slipped out of bed and tip-toed into the kitchen. She did her best to be quiet while she searched for pots and pans and ingredients for the only breakfast she knew how to make.

"Good morning." Matteo walked out shirtless, showing off his sexy chest hair, muscular arms, his abs, and his beautiful broad shoulders. Just like Michelangelo's *David*, Matteo was made to be admired.

Matteo leaned down for a kiss and Danica's body responded, lighting up parts of her body that had been unused, and therefore nearly forgotten, for years.

"What are you making?" he asked her, fixing Lu Lu's breakfast.

"Well." She smiled at him. "I noticed some things in your house."

He raised his eyebrows questioningly.

"I did see the menorah on the bookshelf," she said, "and I found a freshly baked loaf of challah bread."

"So, on one hand, I see some clues that may point to Judaism. However—" she walked over, placed her hand on his chest "—you have a cross tattooed over your heart."

"I'm an international man of mystery." He smiled at her, taking her hand and kissing it.

"Yes, Austin Powers, you are. And I kind of like it."

"I also think you were looking for an excuse to touch me."

That made her blush because he was correct. "Maybe."

"Well," he said, "you don't need any reason to touch me. I give you a lifetime pass."

She was still beaming as Matteo put on his winter coat and rubber boots and headed out to Lu Lu's house with her breakfast. Danica didn't know exactly what had come over her, but she felt, in that moment, lighthearted with a positive outlook. Then again, meeting someone who just "got her," with whom she felt the same, who happened to have Cary Grant's and George Clooney's bone structure, who also was funny and kind and a doctor? Danica surmised that any woman's heart would be in danger of falling for the handsome Dr. Katz.

"How is she?" Danica asked after Lu Lu.

"Same Lu Lu." He smiled as he hung his coat. "Ready for food and love."

Danica was busy slicing the challah bread. "I'd like to see her in her own element after breakfast."

"I can arrange that." He sat down on one of the island stools. "Are you making French toast?"

"Guilty as charged." Danica smiled. "Your kitchen, wait, let me rephrase this, your *house* is set up perfectly. I have found everything I need without having to search."

"Don't go giving me the credit. I had a designer. A woman."

"Well, bless her. She knows what she's doing and is worth every penny you paid."

Sadly, Matteo put a shirt on for breakfast while she set the table and brought a heaping plate of challah French toast. They sat down together, each using butter and the syrup sparingly.

"Mmm." Matteo looked at her with a renewed admiration. "This is a good as my mom's. Not gonna tell her that, or she might never accept you."

Danica's brain temporarily short-circuited when Matteo brought up a possibility of her meeting his parents. She wasn't anywhere near that page; she was still trying to unravel her life with Grant. She simply couldn't see a scenario in which she found herself winding down one serious relationship just to jump into another.

"I'm glad you like it," she said, turning the conversation to safer waters.

She ate one last bite of the French toast, knowing full well that between the alcohol she had consumed and her "throw caution to the wind" diet, there were going to be some pounds to work off in goat yoga.

"So," she said after she dabbed her face with a napkin, "if you don't mind me asking…"

"Shoot."

"Are you Jewish or are you Christian or are you a hybrid?"

That made him smile, and after he finished chewing his bite, he said, "Hybrid."

"Explain yourself, man!"

"Well." Matteo put his napkin on his empty plate, drank a full tall glass of orange juice and said, "My mom, Mariposa, grew up on the island of Puerto Rico. She was bilingual from jump street and a very devout Christian."

He continued while she listened, truly interested in him. "My dad, Ezra, was Jewish by birth and wished that his children also be raised in the faith of Judaism."

"Two religions," she said, and then asked, "How did they navigate that?"

"Well, for my sister and I, we celebrated Christmas and Hanukkah. What kid *doesn't* want more gifts? But beyond that, sometimes the navigation was successful and other times, not so much. It's kind of a miracle that they had my sister and me and it is a testament to their love that they are still married."

"Absolutely."

"So I was raised in both religions and both cultures. I am fluent in Spanish and Hebrew and I did have a bar mitzvah."

"A coming-of-age ritual."

"Yes. Exactly." He nodded, starting to help her clear the table. "And I have a hyphenated name, Dr. Katz-Cortez, for my mother's culture. Most people just use Dr. Katz and that's fine."

Danica laughed, "Actually, I've heard you referred to as *Dr. Drop Dead Gorgeous* more often than Dr. Katz."

Matteo had a surprised expression and then he looked embarrassed.

"Surely you know this?"

"No one calls me that to my face, no."

She wrapped her arms around him, in a casual but completely comfortable manner, and looked up at him with a smile. "You can't blame people, really. You *are* spectacularly handsome."

He hugged her back and seemed more at ease with her light ribbing. He leaned down, kissed her on the lips, and then said, "And you are spectacularly beautiful."

Danica left Matteo's house feeling rejuvenated. Her time with the handsome doctor and his companion pig gave her joy in her life that had been absent for so long that she didn't even recognize that it was missing. And she couldn't blame Grant for that; she had been a dog with a bone when building her career and business and she rarely indulged in extracurricular activities. The only "hobby" she had was strategizing how to beat out her competition in the number of houses she sold and breaking dollars-per-square-foot records for her clients. As she pulled up to the main house on Hideaway Ranch, it did occur to her, upon reflection, that perhaps Grant had been lonely in their relationship. Not that this excused his tryst with Fallon, but did she have any responsibility in the initial breakdown of their relationship? Yes, she did. There were many times, too many to count really, that Grant had asked her to go sailing on his boat and take a mini vacay to the mountains. Her answer to these suggestions? One hundred percent, *no*.

When Danica arrived and parked her rental, she noticed

that Charlie and Ray were standing near the firepit with Wayne and Wayne's brother, Waylon. Just by the body language alone, this didn't seem like a "good" conversation.

She debated whether or not to join them, but then she decided that it might be something to do with the day-to-day operation of the ranch. Waylon was an invaluable member of their team.

"I would've preferred some notice, Waylon," Wayne said in a stern voice she had never heard him use before.

"I gave you notice." Waylon threw a packed duffel bag into the bed of his truck. "I told you I was going to be with Dasi."

Their first guests ever at Hideaway Ranch were a family of three and, as was the way at the ranch, Waylon and Dasi fell in love. The fact that Dasi had a neural diverse Autistic brain, high-functioning, didn't matter to Waylon; he knew that he'd have to take things slow and on a timeline that made sense for all of them. He needed to be in the same city with her, so they could date and get to know each other better.

"This is a hell of a deal." Wayne had his arms crossed in front of his body, his legs planted apart. "One hell of deal."

Charlie said, "Wayne, he did tell us that this winter would be his last in Montana."

"It's still winter the last time I checked. And I still don't know what the gosh darn hurry is all about."

Waylon had packed up the tent that had been his solitude since he came to Hideaway Ranch. Waylon was the second oldest after Wayne with Wade and Wyatt bringing up the rear. They all shared a father who was often absent, and Wayne had stepped into the role of both older brother and fill-in father.

Waylon closed the tailgate of his truck and then walked over to face his brother. "I love her, Wayne. No doubts. And when you find the person you love, being apart from them is an ache that can't be willed away."

Still sour, Wayne accepted his brother's hug before he said, "Keep me in the loop."

"I will," Waylon agreed. "And Wade is heading back here from Texas, so he can pick up any slack."

"What in the hell is going on here?" Wayne asked, exasperated. "When did I become the last person to know anything?"

Waylon hugged Charlie, Ray, and then even hugged Danica. She could see tears forming in Wayne's eyes; he turned on his heel and walked away while his brother climbed behind the wheel.

"I have to do this, Charlie," Waylon said.

"I know you do."

"Help him understand."

"I will," she said. "I promise."

Behind the wheel, Waylon rolled down his window and said, "Oh, one last thing. Wade is bringing his daughter, Phoenix, and Jillian here."

"Here?" Charlie went from completely calm to caught-off-guard in two seconds flat. "He's bringing Jillian *here*?"

"I know it's a shock," Waylon started.

"A shock? That's not a shock, Waylon, it's a dirty bomb! How long have you been sitting on this information?" Charlie asked and then held up her hand. "Never mind. I don't want to know."

"You're the best one to tell him, Charlie. Everyone knows that you are the Wayne Whisperer."

"Don't try to flatter me," Charlie said with a frown, "when you know you just dropped a steaming pile of manure at my feet."

"I'll be in touch." Waylon waved as he shifted into Drive.

When they could no longer see Waylon's taillights, Danica asked, "I take it this isn't good news."

"Nope," Charlie said, hands at her waist, a frustrated expression on her face. "Wade was supposed to get a divorce, but they just can't seem to live *with* each other or *without* each other. And now that drama is heading our way."

"We don't have to have them on the ranch." Danica said the unvarnished, practical thing. "Just because he's a Westbrook doesn't give him a free pass."

"That's tricky," Charlie said.

"Real tricky," Ray echoed.

"I don't see it that way at all," Danica said. "This is *our* land, *our* ranch and *our* livelihood. I don't particularly care that Wade is Wayne's brother and nor should you. If Wade and Jillian can't hold it together, they'll have to go."

"There's my handsome boy!" Journey smiled lovingly at her son, Oakley. "Are you doing all of your homework and listening to G-Ma?"

Her mother, Lucy, had picked out that name, G-Ma, when she found out that her daughter was expecting.

"I'm being good." Oakley grinned at her, and his sweet smile, as it always did, melted her heart.

"And your homework?" she prodded. As Oakley approached the age for him to be enrolled in school, Journey made the decision to homeschool him instead. She found that this format was the best idea for her smart-as-a-whip son, and it gave her a sense of satisfaction that she hadn't expected but loved.

"I'm ahead," her son said proudly, puffing his chest out.

"Good boy," Journey praised him. "Are you excited about coming to Montana?"

Oakley bounced out of his chair and hopped up and down in excitement. "I want to ride a horse!"

"Whoa, there, cowboy! Riding a horse? I'm not ready for that."

"But *why*?" he asked.

She didn't necessarily have a good reason and telling him that he couldn't ride because she had a scary event in her childhood didn't seem like the best idea, so Journey said, "Let's see how it goes. When you meet a horse, you might change your mind."

"Nope!" Oakley shouted. "I'm going to be a cowboy! I'm going to ride a horse!"

Oakley spun around in a circle, making himself dizzy with excitement, while Lucy appeared on the screen.

"It was your idea to write about cowboys." Her mother smiled at her with a wink.

Lucy Lamar was a stunning woman who had worked as a model in her early twenties. She was a Christie Brinkley, girl-next-door type beauty who never lacked work in her chosen industry. She had met Journey's father, Giovanni, in Milan and after a whirlwind romance, Lucy found herself pregnant by a man who was incapable of monogamy or honesty. She returned to the States, modeled as long as she could, and then moved back to her family's farm in Omaha,

Nebraska, far away from the fast-lane life of a model that had taken her around the world.

"Cowboys sell," Journey said, her mind, as it was wont to do, returning to an image of Cody Ty, "and now I know *why* they sell."

They spoke for a few minutes more before Journey put on her outerwear and headed outside. Every day she added to her notes about Montana and ranch life and the way cowboys walked, how they talked and what made them tick. Her plan of getting a head start the first week before her son and mother joined her was nearly over and she felt frustrated and overwhelmed. The option book was due, and she hadn't written her first word.

She opened the door to find Danica about to knock.

"Hey!" Danica smiled at her. "I was just coming to check on you."

"Thank you," she said, stepping out onto the porch. "I think I'm good."

"I know your son and mother are joining you next week. Anything special you need for them? I'm heading into town now."

"I can't think of anything right now," she said, "unless of course you can buy me a couple of extra weeks in Montana at the grocery store."

Danica stopped in her tracks. "Is that what you need?"

Journey cracked a smile. "I'm just behind on my book."

"Do you need an extra week or two here?"

For a moment, Journey wasn't sure they were understanding each other when it hit her. "Can I stay for an extra week or two?"

Could she be that lucky?

"Give me one sec," Danica said, taking her phone out of the back pocket of her jeans. "Hey, Charlie, did anyone book the weeks reserved for family?"

There was a pause and then Danica said, "Okay. Good. Journey would like to stay an extra week or two."

"Two would be great!" Journey interjected.

Danica ended the conversation with Charlie and then said to her, "Ask and you shall receive."

Journey was so excited that she flung herself at Danica, the prickliest of the Brand triplets, and hugged her tightly.

"You have no idea what this means to me!"

"You're welcome," Danica said rather stiffly. "Are you going to attend goat yoga today?"

"Definitely," she said, feeling like the weight of the world had just been lifted off her shoulders. "I had no idea how much I needed goat yoga in my life!"

"Preach," Danica said.

"And thank you again. I can't express what this extra time means to me."

"You're welcome. I'm happy to help," Danica said. "But we're good with just the one hug."

Matteo had become a friend. That meant something to her. They agreed to meet each other at the hiking trail when they had first met as many times as they could manage, and his easygoing, self-assured manner was something she had begun to count on. This wasn't like her at all, but she couldn't regret it.

"Hey there." Matteo found her waiting for him in her rental.

"Hi!" She knew her eyes and face lit up when she saw him, heard his voice, and she didn't try to hide it from him.

She got out of the SUV, hugged him, and then knelt down to give Lu Lu some love. "I see that she's in purple today."

"Yes," he said, "it was a rough start of the day because she doesn't have a purple Frisbee."

"That's a travesty. How dare you?" she teased him. "What was the solution?"

"After a very long talking-to, she decided to forgive me and accept the white Frisbee because, and I'm just assuming this was her logic, the white matches her lace collar."

"I love this pig."

"You love her now," he said. "Just wait until she ruins one of your peaceful mornings. Let me tell you, Lu Lu can ruin a morning, afternoon *or* evening in five seconds flat."

"She's a princess, Matteo. What do you expect?"

"I don't know," he said in a playful manner. "A little more support from you."

"If you want me to take sides, I'd have to go with—" She always seemed to laugh when she was with the doctor and his pet pig.

"Princess Lu Lu," Matteo said in a defeated tone.

"Obviously, Princess Lu Lu."

He offered her his arm and she hooked hers to his.

"You look particularly lovely today," he said.

"Thank you. You, too."

They walked together as a family of three and this stroll through the woods was exactly what she needed to clear her mind. The minute the week started, she had been bombarded with several legal headaches relating to her home and her business. Grant wasn't about to go quietly; he was going to land as many emotional and legal punches as he could, and it made her wonder if she had ever really known the man who had been a fixture in her life for years.

"You're quiet," Matteo noted.

She sighed, not wanting to infect their good time with Grant. If she let him *ruin* every single moment, or any moments for that matter, he would win. And she couldn't allow that to happen.

"It's been challenging, but I don't want to talk about it now. Is that okay?"

"Sure," he said easily. "I'm more interested in making plans for this weekend."

"Oh yeah? What did you have in mind?"

"Do you dance?"

"Not really," she said with a self-effacing laugh. "Two left feet. Do you dance?"

"Do I dance? I salsa, merengue, tango *and* Texas two-step."

"That's way out of my league. I've been known to sway side to side before." She laughed. "That's what two left feet can accomplish."

"I can't hear anything but the sound of Latin music!" He gave a little demonstration of how his hips moved. "Will you let me teach you?"

"Sure," she said. "Why not? I'd follow those hips of yours anywhere you want me to go."

Chapter Seven

Matteo had waited impatiently for Saturday night. He was back to his Friday night Shabbat dinner with his family, which kept the parents and his sister happy, but Saturday night was reserved for Danica. He understood the risk of getting closer and closer to Danica; she was in the middle of a messy breakup, her business was in LA, her entire life was in LA, and one of the last places in the world he would want to live was LA. Day by day, he was giving little pieces of his heart to Danica and there was a very good chance that he might wind up nursing some deep emotional cuts. And yet he couldn't, wouldn't, stop seeing Danica.

"Where are you taking me?" Danica said, letting him lead her to their destination.

"To a magical place," Matteo said, guiding her inside and shutting the door behind them. Then he took off her blindfold and let her see where he had taken her.

"This is your house."

"Yes, it is."

"But this is your house."

"Yes, I know," he said, "but tonight, it's not just my home. No! This is the space where I will teach you to dance."

He swayed his hips, took steps forward, two steps back. "Can you feel the energy in the room, *mi corazon*?"

"I feel something in the air but I'm not sure it's energy."

Matteo laughed, and then swung her into his arms, twirled her several times under his hand and then he captured her, dipped her back, and leaned forward and kissed her exposed neck. He lifted her back upright, spun her several more times, then brought her close, leading her through the basic steps. Her lovely face was alight with joy and fun and, yes, love. He saw it as much as he felt it in his own soul. He loved Danica Brand and she, in turn, loved him.

"Whoo!" Danica's typically perfectly coiffed hair was wispy and mussed in the sexiest of ways. "Now, that was a first."

He held her still in his arms, lifted her chin, and kissed her deeply, trying to tell her, with his lips, that he desired her, that he wanted to make love with her.

"Do you like salsa?"

"Whatever that was? I love it," she said, winded. "I didn't have to do anything but follow your lead."

"And how does that make you feel?"

"Total transparency—" she put her hand on his cheek "—that doesn't come naturally to me."

"But…?"

"I'm willing to give it another go."

Matteo picked her up and then swung her around before putting her down, twirling her again and then slowing down the pace so he could teach her the basic steps.

"Right foot, left foot," he said to encourage her. "You just needed the right teacher."

He could feel her body melting, becoming pliable and

willing. Danica was a quick study and he loved to have her in his arms. He dipped her again, kissing her neck, her ear, her lips. When he lifted her up, her eyes were half-mast, with a mixture of desire and need.

"Danica," he whispered into her ear.

"Yes, Matteo?"

"I want to make love to you."

"Okay."

"Do you want to make love with me?"

"Yes."

Matteo lifted her into his arms and carried her into his large main suite. Layer by layer, he unwrapped her clothing like he was unwrapping a present on Christmas morning or the first night of Hanukkah.

He followed her into the bed, drew the covers over their naked bodies; his hands needed to explore, to touch, to feel. Her skin was silky and warm; her long legs naturally intertwined with his as they kissed, slowly at first.

"Danica?"

"Hmm?"

"Open your eyes, please."

Danica's eyes drifted open.

"Can you see on my face that I am in love with you?"

"Well," she said after a lengthy pause, "I'm really farsighted, so everything close-up is really fuzzy right now."

Matteo lowered his head and shook it. "I was setting this up as a tender moment and you ruined it."

"No, no, no. Let's get it back. Sexy dancing, awesome seduction, the best really, and then you declare…"

And that's when her voice trailed off and it must have

dawned on her as she was recounting the events and what he had confessed.

"You said that you are in love with me."

"Yes," he said, "I am in love with you. I want you to know that yes, of course, my body wants you. How could it not? But so too does my mind, so too does my soul, so too does my heart."

"Oh, God." Danica held his handsome face in her hands, kissed his lips and his neck and his chest. "Where have you been all my life, Matteo?"

He captured her hand, kissed it lovingly. "I've been right here, waiting for you."

Danica awakened in Matteo's bed feeling womanly, well-loved and satiated. They had made love three times, savoring each other until the early hours of the morning. She leaned back against the pillows, stared up at the ceiling, hands behind her head, breasts barely covered with the sheet. This was living. This right here, right now, this was living. So many years she had been living half of a life.

She heard Matteo whistling in the kitchen, and she was lured out of bed by the smell of strong coffee. She picked up his shirt that he had thrown on the back of a chair in the corner, put it on, smelling his scent on the collar, rolled up the sleeves and, feeling decadent, she left the bedroom. She hadn't worn a man's clothing after a night of lovemaking since she was in graduate school. And it darn well felt fabulous.

"Good morning." She padded in her bare feet over to him.

"Good morning to you, my love." Matteo put his arm

around her shoulders, hugged her close and kissed her sweetly.

"I like that shirt on you," he said.

"Would you mind if I keep it?"

"Of course not," then as an afterthought, he said, "As long as it isn't some souvenir."

"Please." She made herself comfortable on one of the stools at the bar. "I put notches in my bedpost for that."

He smiled at her, winked, and then asked, "How did you sleep?"

"Do you mean when you let me sleep?"

Another wink and a smile.

"Like a baby." She smiled back, reaching in her purse for her reading glasses to take a look at her phone. "What are you cooking? It smells divine."

"Plantains. My great-grandmother's recipe."

"I can't wait," she said, turning up the volume on her phone, and that's when emails, text messages and DMs in her social media began to blow up. There were so many dings and pings and chirps, some from the few true allies she had left from her female group, but most from her CPA and her attorney.

"Wanted lady," Matteo said with a question in his voice.

Danica began reading the messages and she stood up, still scrolling, with each message building on bad news on top of more bad news and still more bad news. Matteo was watching her with curious eyes. Under any other circumstances, she would have skipped breakfast, gotten on her phone and focused on the battle with Grant back in California. This time she didn't; that said volumes to her. Matteo appeared to be occupying a space in her heart, her life, that hadn't been occupied before. With Matteo, she was learning how to focus on the moment, finding joy in that moment, and then dealing with business later. The elusive work-life balance.

"Need to talk?" he asked her.

"No." She put her phone down. "No. I don't want to infect our time with this *nonsense* back home."

"I'm here if you need me."

She nodded, watching him take the plantains off the skillet, flatten the slices on a chopping board, then dip them in a bowl of cold water. Then, Matteo turned up the heat on the skillet, cooked the plantains about a minute on each side. He transferred the plantains onto two plates, lightly salted, put the plate in front of her, and then joined her with his own plate.

Her first bite rocked her world. She didn't, as a rule, eat anything battered or fried. And she knew that Matteo avoided greasy or fried food because the man was muscular and fit.

"Well?" he asked her.

She nodded, made a noise while she was chewing to indicate that she was loving what she was tasting.

"Mmm." She nodded again.

That brought a smile to his face as he made short work of his own plantain. A moment later, her plate was clean also.

"Hats off to your great-grandmother!" She patted her stomach, which was rounder than when she had arrived in Montana. Emotional eating was something, over the years, she had deliberately avoided. When she was facing a crisis, she turned to exercise, not food, for the simple fact that her fit body was as much a part of her "uniform" as were her nails, Botox, her perfectly blond hair and her spray tan. The competition was vicious in the LA real estate market, where youth was always prized over wisdom.

"Coffee, tea or me?" he asked.

"Coffee and you," she said with a smile, bringing her plate to the sink.

They took their coffee to the couch where they had their first kiss. Their shared a comfortable silence, something that Danica had only imagined was for couples who had been married for decades.

"Penny for your thoughts," he said.

She put her empty coffee cup on a coaster on the coffee table.

"Nothing earth-shattering," she said. "We've been pretty fast and loose with our food and drinks."

He nodded.

"If I keep going down this road, all of my clothes, which were custom-made to fit me like a glove, won't fit."

"Agreed," he agreed. "I'm not ready for a dad bod just yet."

That made her laugh, and her laugh made him smile at her with so much *love* and admiration that it made her feel self-conscious in the very best of ways. He reached for her hand, and she slipped it into his, a perfect fit.

"Any regrets?" he asked her.

She knew what he was asking, and she gave him her honest answer. "No. Not at all."

He squeezed her hand. "I'm glad. This thing between us seemed to be on overdrive."

Danica had thought something similar, but the time she spent with Matteo had been quality, well-spent time. Could the same be said about her time with Grant? Now that she was experiencing this romance with Matteo, wanting to be in his presence, wanting to soak up all of the way he made her feel inside with his feelings laid bare before her, the answer was no. Matteo had told her he loved her. It had been a shock, yes, but it also enhanced the specialness of their lovemaking. Still, she also felt a sense of being out of control, being swept up in the allure of this whirlwind with Matteo. In her mind, there would be an end to this shooting star relationship with the handsome doctor. Her life was in LA—her house, her business, her connections, and her track record had been built over a decade; yes, things were murky with this conflict with Grant that she was navigating. But she was still going back when the timing was right.

"Do you want to see Lu Lu?" he asked, and she was glad that he had changed the subject.

"Did you really need to ask that question?"

"No," he laughed, giving her his hand in a gentlemanly manner, and helped her up.

Coffee cups in the sink, Danica helped Matteo prepare Lu Lu's breakfast. First, they added pellets to her large breakfast bowl. Then, they added celery, cucumbers and some pumpkin. Matteo cut up some carrots to hide in the yard for Lu Lu to encourage her to forage as was her nature.

They put on winter gear and went into the massive fenced-in area for Lu Lu. Closer to the main house, there was an eight-by-eight tiny house with a front porch and climate control.

"It cracks me up that Lu Lu is a homeowner," she said.

"It's over the top," he said, "but she just can't be inside the house for most of the day. She needs to have more freedom. More stimulation, less boredom. This was the best solution I could think of."

"Well, I love it."

Danica followed Matteo into Lu Lu's house; it was toasty warm, and Lu Lu had a giant, fluffy bed upon which to lie. When Lu Lu saw her, she oinked excitedly and waddled over for a quick chin scratch before she began to devour her breakfast.

"Well, that's another first of many firsts," Matteo said to her as she followed him out the door.

"Lu Lu never goes to anyone else before she comes to me." Matteo had the slightest ring of injury in his voice.

"Are you jealous?"

"A little, yes."

She hugged him spontaneously, loving his honesty. "I'm just the flavor of the month. She still loves you the most."

They hid carrots throughout the yard and then Matteo checked to make sure that a puzzle toy that opened different doors where a pellet was hidden inside was still there. There was also a ball that when rolled by her nose, produced a treat.

"I just love her," Danica said, standing next to Matteo, putting her arm around him as he was putting his arm around her.

"Everyone here loves you," he said, matter-of-factly.

And there it was, a feeling of dread that manifested as a queasy stomach. He was brave, this man, telling her that he loved her without any expectation for a verbal confession of her love for him. It was a gift that he gave freely, no strings attached. It brought joy into her heart but sheer panic to her mind.

"I'd better get going." She moved away from him. "I do need to answer some of these emails."

She said goodbye to Lu Lu, kissing the little pig on her snout, before she followed Matteo inside to the welcoming, warm house he called home. She got dressed with a sense of purpose and then met him at the front door. He drove her back to her condo and at the door, kissed her with a kiss that was over much too quickly.

His hand on her face, he asked, "When will I see you again?"

"On the trail?" she asked. "Tomorrow around seven?"

"It's a date."

"Will Lu Lu join us?"

Matteo looked at her with a very upset expression when he asked, "You aren't just using me to get to my pig, are you?"

That made her laugh. "I don't think so, but *maybe*?"

Matteo returned to her side, kissed her lovingly, and then said, "I love you."

He said it as if they had always said it, with such certainty. She didn't, couldn't, say those words back to him. In her mind, though, the words *te amo, I love you* in Spanish, *were* thought.

Had she fallen in love with Matteo with lightning speed? Was this a rebound? She couldn't answer those questions, so she did what she always did when something in her private life was complicated or emotional: she buried herself in her business. This lucrative distraction was her go-to, but this time, when she began to answer the flurry of emails and placed calls to her CPA and attorney and her Realtors who were struggling without her, it didn't help. And that was the confirmation of her feelings for Matteo that she hadn't really been looking for.

"I love him," Danica said, sitting still at the desk, staring at a large picture of an elk in the snow on the wall in front of her. "I actually do love him. How could I have let that happen?"

She wasn't easily scared, but her feelings for Matteo Katz-Cortez surely did frighten her.

Journey was sitting on the porch at high noon, in a spot where the sun shone down and warmed her up while also melting the snow on the ground. She had her laptop open to Chapter One and there wasn't anything written after that. The more she tried to get out of her block, the worse it seemed to get.

"At this rate, I'll be a one-hit wonder," she grumbled to herself, feeling frustrated and annoyed by her writer's block. One of the authors she admired had said in a podcast that how she dealt with writer's block was to sit at the desk, hands on the keys, and wait. So that's what she had done. Hands on the keyboard awaiting inspiration.

On her character sheet, she had fleshed out the hero of the book, Billy Dean, who had evolved since she had arrived in Montana. That was probably her biggest accomplishment to date; she knew who the hero was now—he made more sense. Billy Dean was older, with some deep lines on his face and around his gray-blue eyes. He had gray hair mixed with brown-black and he was in his mid to late fifties; he definitely had more miles on that speedometer. The hero had completely transformed, a real overhaul to fit more in Cody's image with threadbare jeans and a Stetson hat and boots that needed replacing. And yet even with all of those outward appearance changes, Billy Dean still seemed flat, lifeless, a shell of a man, and she just couldn't seem to fill him in no matter how many hours she had watched Cody go about his business at the ranch. And, yes, of course, she had taken bits and pieces of other men on the ranch, but Cody was still her muse. She was attracted to him in every way a woman could be attracted to a man, and it caught her off guard. Ever since Oakley, she had hardly dated at all. A romantic relationship didn't even make her list of priorities. Now that Oakley was ten, it had, every now and again, hit her that she was lonely for a man. Someone to hold hands with, someone to lean on when times were rough, and someone for her to love. A friend as well as a lover.

Still not inspired to write, Journey's mind went on a winding trip with images of her with Cody and her son in a park, playing and laughing, and loving each other. Did this daydreaming help with the book? Doubtful, but perhaps.

Cody Ty had done his darnedest not to think about Journey. When he saw her, he was cordial as he went about his business. Almost every day, he noticed that she would sit on the porch, in the frigid cold, and watch him work with the horses. He knew that she was at the ranch, doing research on her next book. If she was going to do real research about real life in Montana, she was going to have to get off that porch and get her hands dirty. Cody finished his training with a solid black colt with a frisky, playful personality, and after he put the colt back into the barn, he walked a direct line from the barn to the porch. The closer he got, the wider Journey's eyes were. Big, beautiful eyes, surrounded by a thick fringe of dark eyelashes creating the perfect frame. She was a beauty; rare, mesmerizing, with an electric draw for him that could no longer be ignored.

When he reached the porch, Journey had the look of a skittish filly on her face, and it seemed like she was trying to figure out an avenue of escape.

"Howdy," he said with a tip of his hat.

"Howdy," she said, then immediately chastised herself. "Darn it! I wasn't going to pick that up!"

"You can't cure your fear of horses if I can't get you off this porch."

"Oh," Journey said, and then asked, "You were serious about that?"

"Of course I was."

"Well—" the woman he had nicknamed Palomino in his mind looked around again for some sort of escape "—I appreciate it, Cody, I really do. But I don't really feel like I want to get over my fear. I mean, at least not on this trip."

"If you want to write about cowboy life, you've got to understand the one animal that has allowed cowboys like me to exist. You don't have a cowboy without a horse."

After he said those words, something seemed to dawn in Journey's mind, which showed on her lovely face. With what he read as a newfound resolve, Journey got up out of the rocking chair, crossed to the porch steps and met him on the ground. She had those long legs, and she was darn near close to looking at him eye-to-eye. But he didn't mind. He was drawn to her, and he wanted to get to know her. It was as simple as that.

"Where do we start?" she asked him, matching his purposeful stride.

"Barn work."

She seemed to falter before catching up.

He continued, "You can't know life here without getting your hands dirty."

"Well…" Journey appeared to be having second thoughts.

So he stopped. "If you don't want this kind of training, that's fine by me. But if you want to write about Montana cowboys and cowgirls, life out here in the shadow of mountains, you need to feel it, smell it, experience it, taste it. Experience firsthand what it's like to work in the snow, get up at the crack of dawn to get the animals fed hours before you've had a chance to sit down with your first cup of coffee. It takes true grit, determination, gumption and a whole lot of stupid to choose this life."

"You chose it."

"Yes, ma'am, I surely did. *And* it chose me," he said before he asked, "Question is, will you choose us?"

Chapter Eight

Danica felt like a new woman; her time in Montana, her time with her sisters, and her time, most certainly, with Matteo had given her the space and the break to get in the right headspace and figure out her next steps forward for her business and personal life in California. A renewal had occurred rather quickly. And for the short term, she was able to manage her business remotely but that was not sustainable. The only real dark cloud in her expansive blue Montana sky was, of course, Grant. This Grant was vindictive and angry, and had convinced himself as well as many people in their orbit that he was the victim. He had been forced to seek solace with Fallon. What else could he do? He was in a long-term relationship with an ambitious, driven woman, a cold fish, who was never truly ready for a family, and he had suffered in this state for over a decade. For those who had bought into that narrative, at least she knew who to weed out of her life when she returned to LA.

For now, and at least for the next few weeks she had allotted to be in Montana, she was living her best life, with a thriving ranch business with her sisters, and having a romantic tryst with the most eligible bachelor in a one-hundred-mile radius, who just happened to believe that she was a catch! And even though she still didn't know beyond this day, this hour, these minutes, what that budding relationship would hold for them in the future, she was determined to savor every single moment she had with Matteo.

When Danica arrived at Hideaway, she had been listening to salsa music and doing her best to remember the steps. She got out of her SUV, found a spot of ground near the firepit that wasn't a soggy mess, and then tried to remember the beginning steps Matteo had taught her.

"Okay, legs together, back straight, three count, step forward with the left foot, lift up the right foot, then place it down and return the left foot to its original spot."

She practice that several times, sort of getting it correct. Then she attempted the next six steps by bringing her right foot back. "Four then right foot back, five, lift the left foot, put it down and then bring my right foot back, six."

"What is happening here?" Ray and Charlie came out of the chicken coop together holding a basket of fresh eggs.

"I'm practicing salsa."

Ray and Charlie exchanged questioning looks and then Charlie asked, "Will the real Danica Brand please step forward!"

That made Danica smile and Ray and Charlie laugh.

"Okay," she admitted, "I rarely dance."

"Rarely?" her sisters asked in unison.

Now she was laughing at herself. "Okay, *never*. Until now, I suppose."

"I take it this is the doing of Dr. Dreamboat?" Ray asked.

"Oh, my Lord, that man is chiseled to perfection!" Danica had to admit.

"You're glowing," Charlie noted, then said to Ray, "She's glowing."

"Did you?" Ray stepped forward and lowered her voice.

Danica tried to keep a straight face, but failed miserably. "A lady never tells."

"That's a big fat *yes*," Charlie said.

"I can't affirm or deny," she teased them, but she knew her broad, happy smile, combined with her unusual, relaxed vibe, answered the question without any words needed.

"But—" she wiggled her eyebrows suggestively "—we have had hours and hours of riveting, amazing, mind-blowing, life-altering…"

Her sisters leaned in, waiting for some saucy secret to be shared.

"…conversations."

"What?!" Charlie shook her head with a frown.

Ray elbowed Charlie. "I suppose *conversation* is a new euphemism for sex."

Danica shrugged with a very happy smile. "I suppose it could be."

"You go girl." Ray gave her a high five. "You damn well deserved it."

Danica had to agree. This romance with Matteo was what she needed to repair her deflated ego, but she knew, in her heart, that this connection to Matteo ran deeper than a fling. He had captured her heart, along with her body and her soul. Even if they couldn't make a full-time relationship work, how she felt inside would not change. In fact, Danica was absolutely certain that this love she had for Matteo would never fade, that even if she met another man in LA, she would always carry Matteo in her heart.

They headed toward Charlie's renovated cottage that had been the cabin their great-great-grandparents had built and with Wayne's help, Charlie had lovingly restored. She lived in that cabin now and everyone who knew Charlie knew that she would live the rest of her life in that cabin.

Bowie, Charlie's beefy, muscular pit bull–rottweiler mix, met them at the door, wearing a plastic collar around his neck.

"Hi, good boy." Ray leaned down to pat Bowie on his head. "He looks so miserable."

"I know." Charlie stripped off her coat and hung it on the horseshoe-themed coatrack that Wayne had built for her. "He's always been so active, this surgery on his leg has been really hard on him, and it's been hard on us. He whines, he barks, I think he feels that if he has to be miserable, then so too should everyone else in his orbit!"

"Hi, there, Hitch." Danica reached down to pick up the older cat that Wayne had with him for several years while he traveled from job to job, never settling anywhere until he found a forever home with Charlie at Hideaway Ranch.

"Hitch is the only one who can suffer Bowie now." Charlie let them into the small quaint entryway. There were many parts of the cabin that were original, including the stone hearth built by their ancestors, and much of the wood on the walls was salvaged.

"It amazes me what you've done here, Charlie." Danica sat down at the small square table that Wayne built using some of the wood from felled trees. At one time, this cabin was in horrid condition, taken over by trees, animals, vines and weeds.

"Coming from you," her sister said, "that's high praise."

"I mean—" Danica ran her hand over the butcher-block table handmade for the home "—Wayne is a master carpenter."

"Coffee?" Charlie asked them.

They nodded yes, so Charlie put on a pot before joining them at the table. Bowie, looking depressed about his collar, lay down on the floor and Hitch sat in a bread loaf position next to him.

"Good boys," Charlie said. "Such good boys."

When the coffee was ready, Charlie delivered three piping-hot coffees in chunky mugs for her sisters to enjoy.

"Now it's time to discuss some business," Danica said. "I've been looking at real estate prices in Big Sky, and I can't believe what I'm seeing. There have to be more multimillionaires *here* than in California, period."

"What?" Ray asked, looking stunned.

"Take a look at this." Danica pulled up one of the popular sites for advertising homes for sale. "Fourteen million, twenty-two million. The only property under one million is a studio condo. I can only imagine what our ranch is worth."

"No," Charlie frowned severely. "No."

"I'm not saying sell, Charlie," Danica said firmly, "but we must raise our prices. We are leaving money on the table, and we can't."

"Okay," Charlie said.

"And we have to build more cabins," Danica added.

"Summer is really short," Ray said, "so we'll have to be ready the minute the weather takes a turn toward spring."

"Let's get set up with our architect and figure out locations, layouts, designs," Danica said.

"It makes sense." Charlie uncrossed her arms.

"I promise you, Charlie," Danica said, "I'm not angling to sell. I just want us to be profitable, and looking at what's available, with these celebrity mansions eating up the small amount of land there is to be had around the ski resort, we can ask for more. We've got to be competitive."

All three of them agreed on that and then tied up any loose ends regarding the ranch.

"I'm excited to have Journey's son and mother to arrive at the beginning of next week," Charlie said, "and they have extended their stay for two weeks."

"Oh!" Ray exclaimed. "I ordered her book! It's really good. I'm going to ask for her to autograph it."

"She's our first author, so that's supercool," Charlie said. "A feather in our cap."

They closed the minutes for the ranch; after their business was completed, and after a coffee refill, Danica asked, "How's Dean?"

Ray sighed heavily. "Devastated. He just seems *lost*. The girls, especially Paisley, are taking it very hard. We've lost both of our parents, and we know how it feels."

"Horrible," Danica said.

"Unmoored," Charlie added.

"Nothing I say seems to help," Ray admitted. "He's barely eating. He's barely sleeping. He's lost a lot of weight."

"Do you think he'd seek help?" Danica asked.

Charlie nodded and added, "I was thinking the same thing, Ray."

Another deep breath in, Ray said, "I've thought about that, and if he doesn't rebound—I just want him to mourn the loss of his father without losing touch with his own life."

"Of course not," Charlie interjected.

"I think we will have to figure something out. He needs to be there for the girls. As much as I love them and they love me, they need their father. This is the first major loss his girls have experienced. Paisley was two and Luna was still in the oven cooking when they lost Dean's mother."

"It's so hard," Danica said. "I just hope that Dean can find a path back."

"Let us know if there's anything we can do to help," Charlie said.

"Yes, please do," she agreed.

They finished their coffees, put on their winter gear, and then headed back outside. Ray asked, "When are you heading back to California?"

"Kicking me to the curb already?" Danica laughed.

Ray put her arm around her shoulders, "Never. I would actually like for you to move back. It would be wonderful to have all of us back in the same zip code."

"Well, I don't imagine that will happen," she said. "I think that I will have to head back in a week or two. Grant is being awful, just awful, and I have to show up and show him that I'm not afraid of him or his lawyers. I have to get into the ring so I can pull a Rocky move and knock him out!"

"You can do it, Danny," Charlie said encouragingly.

"Not even a fair fight, really," Ray agreed. "You can run circles around him while wearing stilettos and a pencil skirt."

Danica stopped, asked for a group triplet hug, and realized in that exact moment that she had built what she still loved in California, but Hideaway Ranch, for the first time in the longest time, felt like home to her. Her sisters felt like home. And so too did Matteo Katz-Cortez.

Journey felt sweaty underneath her winter clothing and when that cold Montana air hit her exposed skin on her neck or her nose, it actually hurt. She hadn't been exactly sure what Cody would be like up close and personal, and now she knew. He was serious, goal-oriented, often abrupt and unsmiling, and he was proud of his cowboy lifestyle.

"Let me show you how to use that pitchfork," Cody said, reaching out for the rather heavy pitchfork in her hand. "You've got to put some muscle behind it."

"I was putting muscle behind it," she objected to his characterization.

"You've got to be efficient and quick, because all of these here animals are eating and getting ready to make some manure and you'll still be on the first go-around."

Journey frowned at him. "I think I was doing the exact same thing you were just doing."

"Nope."

She took back the pitchfork and did the *exact same thing* she was doing before the demonstration, and scooped up some manure from the goats' stalls, put it into a wheel-barrow, and wished she had chosen a different muse. As it turned out, Cody Ty could be grumpy, annoying *and* bossy. He was, admittedly, very handsome in a rugged, rough-around-the-edges cowboy way; she liked the experience on his face. His hands were often ungloved, large, and calloused. But—and this was very important—he was a royal pain in the backside.

"What now?" she asked with an attitude that would rival her ten-year-old when he didn't want to pick up his room.

"Water buckets need to be dumped and cleaned."

She was already tired, but now it was a challenge and she refused to give in to the need to take a hot shower and crawl into bed for the rest of the day.

She went back into the goat stalls, grabbed the water buckets, which were heavier than they looked, groaned when she lifted one up, waddled toward the gate, spilling water along the way, and then she tripped over the water hose, dropped said bucket, and the dirty water in the bucket spilled out on the gravel aisle of the barn.

Cody gave her the side-eye and she really, truly and honestly wanted to throw that bucket at him. No one, not even her ex-husband, had gotten under her skin as quickly as Cody Ty had managed to do.

When he came over to help her, she held out her hand, and said, "Back off, cowboy, I've been given a job to do and I'm gonna gosh darn do it!"

That was when the tiniest glint of respect came into his deep-set eyes as he held up his hands in surrender. She had put a point on the imaginary scoreboard as she little by little, inch by inch, cleaned all of the buckets and put them back, and then filled them with water. By the time she was done with that chore, the goats had already left her some manure and urine. And then that was when she broke down.

"What kind of life is this, anyway?" she asked no one in particular. "This isn't romantic! This is dirty and smelly and exhausting."

In her moment of frustration, she had backed up and then she felt a nibble on her ear. She screamed, jumped, spun around, and realized that one of the horses had tried to turn her into a snack.

"Okay! That's it. You win." She leveled Cody with her best stern mother look that she had honed over the years. "I'm out of here!"

"Whoa, whoa, whoa," Cody said. "Don't go."

She crossed her arms. "Why should I stay? I'm not here to be the butt of your jokes. I have a book to write—my son and my mother are coming at the beginning of next week and I haven't written one word!"

"Now, just take a minute to cool off. I was just giving you a taste of reality."

"Okay. I get it," she said sourly. "Nothing but hard work, more hard work and more hard work."

"That's the life," Cody said, "but is that all you got?"

"What do you mean?"

"What do you smell?"

"Seriously?"

He nodded. "What do you smell?"

"Besides manure?" she asked. "A sweet smell."

"Alfalfa," he said. "Good fiber for the horses and the goats. What do you hear?"

"Other than you bark at me?"

"Yes. Other than that."

She closed her eyes and listened, and then opened her eyes. "Chewing. The sounds of the animals—the horses blowing air through their noses, the goats talking to each other."

"What do you see?"

"Beauty everywhere," she said softly. "The horses are

beautiful, the goats are adorable, and the donkeys have those amazing ears."

"What do you feel?"

She thought about it, and then she realized, besides exhausted, sweaty, cold and frustrated, she felt "free."

"That's right." Cody nodded, and he seemed pleased with her thoughts. "It's a hard life, but it's a good life. This is one of the last places in this country that a man—or a woman—can feel *free*."

Journey felt oddly *changed* from this exercise with Cody. This was impactful and while she certainly wasn't going to puff up his already high self-esteem by telling him this, ranch life felt four-dimensional, not one-dimensional.

"I suppose I should thank you," she said begrudgingly.

That was when he smiled at her and she could see that smile reach his eyes. "Don't thank me if you don't want to."

"Okay," she said, "I take it back."

Then he laughed and she liked the sound of it, but she now was pretty sure she needed a different muse.

"That's all right." He nodded, leaning against the pitchfork. "If you learned something that helps you along the way, that's good enough for me. I've always loved to read and being that you are an author, that's impressive to me."

And there it was, Cody flipping the script and making her feel bad for being salty.

"Well, thank you."

They stood in silence for a second or two and then Cody asked her, "Was this a onetime deal or do you want to learn more?"

The next words came out of her mouth without much

thought behind it. "Actually, I'd like to learn more about you."

He stared at her, and she stared at him, and then he broke eye contact, coughed a couple of times and said, "Well, I'm flattered. But you can probably find out all you need to know about me on the internet."

"No. I can't."

Cody looked down at the toe of his boot, seeming to mull something over. "If you need to know more, you'll have to get to know horses."

"I know that this one—" she pointed to the small sorrel horse that had tried to take a bite out of her ear "—tried to bite me."

"Rose?" he scoffed. "She wasn't trying to bite you. She was saying 'hi.'"

Journey didn't believe that for a second, so she just shook her head.

"They're herbivores."

"Okay, so maybe she didn't try to bite me—"

"She most definitely didn't try to bite you."

"Why is it so important for me to learn horses to know you?"

"Because," Cody said sincerely as he rubbed Rose's ears affectionately, "they are as much a part of who I am as my name, the color of my eyes or the wrinkles on my face."

"One doesn't go without the other."

"That's right."

Journey said, "Okay. How do I get started?"

"You already did," he said. "I just wanted you to be with them, look at them, see how they moved, how they spoke to you and to each other."

"Impressive," she said. "You got me to start without the anxiety."

"Yes, ma'am," he said. "You'll need steel-toed boots."

"Okay."

"Then I'll see you tomorrow," he said, "not on the porch."

"Yes." She nodded, feeling that she had just been in the company of greatness. "Thank you."

"It was my pleasure."

She raised an eyebrow at him and asked, "But was it, though?"

Cody felt like a real heel. All of his defenses were on high alert. He hadn't been involved with a woman in a very long time, not that he hadn't had options. There were always plenty of options. And he'd even tried his hand at marriage a time or two. Even though most people would assume that champion cowboy Cody Ty Hawkins was a ladies' man, sleeping his way through the women at the rodeo circuit who just seemed to get younger and younger with each passing year—that wasn't him. He was a romantic, in it for love, and he had his heart squashed by a woman he had loved from the time he was a teenager in Tennessee. Lola Wilson, his second wife, had run off with his best friend while he was on the rodeo circuit. He lost his best friend and his wife all in one shot. So he did what he did best— he cut ties with the past and moved on into his future. The divorce was quick, and he didn't get invited to their wedding. He supposed he drank himself into a stupor a time or two until he finally dried out and a chance meeting with Wayne Westbrook, one of the finest cowboys he had ever met, changed the direction of his life.

"How are the babies coming along?" Wayne stopped by the barn to say hi.

"They're a fine group," Cody said. "I've given my heart to too many women, but I have to say, this little filly right here? I've gone and done it again."

"Love's like that, isn't it?" Wayne said. "You don't know when it's going to strike."

Cody's mind immediately went to Journey Lamar. That woman had run over him with a steamroller and flattened him but good. "It sure does."

"Well," Wayne said, "if you've got to have her, just let me know. We'll work something out for you."

"I just might," Cody said. "I just might."

Wayne shook his hand and then headed off, but Cody called him back. "I've offered to work with the author."

"Journey?"

Cody nodded. "She's researching ranch life."

"I heard that," Wayne said, his expression registering confused. "If you have time, I've got no objection."

"I just wanted to keep you in the loop, is all."

Wayne gave him a nod. "Consider me in the loop."

Cody put a harness on the little filly that had caught his eye and walked her out to the round pen. She was a real good-looking horse, and she was willing, curious and intelligent. In the best of ways, this little filly reminded him of Journey. She had some grit; he wasn't so sure there for a minute or two, but when she was getting hot under the collar, he saw a woman who would fight her way to the top, like the cream that she was.

She was dangerous to him; he didn't need another heartbreak. And yet he was drawn to her like that bee to honey.

When Charlie told him that the author wanted to get to know him better, to understand cowboy life, he had been flattered but not at all interested. He'd already had his life dissected, shredded and thrown out to the sharks who took a kernel of truth and turned it into a scandal. He was famous; had been for more than half of his life. But fame was an illusion, and he never found any happiness in it. So, it was a "thank you but no thank you" situation. And then she caught his eye and, yes, of course, she was beautiful. He saw her outer beauty; he was more impressed with the kindness, the honesty, the vulnerability in her eyes. She was, to his mind, an open book. She wore her heart on her sleeve, and it made perfect sense that she was a romance author. Journey Lamar wasn't jaded like him; in fact, he believed they were polar opposites. He believed she was resilient in a way that he could never be.

When they reached the round pen, Cody forced his mind to the present moment so he could give his full attention to the lovely filly prancing about, snorting, kicking up her heels and then racing around him while he waited patiently for her to get her abundant energy out. When she slowed down, he caught her eye, and then backed up, giving the filly an opportunity to willingly come to him as he stepped back slowly. Horses were herd animals with a hierarchy; in the round pen, it was his job to show the horse with him that he was the leader of the herd.

"Good girl," Cody praised the filly when she stopped, looked at him, and then turned her body toward him, and then she walked over to him.

"There you are, sweet one." Cody scratched her behind her ears, speaking to her in soft tones.

"I think I'm going to have to declare my love for you, my beauty," Cody whispered to the young horse. "I'd rather give up a month's pay than lose you."

And that was settled; he would claim her tomorrow and then he would be thinking on a name. The filly rubbed her head against him; for him, that was her accepting him into her life.

"We belong to each other," he told her as he put the halter back on her slender head. "I promise to take care of you for the rest of your life."

Chapter Nine

"I love her," Matteo told his sister. For as long as he could remember, Estrella was the one person he told his deepest thoughts and secrets.

"I'm sorry, what?" his sister asked in a raised voice. "That's too fast, Matteo. Way too fast."

"You said that you fell in love with Lars the first time you met."

"Well, yeah, I did," she admitted, "but I…"

She stopped, thought for a moment, and then said, "Okay, you have me there. But this feels different. Lars and I hadn't built lives on polar opposite coasts."

"And what if you had?"

Estrella thought for another moment. "One of us would have to move. Are you willing to give up your practice, something you have built for nearly two decades?"

"I don't know. I'll cross that bridge when I get to it," he said. "For now, I just want to enjoy this feeling I have for Danica without putting a bunch of obstacles in our way."

"You know I support you. I always support you. I'm just worried," Estrella said. "What do you think the folks will think?"

"They'll love her."

"I hope so."

"They'll love her," he said again, "because *I* love her."

He said goodbye to his sister, understanding Estrella's concerns, and thinking maybe he should discuss moving the relationship forward; maybe he should consider moving this relationship with Danica to a more defined place. Yes, it was very early, and yes, Danica was in the midst of a messy breakup. But they had a soul-to-soul connection, one that he had never experienced before. And he believed that Danica, while perhaps less certain, returned his feelings.

Matteo prepared a health-conscious meal, a cauliflower steak with Thai-inspired sauces cooked in a skillet, flavored with olive oil, cilantro, a pinch of brown sugar and, for a taste bud surprise, finely chopped peanuts.

When the doorbell rang, he felt unusual nerves in his stomach; his sister, who historically had been correct in all things, had gotten into his head. He did feel rushed in that Danica's stay in Big Sky was most likely coming to an end sooner rather than later, and he felt compelled to formalize their relationship because, in his experience, distance did not make the heart grow fonder. He opened the door and was greeted with the woman who had stolen his heart. Matteo could see in her face that she was as excited to see him as he was to see her. The moment she stepped out of the cold into the warmth of his home fueled by a lovely, romantic fire, he took her in his arms and kissed her.

"I'm glad to see you," he said, helping her out of her coat.

Once free of it, she turned back to him, put her hand on his face, looked at him with an expression that he read as budding love, and she kissed him, with the same passion he had just kissed her with.

"I'm glad to see you, too," Danica said, walking into the living room. "It smells delicious. And the fire. Thank you."

"Of course," he replied. "I want to keep you coming back for more."

"Between the ranch and your place, I've barely spent any time at the rental," she said, then added, "Not that I'm complaining."

"I'm glad to hear that." He poured her a glass of wine.

Danica picked up the wineglass, swirled the white wine around, sniffed it and then gave it the tiniest of tastes. "It's dry. It's a bit spicy. Austrian gruner vletliner?"

Matteo laughed, amazed at her palate. "Ten for ten, currently undefeated.

"Here's to you, Danica." He held out his glass to her.

"Here's to us," his date said, gently touching her glass to his.

It was a moment like this, a phrase such as this, using the word *us,* that gave him hope that he wasn't rushing things. And yes, he had said the L-word already, but it hadn't scared her off. They had met regularly for a hike on the trail where they first met, she absolutely adored Lu Lu, and Lu Lu returned that feeling to Danica. They texted several times during the day and they had shared a *physical* chemistry unlike anything he had experienced before.

"Dinner is served," he said after he plated the dinner fare.

"Matteo," his date said, "this is beautiful."

"I hope it tastes as it looks." He joined her.

Neither of them wanted to overindulge on the wine, so after one glass, they both switched to water with lemon.

"Mmm." Danica took her first bite. "Mmm!"

He took his first bite and he had to agree; this was one of his best meals.

Danica laughed and he loved to look at her beautiful face with the deepest ocean-blue eyes, a pert nose, and her signature ice-blond hair. She was stunning, a knockout, but her looks were only a small part of why he loved her. He loved her kindness, her intelligence, and yes, her ambition. She loved her work and so did he. And she loved Lu Lu. She understood why the adorable, but naughty and difficult-to-raise, pig held a special place in his heart. And because he had a lot of first dates that never turned into second dates, meeting Danica was the lightning bolt he had been waiting for. A big flashing sign with blinking lights and a red arrow pointing to Danica, saying *this is the one*, *Matteo*.

They finished their meals and transitioned to the living room to sit in front of the fire. Danica naturally sat close to him and leaned her back against his body. He kissed her cheek, and held her in his arms, and it felt like the right time to express his desire to define their relationship. But Estrella was in his head, holding up a yellow caution light, and that gave him pause. Estrella was his biggest fan, and she was never one to deliberately put up stumbling blocks in his way. Perhaps he *should* slow down, enjoy each moment with Danica without the added pressure of formalizing a relationship. She was, after all, going through a stressful breakup. And while Danica preferred to keep her legal and financial wranglings with Grant away from their time together, he was noticing subtle signs of frustration and anger that gave him a clue to her inner thoughts when it came to her relationship with Grant imploding.

Danica sighed happily in his arms, and he kissed her on the top of her head and drew her in closer.

"Thank you," she said to him.

"What for?"

"Everything, really," she said. "When I walk through that door, I can leave everything in my life in California at the doorstep. Your home, your arms, are safe places for me."

"You're welcome," he said, his mind circling back to what Estrella had said to him just a couple of hours ago. He felt ready to take things to the next level, but now, hearing how Danica felt about him, about his house, about his company, it didn't sound like a permanent home for her. In fact, it sounded as if she wasn't thinking of him seriously at all.

That night they cuddled, he held her in his arms until she fell asleep, and then he got out of bed, feeling like a lovesick fool. He needed to slow down, way down. And he might as well get started with that new leaf right away. He had told Danica that he loved her, but she had never returned that sentiment. He had put his heart out there, but he was alone in that risk.

Matteo donned his winter clothes, walked out to the small cottage built just for Lu Lu. He opened the door, walked into the warmth, and then sat down on the ground. Lu Lu, always willing for snuggles, got up, came over to him, and then plopped down next to him, rolled to the side, and asked for belly scratches.

"You've always been my girl, haven't you, Lu Lu?"

As if she understood him perfectly, she oinked a couple of times and then took her scratches quietly. After an hour of belly scratches, Matteo returned to his own bed, without a clue how to move forward with Danica but knowing that it was time for them to at least have a conversation about whether a long-term relationship was even on the list of possibilities. Or was he just a diversion for Danica while she ended her relationship with Grant? Either way, the dawn of the next morning would be, quite possibly, a pivotal one.

Danica awakened feeling refreshed from a night of sleeping in Matteo's king bed. They hadn't made love but that didn't matter. Her feelings for Matteo certainly went beyond the physical, but admittedly, the handsome doctor did have an incredible physique and she liked it particularly when he wore a form-fitting T-shirt that showed off every bulge of the biceps and the curves of his pecs. He was a truly fine example of a chiseled man from his face to his form. She swung her legs out of bed, ran her fingers through her hair, put on his pajama top as was a new habit for her, and then padded out to the kitchen, lured by the smell of strong coffee.

"Good morning," she said to Matteo, walking over to him with a hug and kiss.

"Morning," he said, but seemed a tad standoffish. "How'd you sleep?"

"Like a very happy log." She took the offered coffee with a spritz of cream and no sugar. "But I suppose, technically, a log doesn't have feelings."

Matteo laughed at her joke, but that smile disappeared in record time. "Is everything okay?"

"Well, there is something I need to speak with you about."

"Oh, God." Her fingers on the mug tightened noticeably. "You're married."

"No," he said, and then repeated, "No."

"You got someone pregnant?"

The expression on Matteo's face made her immediately want to take that back.

"No," he said, "I'm not Grant."

She looked down at her coffee for a moment and then met his gaze. "Sorry. That was so…wrong."

He nodded, but there was definitely something serious on his mind and her body defaulted to the recent trauma of Grant and Fallon, and she just wished that Matteo would cut to the chase.

"There is something I want to discuss, but it doesn't involve another woman. Or another man, I suppose I should say."

She breathed in deeply, let it out, and then sat up straight, shoulders back, prepared to hear something she did not want to hear.

Matteo was about to tell her what was on her mind when her phone started buzzing and moving across the marble island. She looked at it and so did Matteo.

"I'm sorry," she said, "I have to take this."

She answered the phone, stood up, and listened to her attorney tell her the latest in the negotiations with Grant regarding the business and her estate.

"What are you saying?" she asked, pacing now. "Are you telling me that he isn't willing to let me buy him out?"

"Yes," her attorney said.

She felt her throat closing, her temperature rising and her mind short-circuiting. "Why?"

"He believes that the business has been undervalued and he wants more."

"He wants more?!" she asked, her voice raised. "He wants more?! Well, I would like him to be out of my life! That's what I want."

"Danica," her longtime attorney said calmly, "you need to be here, in LA, so we can fight this together. The longer you are away, the longer Grant seems to be digging in his heels."

"He wants a face-to-face with me?"

"Yes," he said, "and so does the arbitration judge. You need to fly back today."

Danica was quiet while her brain tried to digest what her attorney had said. Every day seemed to bring her one step closer to her return to California, but there was a part of her that didn't want to go back to that life. There was so much pain attached to it: feelings of betrayal, heartbreak, disbelief and pain without description for the children that they had planned to have with each other. How many people did she have to "unfriend" or "unfollow" on social media when they "liked" pictures of Grant's sonograms of the baby he was now having with Fallon? It was a kick in the gut, and it caused a new level of emotional pain that she hadn't known existed.

"Okay," she finally said, sinking into Matteo's couch. "I'll catch a flight today."

"None available," he said, "I already checked. I've arranged for a private jet. A driver will take you from Big Sky to Bozeman. You'll catch your jet there. Paramount Business Jets."

"Okay." She sounded as deflated as she felt.

"I'll send a driver to pick you up when you arrive in LA."

The call ended, and Danica just sat still, knowing that

she had to move quickly, go to the condo, pack up her necessities and then head off to Bozeman.

She was staring at her phone, dazed, when Matteo joined her on the couch and put his strong arm around her, giving her the comfort she so desperately needed.

"What can I do?"

She shook her head, wanting to stay in this moment instead of heading back to LA. "Nothing."

Matteo was a man, a doctor, who was used to being able to solve problems. But this was a problem only she could solve, along with her team of attorneys and CPAs. She stood up, as did he, and she accepted his hug for a few minutes before she stepped away.

"I…" she began, and stopped. Then started again. "I can't—" she pointed to him "—be…" She stopped again, and then she shook her head, with what she knew was a sorrowful expression. "I have to go. I'm sorry. I am."

Danica raced to the bedroom, stripped off the pajama top and quickly dressed. She ran out of the bedroom, looked at Matteo, before she pivoted, returned for the pajama top that still smelled like him, and asked, "Can I take this with me?"

Until that moment, until that question, Danica could see Matteo drawing back from her. Her life was a mess, but the times with him were small pockets of joy and she didn't want this *entanglement* with Grant, a man who she now understood had an axe to grind with her, to ruin her relationship with Matteo. Their relationship was pure and lovely and uncomplicated and other than her sisters, Matteo was the only one she felt that she could trust. That made him invaluable to her.

"Will you come back?" Matteo asked as he enveloped her in one of his amazing hugs.

"Yes," she said. "I'm only packing a carry-on. Grant is still living in my house, and we have yet to agree to the terms on that property.

"I have to go," she said, fighting back tears. "I will miss you."

Matteo took her face in his hands and stared into her eyes with nothing but care and acceptance. "I am only a phone call away. If you need me, call, text, video chat."

"You promise that you're okay to drive?" Matteo asked. "I can drive you to Bozeman if you'd like."

"Thank you, Matteo, You are such a thoughtful man. My CPA is sending me a driver."

He helped her into her thick coat and scarf before she put the strap of her purse over her shoulder.

"Until next time," she said, accepting one last sweet kiss from her charming doctor.

"Let me know that you've arrived safely," Matteo said.

"I will," she promised before she backed out of his drive, then she stopped, remembering something important.

She rolled down the driver's window, and called out to him, "Give Lu Lu kisses for me! And please send videos!"

That was the moment when Matteo appeared to be his normal self. Whatever subject he wanted to raise had seemed to disappear when she needed comfort. And once she mentioned Lu Lu, his smile returned to his face.

"I will," he promised, standing in his driveway until she could no longer see him in the rearview mirror.

Even though she hadn't been able to put voice to it, she did feel genuine love for Matteo. It was too soon to know how things would pan out between them, but that didn't take away the feeling she had for him in her very bruised and trampled heart.

"As soon as humanly possible, I will be back." She said aloud to herself the words she hadn't been able to say to him. "And next time, I hope to have excised Grant from my house, my business, my mind *and* my heart. I deserve that. And so does Matteo."

"Hi, my handsome boy!" Journey said when Oakley answered her video call.

"Hi, Mom." Oakley grinned at her. "Three more days!"

"I can't wait. I miss you too much."

"I miss you!"

"Do you know what you want to do when you get here?"

Oakley jumped out of his chair and hopped up and down in excitement. "I want to ride a horse!"

"No," she said quickly and emphatically.

"Hi, sweetie." Her mom came into view. "How's the book coming along?"

"Okay. At least I've got some words on the page."

"That's awesome! I'm proud of you."

"Thanks, Mom," she said. "What's up with Oakley's idea to ride a horse?"

"Well, I made an error," her mom said with a guilty look on her face. "I might have mentioned Cody Ty's name."

"He's incredible, Mom," Oakley said, squeezing in between her grandmother and the iPad. "I've watched almost all of his videos!"

Journey didn't know quite what to say. She was happy that Oakley was still excited to come to Montana, but the idea of him wanting to ride a horse because of Cody Ty made her ill.

"G-Ma! Can I go play video games next door with Misty?"

"You've finished your schoolwork, so yes."

"Bye, Mom!" Oakley said with his endless well of energy.

"I'll see you soon!"

"Okay!" he yelled out of the frame.

"I love you!" she called out just before she heard the front door slam.

"Mom—" she dropped her head into her hands "—I don't want him on a horse."

"Look," her mother said, "I'm sorry that I mentioned Cody Ty and now he's Oakley's hero. But I don't think it's a good idea to make him afraid of horses because you had a traumatic event."

Journey breathed in through her nose and then blew it out slowly from her mouth. "I suppose you have a point…"

"I know you want to put him into a hermetically sealed bubble. But you can't. He's got to navigate this world just like anybody else."

"I suppose."

"He'll be fine, sweetie. And I could think of tons of people he could look up to that we'd disapprove of. From what I've seen of Cody Ty, he promotes the value of hard work, perseverance and family."

"He's not a saint," Journey said, now having mixed feelings about the champion cowboy.

Her mother had a keen eye and asked, "So no longer your muse?"

"Well, I wouldn't go that far."

"How far would you go? Is this still a safe place for Oakley?"

"Yes, of course it is," she said quickly, "and spending time with Cody has helped me break through my writer's block for now."

"So what's the problem?"

She shrugged, wishing she hadn't even given her mom an inkling of her feelings for, and about, Cody.

"He can be..." She paused, and then said, "Abrupt."

"Okay."

"And bossy."

Her mom raised an eyebrow at her, and no words were needed.

"And he's always pushing me to get my hands dirty, get a full picture of ranch life, etc., etc.!"

"He sounds like a good man who's trying to help you out."

"How can I be losing this contest with a man you've never even met!"

"I didn't raise you to be a snowflake, Journey."

"How do you even know that term?"

"I know things," her mom said with a wink. "Now get back on that book."

"I will. I am. But..."

"But what?"

"I think it sounds stupid."

"Journey?!" her mom exclaimed. "Why would you even think that?"

Journey didn't want to admit that the reader reviews had been so harsh. Her first book felt like the best she could have written; she wanted her characters to feel as if they could be the reader's best friend, or sister, or mother.

"I just have lost my confidence, I suppose."

"No," her mother said. "No, ma'am. I know exactly what is getting into your head and you need to put those reviews in the trash where they belong. Your editor loved your first book, so much that she's willing to buy another!"

Journey nodded, and she knew that her mother had a point, but the reviews were stuck in her mind, and it was difficult to eject them from her brain.

"Don't let people live in your mind rent-free, Journey." Her mother added, "This is your chance to live your dream and write for Harlequin. If you give the power to these unknown people, who may have motives for rating your first book so low that have nothing to do with the quality of your book and everything to do with their own jealousy, they win and you lose!"

After a moment of reflecting on her mother's words, she looked up, nodded her agreement, and said, "You're right, Mom."

That made her mother laugh. "Boy, would I love to have pushed Record on this conversation!"

"I'll never admit to it, Mom. I'll take this conversation to the grave."

"Well," her mother said with the unconditional love she had always given to her and to Oakley, "just as long as you take it to your heart first."

Chapter Ten

"Where are your steel-toed boots?" Cody asked her in that razor-sharp tone that he used all of the time.

"Still at the store, I suppose," she replied, chin up, hands resting on her hips, and looking him right in the eye.

Her stance only served to tickle him, not annoy him, and Cody surprised her, as he often did, when he said, "Come on, then. I'll take you to Bozeman."

Now frozen in her spot, she couldn't quite figure her next move. Yes, he was bossy, annoying, frustrating, but he was a nice man underneath his gruff way of being in the world. She did have him at a disadvantage because she knew more about him from researching him online than he most likely would ever know about her.

He waved at her to follow him, and she decided to accept the ride. Steel-toed boots weren't a regular fashion need in her wardrobe. Also, whenever she spent time with Cody, no matter how prickly he could be, she was given insight into her cowboy character. That was invaluable to her.

Cody walked with a slight limp and his legs were more bowed than she'd ever seen. You could imagine a life in the saddle for a man with that bow at the knee. His eyes crinkled deeply when he thought something was funny, and his bushy handlebar mustache, a relic of the past, seemed to suit him particularly well. He was brutally honest, up early, to bed late, and he had a connection with the animals in his care that she had never witnessed before. She had tried to piece together a whole picture of Cody with the man she was getting to know now with the man she had researched online. But Cody was still a mystery that kept her intrigued and coming back for more.

"This is an impressive truck." She climbed up into the passenger seat.

"Thank you kindly."

His truck was a forest-green GMC Sierra 3500 Duramax Diesel V8; the inside was luxury from the stitching to the power seats that offered a massage. Cody Ty seemed to her to have few worldly desires and he certainly didn't match the glitz and glamour country celebrity he had apparently been in his younger years. He was humble in that way, but when it came to creature comforts, that's where the money was spent. His decked-out travel trailer was impressive from the outside and if it had any upgrades similar to the truck that hauled it from place to place, it had to be impressive on the inside.

"Are you sure you have the time to take me?"

"I've got all the time in the world if I say it's so," Cody said. "I don't punch a time clock. Never have—if God blesses me, I never will.

"How's the book coming?" he asked.

She breathed in and said on a sigh, "I started, so that's an improvement."

"Have I been helpful?"

Journey glanced over at him, wondering how honest she needed to be.

Then he chuckled at her silent thought process, and he added, "Besides the fact that I'm a pain in your hind parts."

"You are," she said, "a pain in the hind parts. In more ways than one."

He went straight from a chuckle to full laugh. "I knew you had it in you."

"Had what?"

"Fight, gumption, whatever you want to call it." He clarified, "A cowboy—or cowgirl—can't make it in life if they don't have it. Make sure your characters have it."

"I will."

They rode in silence for a mile or two, listening to a country music station that she wouldn't have listened to on her own, but she discovered that she liked it, and she said as much to Cody.

"It's good music. I was raised on it," he said, "but I like symphonies and operas the most."

Now she was actually staring at his profile.

He glanced over at her with a smile, and said, "Doesn't fit the image?"

"No," she agreed, "but it makes you even more interesting."

"Happy to help."

And she could tell that he meant it. The more depth she could find with Cody, the more round, balanced and believable her character could be.

"My son, Oakley, he's coming out with my mom next week."

"That's real nice."

She hesitated and then added, "You are his latest idol."

Cody Ty considered this information and looked at her with an expression she hadn't seen before. He was pleased.

"Well, how 'bout that?"

"He's watched all of your videos."

"Well, that's real nice," the cowboy said. "I look forward to meeting him."

"He wants to ride."

"And that doesn't sit well with you."

"No," she acknowledged, "but my mom doesn't want me to put my trauma on him."

"She's got a point."

"Yes, she does," she said, "but that doesn't mean that I want him to climb on the back of an animal, while admittedly beautiful and magical and graceful, that runs first and asks questions later."

He listened without much response, until she asked, "Why do you love them so much? Maybe hearing it from you would help me understand my son better."

"Horses gave me my career and a purpose. So many people say they love these animals, who are, from my view, one of the most beautiful creatures made by our God in heaven, but they fear them. And because they fear them, they handle them roughly or cruelly. They'll speak to you if someone is patient enough to listen."

Journey wanted to believe Cody; she wanted to understand the draw the animals had because now her son seemed to have the same pull to these animals. But she hadn't lost her fear, even though she did feel less fearful than when she started working with Cody in the barn. And this turn in her thinking to her own son made her curious about Cody's childhood. From what she picked up online, it wasn't an easy one.

"You grew up in Alabama?"

"True."

"Is that when you developed this love for horses?"

"I didn't develop much love for anything back then. Alabama was poor in general, but my family was dirt poor. I worked when I was a kid for peanuts. Scorching hot and dry as a dust bowl during the summer, and all I knew is that I wanted out. I didn't have much use for school, and my mom, raising a pack of kids while working a couple of jobs, didn't mind me working instead of learning."

The minute Cody began to tell her about his past, all of those tidbits she had learned seemed woefully bland or full of too many holes.

"It sounds like a hard upbringing."

"I 'spect so, but it made me who I am today. I understand the meaning of hard work. Watching my mother struggle, while my dad spent too much money on booze, and going without meals or missing school so many days that you could never catch up," he said. "That has kept me humble, no matter how famous I got. No matter how many years go by, I'm still that kid who had one pair of pants that my granny sewed material onto the ends of while I grew. My shoes had holes in them, but I was grateful to have them."

Journey turned her body toward Cody. "So when did horses come in?"

"Well," the cowboy said, "I loved Clint Eastwood, and so did my daddy. My brother and I used to sneak into the movie theater and watch him on the screen. Bigger than life, in the saddle more than he walked on the ground. That was what I wanted to be. A cowboy. Just like John Wayne."

"And now my son wants to be a cowboy, just like you."

Cody parked in the lot outside of a country-western store; he shut off the engine and looked her over with a keen expression in his eyes. "You remember the wisdom of Willie Nelson?"

"Yes, I do know. But the way Oakley is talking, I may not have much of a choice."

He winked at her with a smile. "Let's go get you some real cowgirl boots."

Danica had been in LA for a couple of days; she had opted to take a suite at a hotel; Grant still lived in her house, and even though the early agreement between them barred him from moving Fallon in, her ex's desire to move his now-fiancée into the house and set up a baby room in one of the guest rooms was common knowledge. As much as she loved that house, she could not, would not, live beneath the same roof as Grant.

After a long day of negotiations, Danica could not stomach any of the offers proposed by the other side.

"This is my home!" she said to Ray and Charlie on a video call. "I built it. Every single tile, every single fixture, every window, stone, door handle, came from my brain! All he did was show up later and now he wants it for Fallon? I can't." She tried to locate a clean tissue. She had been crying so much that she had already run through one box.

"I'm sorry," Charlie said.

"We are." Ray nodded.

"But once the emotions settle, what is the best path forward for you?"

Danica blew her nose loudly. "I don't know. I'm still shocked that I could lose my home and my business."

"Okay, don't kill me for asking this," Charlie said. "Is there a possibility that you could work with Grant?"

Danica looked horrified and then furious as she shouted, "No! No! *No!* I will not work with that womanizing coward." She pointed to her chest. "I'm the one who started the business. He was just another pretty face that I hired."

She yanked another Kleenex from the box. "How could this be? How could I lose everything I worked so hard to build? I've lost friends…"

"Not actual friends," Ray interjected.

"Okay, yes, you're right. But those were close contacts that greased the wheels of my business. And now they are raving over Fallon's perfect little baby bump?"

There wasn't much her sisters could say in general, and nothing they could say to make it better. Nothing would ever make this better; it was a wound that would leave an emotional scar and that would last a lifetime. She would never forget this for as long as she lived.

"I need to stop crying," she said through her tears, "pick myself up by my bootstraps and figure out what to do next."

"We're here for you, Danny. We're always in your corner."

"Thank you," Danica said. "I'll call you guys later."

When she hung up, she rolled into the bed, covered her head with the comforter and tried to put the horrible news of the day out of her mind. When she heard the ringtone she had programmed in her phone just for Matteo, she reached her arm out from under the comforter, grabbed it and brought it into her cave.

"Hello?"

"Hi." The deep timbre of Matteo's voice washed her body with a feeling similar to sinking down into a hot tub.

"Hi."

"How are you?"

She sounded stuffy like she had come down with a bad cold. "Terrible."

"Tell me what's wrong, Danica."

And so she did, every last horrible thing. Her business, her contacts, her home, were all on the line. And it was inconceivable to her that she, the victim, was ending up on the losing side.

"I need to see you," Matteo said. "I'm going to switch to video. Pick up."

This was a new level of intimacy for her with anyone other than Grant and her sisters. She had worked for decades to cultivate and curate a very polished image of Danica Brand, business owner, Realtor to the rich and famous, "it" woman. Flawless makeup, age lines erased with any and every trick in her plastic surgeon's toolkit. And she had been fighting and winning the race against the clock; many women who had youth on their side had not been able to beat her. Had it been increasingly difficult to stay at the top? Yes, it had. But she had still been able to hold onto that crown she had fought to earn.

A few moments later, Matteo video-called and when she answered, she was greeted by an enthusiastic oink from Lu Lu.

"Oh, Lu Lu!" Danica forgot about her appearance and

just focused on her adorable friend, Princess Lu Lu. "I miss you."

"She misses you," Matteo said, "and I miss you."

Danica caught her picture in the small square; her eyes were swollen and red, her waterproof mascara had run and looked like she tried to imitate Cleopatra. Her hair had been pulled up into a clip, but most had escaped while she was hiding under the covers, so she looked like she had porcupine quills.

"How can I help?" Matteo asked her.

"I don't think anyone can help, really," she said, downtrodden. "I either accept working with Grant for the rest of my career and split the house in two and live with him while he raises his baby. The baby *we* were going to have together…"

"That wouldn't be healthy for anyone."

"Or, I can just hand him the key to the castle and the business! How is any of that remotely fair?"

Danica reached out from under the comforter again, searching for that box of Kleenex. She blew her nose without any concern about how it sounded; Matteo had already seen behind the curtain. This was her as a hot mess.

"I need you to sit up and get yourself into a shower," he said with a layer of authority in his tone.

"Are those doctor's orders?" She couldn't believe she had it in her to actually flirt with Dr. Dashingly Handsome.

"Yes."

She frowned at him, thought it over, and then threw the comforter off of her body and pushed herself upright.

"Listen to me, Danica," Matteo said, "you are the strongest woman I have ever met."

"I thought you were going to say beautiful."

"That goes without saying."

"Well," she said, moving her hand in a circle around her puffy face, "if you think this is attractive, you must truly love me."

"I do," he said without a moment of pause. "Love you. And I need you to get out of bed and rinse yourself off. You're too good for this, *mi amor*, and you're a damn sight too good for this Grant guy."

"Mi amor," she repeated the sentiment. "I like that."

"Well, we like you," he answered. "I'll call you later."

Danica hung up with Matteo and actually felt better. So she did get out of bed and she did get into the shower. And afterward, things didn't look so grim. She had her sisters' love and support and she had Matteo and Lu Lu's love and support. With their help, she could find a way to step back into the light after coming through a dark tunnel.

With her hair in a towel, wearing a thick white hotel robe, Danica ordered a healthy meal and then watched back episodes of *Star Trek: Discovery*. And she was just getting ready to watch season three when Matteo video-called back as he said he would.

"What are you doing?" he asked, "besides being gorgeous."

She smiled shyly; her face completely devoid of any makeup under bright lights made her feel almost more naked than when she was actually naked with him in low light. She turned the camera around so he could see what she was watching.

"Are you serious right now?" he asked her.

"What?"

"You're a Trekkie?"

Danica nodded.

"How did I not know this about you?" Matteo seemed rather shocked.

"Well, we haven't known each other long enough to know so much."

"You should have started with this first." He held up his hand in the Spock salutation.

She held up her hand also and said, "Live long and prosper."

"Lu Lu loves *Star Trek* too. All of them except for *Star Trek: Enterprise*. She thinks it's super chauvinistic."

"And gives real pigs a bad name." She laughed. "It's hard to believe that it was made on 2001. There is some truly cringe-worthy dialogue."

"Agreed."

Danica, Matteo and Lu Lu watched the entire season three of *Discovery* and when she was unable to keep her eyes open, and Lu Lu's rhythmic snoring lulled her to sleep, Matteo ended the call and she groggily turned off the TV and then fell into a deep, restful sleep and didn't open her eyes again until her alarm went off at five in the morning.

As she got ready to hit the gym, she thought to send Matteo a good morning text, knowing that he would already be awake to exercise as well.

"Good morning, Matteo," she wrote, and then added an emoji blowing him a kiss.

"Good morning, *mi amor*," he texted right back.

Danica left her hotel room feeling upbeat, grateful that she had met Matteo. No matter what happened in the future, she would never forget his support and kindness during this most difficult time in her life.

Journey was walking beside her cowboy muse in the town of Bozeman, and at first, she didn't really notice anything different. But then people were pointing at Cody, taking pictures and videos of him. Cody took it in stride, nodding his head, waving a bit, while he kept on moving along.

"Man, you're amazing." One man walked right up to Cody, shook his hand and then asked for a selfie.

And then it was just a *thing* that happened. Kids, parents, *grand*parents, saw Cody, recognized Cody, and then wanted attention from him.

"Sorry 'bout this," he said sincerely. "I was a pretty big deal here in Bozeman at one time."

"It looks like you're still a big deal here."

Journey stood back and watched Cody with his public. They were dedicated to him; generations of family members knew him, respected him and wanted to thank him for the years of entertainment. Then she noticed that some of his fans just happened to have Cody Ty hats on and T-shirts with his face or a scene when he was riding a bull. She knew that Cody had been popular back in the day and she supposed she thought of him as sort of washed up; she couldn't have been more wrong if she put some effort into it.

After he had given the group of fans autographs on their shirts or hats, took a bunch of selfies and said his catchphrase, new to her, into the videos, "Cody Ty wild," he put his arm around her shoulders so he could move both of them forward from the crowd.

"Does that happen everywhere you go?"

"Nah." He took his arm away. "Some places more than others."

"When's the last time you rodeoed? Is that even a word? Rodeoed?"

He chuckled and smiled at her. "It is a word and it's been too many years to count."

"And still." Journey couldn't help it, seeing all of his fans dedicated to Cody years after the peak of his career, that was something special. This man had something special and maybe that "it" factor that a person either had or didn't have, Cody Ty had in spades. And now her laser focus on Cody as her muse made all of the sense in the world.

"Here we are." Cody opened the door for her. "We can find you boots here for when you're working with the horses, and they step on your foot, and they will step on your foot because it's gonna take a minute or two for you to know how to not get your foot stepped on."

"You just said a whole lot of words without making a whole lot of sense."

He laughed, a nice, robust laugh, as he followed her inside the store.

"Cody Ty Hawkins!" The owner of the shop spotted him, rounded the counter and stuck his hand out for Cody to shake. "Welcome!"

Cody posed for yet another picture and then said to the owner, "My friend needs a pair of steel-toed boots."

"I am tickled, truly tickled that you have brought her to us," the owner said, beaming with what Journey could only describe in her head as a fanboy moment.

The owner of the store left them in the hands of a salesperson who didn't know Cody, which was nice because she wasn't trying to take pictures that would capture her trying on boots. She always had giant feet and it took a while for her legs to catch up with those feet; she was teased mercilessly in junior high school. And when she got her first catalog spread in the local newspaper, instead of making her "cool," the teasing only got worse. So she was sensitive and didn't want her feet spread all over social media as the backdrop for a pic of Cody.

"How do you deal with this?" she asked, pushing her foot into a boot.

"Oh, I don't mind it, really," Cody said, sizing up the boots she had on. "My fans are dedicated to me, and I'm dedicated to them. When I was down on my luck, and there's been a few occasions of that, they've done what they could to lift me up and not tear me to pieces.

"How do those feel?" he asked, watching her walk.

Journey stood in the boots, kicked the heels, pushed her foot forward in the toe of the boots. "Pretty good, actually. I can definitely feel that there isn't any give in the toe of the boot, but I think it works."

"Good."

"I still don't think I need them because I'm not going to be close enough to a horse for it to squish my toe."

"Humor me."

"Okay," she said, "I'll humor you."

"Thank you." Cody stood up, got a bit creaky halfway up, put his hand on his knee and then pushed through what looked like a flash of pain on his face.

There was a moment when no one was trying to take a video or a picture; no one was asking him to say his catchphrase. And Journey was glad for the reprieve. She had a short-lived career in modeling and had landed some big campaigns before she got pregnant. But she had certainly not achieved notoriety in that profession. Seeing Cody's fans, it was both annoying and impressive all in one bundle.

"Cody Ty!" the owner said, coming through the front door of the store with a chubby woman with an amazed look on her face and her hand over her mouth as if she was rendered speechless.

"This is my wife, Mary. She's your biggest fan," the owner said. "I'd really appreciate it if you'd let us get a picture with you."

Cody agreed and took the picture while she paid for her boots. The salesperson handed her the receipt and the bag. The salesperson leaned forward and asked, "Who is that guy, anyway?"

"That's *the* Cody Ty Hawkins," she said with an unexpected defensiveness in her voice. "Rodeo royalty."

Chapter Eleven

Danica awakened feeling a mixture of emotions. She had a meeting with her team of attorneys; she was a wealthy woman, yes, but there were limits. Having this many attorneys on retainer, sending a bill every month for a file review, needed to stop.

"Good morning," she said to the new receptionist, Brindle Huckabee, when she walked through the door of her business for the first time since the day she left for Big Sky.

"Good morning, Ms. Brand!" Brindle jumped up, closed the gap between them, grabbed her lightweight coat and her floral motif blue-and-white Prada bag.

"I'll keep my bag," Danica said, rather curtly. It felt odd to be back. It had been a relatively short time away but this, somehow, no longer felt like her home away from home. It was seventy degrees and it felt too hot!

"Any messages?" she asked Brindle.

"No, ma'am." The earnest young woman, seemingly starstruck, was shaking with excitement or fear and maybe she needed the restroom. Either way, Danica put her out of her misery.

"That will be all," she said to Brindle, and then walked the long hallway to her expansive office.

On her way back, she stopped by the room, a shared space, meant for the junior Realtors.

"Oh! Ms. Brand," Leena exclaimed, flew out of her chair, and flung herself at her. "I've been so worried!"

After Danica extracted her body from Leena, she said, "I'd like to meet with you in my office in ten minutes."

"Yes, ma'am, of course."

Now that she was in town, through their lawyers, Grant and Danica had come up with a schedule at the office until they could decide on a course of action. Today was her day and she fully intended to make the most of it.

"Brindle!"

"Yes?" The young woman popped her head in her office door.

"Do we have some sort of disinfectant wipe?"

Brindle nodded. "Yes, we do."

The office manager was back in a flash and tried to wipe down the desk for her; Danica thanked her and then did the deed herself. Nothing in the office looked disturbed, but she knew every centimeter of her office. Every knick-knack, every picture, every pen, she knew the placement. And she knew that Grant had been using her office while she was away. And Fallon and he might have been doing dirty things on her desk and the thought made her nauseous. She wasn't a germaphobe really, but some things were a bridge too far.

Leena knocked on the doorframe to her office and Danica waved her in. After she had disinfected her desk, her chair, and any other surface that may have been used by Grant and his new fiancée, Danica sat down at her desk chair, annoyed that she had to adjust the settings to fit her needs, and then asked, "Fill me in."

And Leena did.

"I've had three open houses this week," Leena told her.

"Good," Danica said. "Are you feeling more confident?"

"Yes, I am."

"Glad to hear it. What else?"

There was a pregnant pause before Leena asked, "Can I speak candidly?"

"Of course."

"I don't like working for Grant."

Danica sat forward and listened.

"He's really harsh in his critiques of my job."

She raised her eyebrows, letting Leena know that she was listening.

"And he lets Fallon boss me around."

Danica had never felt firsthand the meaning behind the phrase "hot under the collar." But she did now. She did her very best to hide her frustration and focus on the work. Leena was going to make an excellent Realtor; she had the look, the brains and the enthusiasm for the job. And Danica wanted to make sure that Leena had the best chance, the well-deserved chance, to transition from a Realtor in training to a full-blown Realtor.

"Do you think you'll come back?" Leena asked her. But the honest truth that she shared with Leena was, *I don't know.*

After her meeting with Leena and touching base with the other Realtor in training, Aditya, who was rather cold and distant, which signaled to her that Aditya had hitched his wagon to Grant's fading star, she began to answer messages that had been neglected while she separated herself from reality in California. The Montana time in her life was bizarre to her and would be for those who knew her in the California setting. Would they recognize the pig-loving, salsa-learning, throw-caution-to-the-wind and canoodling-with-the-most-eligible-bachelor-in-Big-Sky-and-beyond woman?

No, they wouldn't. She was known as the ice queen in her Realtor circles; not only for her ice-blond signature hair, but because she never cracked during negotiations, and she always picked closing the deal over building potential friendships. Danica wasn't proud of that label anymore. She had been until she had time to reflect in a setting polar opposite to LA. Watching so many of her contacts align their loyalties with Grant was a slap in the face. And it occurred to her that perhaps pouring her entire self into her career and chasing that epic closing that kept on propelling her to the top of the LA heap was misguided.

Everyone had left for the day, and she was alone in the empty office that she had built from a one-room business to an empire that was housed in one of the most prestigious office buildings in LA. That meant she had arrived.

She was standing in her office, looking out of the floor-to-ceiling windows, feeling melancholy. She had brought a box with her; just a plain moving box that would be used to take her most valued personal items with her. Even this had been agreed upon by arbitration.

Her phone rang while she was catching tears with a Kleenex under her lower eyelashes.

"There she is!" It was Matteo. God bless his excellent timing.

"Hi."

"What are you doing?"

"Just wrapping up some loose ends at work." She leaned back against her massive desk.

"Any news?"

"No," she said, "not yet."

"Okay," he sounded in a hurry. "I'll call you later."

"Please do," she said, feeling a calm wash over her just by hearing his voice.

He had become important to her and being in LA had made the depth of her feelings easier to understand.

After she hung up with Matteo, she carefully wrapped the awards that had come down off the wall. She took Swarovski crystal animals out of the curio cabinet, something she had been collecting since her midtwenties. And besides that, everything else could stay. It was difficult to see her life distilled down to one cardboard box. But like it or not, this was her new reality until she came to terms with Grant. When she had retreated to Montana to get her head screwed on straight, the idea of *not* going back to her business and her estate had seemed so implausible that she hadn't even considered it.

With her box in her arms, she waited for the elevator to arrive and then pushed the button to the main floor. Her head was lowered, and she was feeling very blue, but when the door slid open, she put on her social mask and walked out of that elevator like a woman on top of the world. Then she saw Dr. Matteo Katz-Cortez standing in the lobby, awaiting her arrival, holding a bouquet of red roses.

And that made her mask crumble as they walked toward each other to meet somewhere in the middle. He took her into his arms, strong, muscular arms that made her feel safe and protected, something she hadn't imagined she needed since she was a little girl in her father's safe arms. But right now, in this moment, she did need that comfort and Matteo gave it to her without question.

"I can't believe you're here!" Danica held the red roses, breathing in their sweet scent.

Matteo picked up the box of her belongings and walked beside her, past the lobby desk and into the revolving door and the light of a sunny California day.

"Do you have a car?" she asked.

"No." He smiled at her. "I could use a lift."

Matteo didn't take leaving Big Sky to show support to Danica lightly—not even when he knew that his partner, Dr. Brown, who typically covered the Bozeman area, could see his patients. This was something he hadn't done since he helped his ex-fiancée and her daughter move out of his house. He didn't think anything else could be more important than his track record; at that time, he hadn't known Danica was going to come into his life and turn things on its head.

"I took a room in the hotel," Matteo told her in the hotel elevator.

"No."

"No?"

"Yes. No," she repeated, "I'd like you to stay with me. I've taken the penthouse."

"I didn't want to assume."

"I understand, thank you," Danica said, "but you came all this way to be with me."

He had.

"So, be with me."

"Okay."

Matteo got off at his floor to gather up his belongings and then rode the elevator up to the penthouse, used the spare key and walked into luxury that was not his norm. He was comfortable financially, but he wasn't so wealthy that taking this penthouse would be a regular occasion. Seeing this penthouse helped him understand Danica outside of Montana.

"Hello, *bonita*." He put his arms around her, called her pretty in Spanish and kissed the side of her neck. She put her hands on his hands and leaned back on his body. This was more than just a body movement for her; she was leaning on him both physically as well as figuratively. And he felt honored to have gained Danica's trust.

She turned in his arms, arms that had ached for her after only a few days apart, and he saw her lovely face bathed in the sunlight, her ice-blond hair recently trimmed and tucked behind her ears. Large glinting diamond studs adorned her ears and a collar of diamonds hung around her slender neck. Her makeup was flawless and so too was her suit, which appeared to have been made for her, it fit so perfectly. Montana Danica was more relaxed, comfortable, with less makeup and no flashy jewelry. LA Danica was different, quite a bit different. But Matteo believed that his Danica, Montana Danica, was a truer version of herself.

"Thank you." She looked up at him with her large blue eyes. "It must have been so difficult for you to get away on short notice."

"It was a challenge, but one that I believe was worth it,"

he said, running his hand over her silky hair. "I hope you are happy that I'm here. This could have given off a weird vibe showing up unannounced."

"No." She put her hand on his chest. "You showing up here when I was feeling so alone was exactly what I needed."

Grateful to hear that his big, romantic gesture was received in the manner it had been offered, he leaned down and kissed her, drawing her closer into his orbit.

"Mmm," she murmured against his lips, "I've missed these lips."

"They have missed you."

Danica took his hand and led him to the main bedroom and closed the double doors to block out LA. They stripped out of their clothing, met in the middle of the bed, and their bodies naturally intertwined, lips upon lips, hands exploring, until their union created one body, one soul, one mind. Making love with Danica had been something he didn't even know was absent in his world. Of course, he had made love since his breakup, but it wasn't as frequent as folks outside looking in would think. Lu Lu was frequently his late-night date after all of the first dates ended without a connection. It was notable that so many women wanted to move fast with him; first date, then hop into bed and then get engaged, and now he wanted to move fast with Danica. However, seeing her on her own turf, seeing her dressed in her armor, threw ice-cold water over him. In spite of his drive to lock her down and commit, he could see her devastation, live and in person, and he knew, down to the core of his being, that Danica didn't need any more pressure on her, especially from a man she counted on as a safe, un-complicated space.

After they made love, they showered and donned the plush bathrobes, and ordered room service. They feasted on relatively healthy food, with a promise to hit the gym before the crack of dawn the next day.

"I'm stuffed." Danica flopped backward on the bed.

"Stuffed. Yes."

She rolled over, propped herself up onto her elbow and smiled at him with what he was sure was love, and kissed him on the lips.

"Gosh darn it, Matteo, you are so handsome."

He reached up to put her hair behind her ear. "Gosh darn it, Danica, you are so beautiful."

They went out onto the terrace with a glass of wine and kissed with the bustling cityscape in the background as dusk gave way to night.

"I do have a present for you," he said, kissing her neck, feeling the need to make love to her again.

"A present?" she asked, and that's when he saw the tini-est of slivers of the kid in her.

He laughed, put down his empty wineglass and walked over to his carry-on bag. She followed him, curious. He pulled out a wrapped present and handed it to her.

"I saw this, and I couldn't pass it by."

Excitedly, she started unwrapping the small box.

"It's not an engagement ring," he added, "just in case you were worried."

"I wasn't."

Matteo waited patiently for her to slowly unwrap the present, put the bow on the table, along with the ribbon, and then the paper was methodically removed, folded and put next to the bow and ribbon. *Finally*, she opened the box, stared at its contents, while a smile began with her lips, broadened and then reached her eyes.

"What a perfect gift," she said, emotionally, while she carefully took the crystal animal out of the protective foam.

"It's Lu Lu!" Danica said. "I only told you about my collection one time."

"I only need one time."

Danica admired the chubby crystal pig with a metal curlicue tail and black eyes.

"Thank you," she said, "for the gift, of course, but also for *seeing* me."

Journey had developed a routine of helping Cody in the barns—there were other cowboys available to handle the mundane chores of cleaning buckets, mucking, turning over stalls with fresh bedding and refilling hay bins—but he still wanted to keep his hands in the pie and, as far as she could see, he didn't shy away from those chores. In fact, now that she knew him better, Cody kept himself humble and grateful by doing the jobs typically handled by the cowboy, or cowgirl, last in line to eat at the trough.

"I just figured out something." She leaned on her pitchfork, an implement she had recently developed a relationship with.

"Oh yeah?" Cody hoisted a new bale of hay into a cart. "What's that?"

"You've been desensitizing me."

Cody stood upright, sweat on his brow, and asked her, "How do you figure?"

"This entire time, I've been under the impression that you wanted me to experience true ranch life, so I can taste it and smell it and feel it."

"Sounds about right."

"But," she said as if she was about to solve a mystery, "you've been getting me to work around the horses, so I could feel relaxed around them."

Cody chuckled, and she loved to hear that rare sound from a man she had grown to both like and respect. So much so that she was tempted to buy some Cody Ty swag and get him to sign it for Oakley.

"Did I get it right?" she asked.

He looked up at her, head cocked to the side, looking a smidge guilty.

"I did get it right!"

"Did it work?"

Journey sat down in a nearby chair, looked at the sweet-faced mare across the aisle, and realized that she *could be* calm around a horse. This was a huge leap for her, and she couldn't believe Cody had masterfully gotten her to this point while distracting her by giving her grunt work in the barn.

"Yes." She smiled at him. "It did, actually."

He smiled with a nod. "Well, that's all right."

Cody sat down in another chair, slumped down a bit, legs out in front of him, his ankles crossed. Completely comfortable in his own skin.

"Can I ask you something?"

"You can ask, but that don't mean I'm gonna answer."

She smiled, knowing that about him already. "How old are you?"

He looked down at his crossed hands resting on his flat stomach before he lifted his head just enough to see her, she suspected, without allowing her to see his eyes. "You can't figure that out on your fancy phone?"

"First, it's a smartphone, not a fancy phone," she said.

"I don't have any use for them."

"Second," she continued, "I have looked you up on my fancy phone and you have way too many birth dates floating out there. Why is that?"

He pushed his hat back on his head with his forefinger so he could look at her. "No one knows, that's the short version."

"And the long version?"

He took off his hat, raked his hand through his salt-and-pepper hair, then put the hat back in place. "The long version? I was born at home, parents couldn't afford a doctor. Mom nearly died while my daddy was out doing only the good Lord above knows what. Time got the best of us sometimes. One hard day would blend into the next hard day. We didn't celebrate our birthdays and Mom had so many youngsters roaming around that she couldn't remember who was who and which was which. My birthday is just a guess. That's all. Just a guess."

"I'm sorry."

"Don't be." Cody's shoulders tensed along with the muscles on his face. "My life has turned out as it was meant to and I don't have one ounce of regret about anything I did or anything that was done to me," he continued, "and with everything my mama had to endure, and every dawn-'til-dusk job she had to work, and every beatdown my pa gave her when he came home drunk, I'm lucky to be alive.

I don't much give a damn if anyone knows my real birth-date. Makes no difference to me."

"I've upset you," Journey said. "I'm sorry."

"Don't spend another second worrying about it." Cody stood up. "I've already forgotten it."

"Okay," she said, also standing up. "How old do you *think* you are?"

"Relentless, aren't you?"

She nodded. "When something's important to me, yes."

"My age is important to you?"

Again, she nodded.

"How about this, I'm stove-up and beat down," he said in blunt manner, "and if that don't satisfy you, I'm sure as heck old enough to know better."

Cody didn't want to admit it, but Journey had hit a sore spot with all of her questions. He'd been asked before in a multitude of venues, but she was the first to truly get under his skin. He liked Journey, more than he should, actually. She was a big-city girl, still young with her whole life ahead of her. The die had set on his life, and he accepted it. No matter how attracted he was to her, and he was plenty attracted, he had to keep her at a distance. Admire her from afar was his way of thinking about it.

But it was tough. Damn tough. Every day he told himself that he was going to spend less time with the beautiful blonde palomino, but when the next day arrived, he'd end up spending more time, not less. He'd let her lead him down a path, asking him questions about things in his life that he'd long since forgotten. And in those moments, he remembered why he could never be with a woman like Journey. He'd led a reckless life full of fame, fortune, beautiful women, and all of the trappings of success that a boatload of money could buy. But all of that had come with a cost; he was stiff as a board, rickety and crotchety. He'd made a life on his own terms without having to ask anyone for permission.

He'd given up on finding love. And he had made his peace with it. A woman like Journey—lovely, intelligent, educated, a single mother who adored her son and was trying to live her dream of being a successful romance author— was not in his wheelhouse. He admired her and he wanted to help; she was the type of woman not found in country dive bars while moving from one town to the next. And, yes, he had seen some feelings for him in her eyes, but when the balance sheet was completed, Journey Lamar was just too damn good for him.

Journey sat down at the desk and began typing. At times, the words poured out of her, but more often than not, she ended up with her head in her hands, trying to figure out what needed to be said next.

"Stubborn man," she muttered, walking over to the window to watch Cody working with one of his young horses.

Why did she care two hoots about his age? She could answer that question easily. She liked Cody. She respected him. And he was the first man since her divorce from Oakley's father that she had any interest in whatsoever!

She pinned him somewhere in his late fifties, but he was more alive and vibrant and talented than any of the men in her age range. And she found herself falling for him without any way to resolve their Grand Canyon–sized differences. It wasn't just about age.

"Damn it, Journey, *focus* on the book."

Sitting down at the desk again, Journey did realize that the more time she spent with Cody, the more her hero of the new book resembled the famous cowboy. The way he walked, the way he talked, the clothes that he wore. Her hero was being shaped to resemble Cody because of her own attraction to him. She had a secret, one that she didn't know if she would share with her best friend and mother. Oakley wasn't the only admirer of Cody Ty Hawkins in the family; she had become a total fangirl, too.

Chapter Twelve

Matteo was going to be with her over the weekend and Danica felt grateful for his support. She had contacted several of the friends in her corner, which made LA seem less lonely, less isolated. But no matter who the small handful of people standing by her were, she was the one who had to ultimately decide what to do with her entanglements with Grant. Sitting across from Grant for the last several days had been painful. This was to be the father of her children; now she realized that her slow walk to children with Grant had been a gift. As horrible all of this was, and how unfair it seemed, at least they weren't fighting over custody of a child.

"You look beat." Matteo had been working at one of the three desks in the penthouse suite, but he stopped to greet her.

"I am."

"Do you want to talk about it?"

She breathed in deeply and then after a long exhale, she said, "No. Maybe later. Just not now."

"That's okay," he said. "Why don't you sit out on the terrace, and I'll bring you a healthy juice. Crafted just for you by these hands." Matteo managed to make her smile, even in her worn-down, exhausted state, no matter how weakly. She changed her clothing, putting on shorts, a tank top, and a headband to hold her hair away from her face. After some sunscreen on her face, arms, hands, and neck, she slipped on designer sunglasses and leaned back in one of the lounge chairs and shut her eyes. This was exactly what she needed; a sunny day, relaxed clothing, with *Dr. Dangerously Handsome* making her a healthy juice.

Matteo's button-down shirt was left open, showing off his developed pecs and six-pack abs. Eye candy.

"Hope you like it." He handed her a tall glass filled with a green concoction.

While he took off his shirt and took the chair next to her, she tasted a tiny bit first. "Mmm!"

"You like?"

"How do you do this, Matteo? You're so talented!"

"Thank you."

"No, Matteo, thank you," she said, "for being here for me."

"That's what friends are for."

"Well—" she frowned at him "—I hope we're more than friends."

He reached out, took her hand, gave it a gentle squeeze. "We have time to figure that out later."

"Okay," she agreed, "you're right. My mind seems to be scattered, like a one-thousand-piece puzzle thrown into the air with pieces flying everywhere."

"Well," he said, letting the rays of the sun turn his skin a golden brown, "I do have one thing that may help get your head back in the game."

"What's that?"

"Salsa."

"Salsa?"

"Salsa," he confirmed. "I found a club where we can dance. I'd like to get you out of my living room and onto a real dance floor."

"Do you know what?" she asked. "A couple of months ago, you couldn't get me into a club, much less for dancing. But I like the idea."

"Good."

"I don't have anything to wear, I don't think. I brought casual and business."

"Hold that thought." He got up and went back inside. When he returned, he had a bag with him.

"Is this a dress?"

"Open it."

So she did. Inside the bag was a slinky little black dress with an open, plunging back and a tulip skirt meant to create a dramatic flair with the movement of her hips.

"It's gorgeous," she said, not sure that this was her type of dress or not.

"Full disclosure," he said, "I did consult with your sisters."

"It's…" She paused and then said, "Thank you. It's very thoughtful."

"Uh-oh." He frowned. "Not sure I like all of this thanks for being so thoughtful. What's wrong?"

She looked down at the dress in her lap. "Do you mean besides the ten slices of cheesecake I've eaten since I've been here?"

"Wish I'd been here to join you," he said. "I love cheesecake."

"Me too, obviously," she said, shrugging, "but that's not it, really. I'm just not…"

Matteo watched her and waited for her to continue.

"I'm not really the sexy type," she said, feeling rather shy. "Tough businesswoman, check, Realtor to the stars, check, and a decent sister, check, check. But, sexy? No."

Matteo looked at her as if she had just confessed to being an alien from a faraway galaxy.

"Okay, first, you *are* sexy, and two, you can be all those things you just listed. Only now, you can add sexy salsa dancer to the list."

Danica told him that she would at least try on the dress, put on some strappy heels and then decide if salsa dancing was going to be in her immediate future. It was strange how she had compartmentalized her life—sister, Realtor, community leader, businesswoman, globe-trotter. Matteo may have pointed out something important for her; who was she without those rigid frameworks she had erected around herself? And who would she be if one of those narrow definitions went away? Honestly, she just didn't know.

Journey had made progress on her unexpected quest to get over her fear of horses. That didn't mean she was going to ride one, but being able to lead them, groom them and be in the stall with them to muck seemed like reachable goals. She wanted to show her son that it was never too late to grow and change. And that if she overcame her fears, then he could also conquer his.

"How does that feel, sweet girl?" she asked Rose, an older mare who was petite in stature, calm and gentle.

Cody was standing nearby, working with a colt, while she brushed Rose. And while she brushed the horse, she found herself talking to her. The mare, as she had soon discovered, loved to be spoken to in a soft, gentle manner. And when she was successful in making the mare feel relaxed around her, the mare would lick and chew and then her large brown eyes would droop to half-mast. There was a sense of self-pride that she was able to be near a horse and feel safe, confident and knowledgeable.

"These animals are a reflection of who we are," Cody had told her. "They read energy, they read your heart, and some folks don't like what they see reflected in a horse's eyes."

Journey did her best to keep her toes out of the line the horse would step on should it need to change position or if it was spooked by something.

"These here animals are prey; that's why they have eyes on the side of their heads so they can see predators. If your energy is off, if you approach them with fear, they're gonna think that *you* are a predator, and you'll see the horse get real animated."

Cody had continued, "If a horse is nervous, edgy, worried, that's on you and your energy. Most folks want to blame the horse, but there's a whole lot of idiots out there."

Journey did her best to be a good student, enjoying her time with Rose. She learned how to groom her, pick out her hooves, comb her mane and tail, put the halter on her head, and lead her to and from the stall. And she couldn't deny that this relationship with Rose had changed her for the better; it had also given her writing a sense of authenticity. She now knew how a horse's body moved, why they shook their heads, what to look for when picking out the hooves, and she had become a talented manure mucker. She had to thank Cody for this; he was the one who basically booted her off the porch and into the barn.

"My mom and son are arriving tomorrow," she said, combing Rose's long mane.

"I've heard." Cody smiled at her.

"At least two times from me today." She smiled fondly at him. "Just fair warning, Oakley is going to want to tag along with you. Lately, all he wants to talk about is you."

"I don't mind if your son wants to learn how to be a cowboy. But I won't have you micromanaging the situation. If you don't trust me with your boy, then best not get started in the first place."

She stopped combing and frowned at him. "What makes you think I would micromanage?"

He looked at her and she looked at him and then she said, "Fine, you have a point."

"I know I did," he chuckled.

After she combed Rose's mane free of knots and tangles, she moved on to the tail. She loved brushing that tail, starting at the end and working her way up. She had wanted a girl because she had always been a girlie girl. But she was blessed with a son, and she embraced it with her whole heart. And yet she still longed to comb a little girl's hair, sweep it up into a ponytail or French braid it. Rose was the closest to that experience, and she was grateful for it.

While she was slowly working her way through the tangled tail, she did broach a subject that had been on her mind. If Cody did work with Oakley, she needed to warn him about something many people couldn't seem to overcome.

"I did want to share something with you," she started, still, after ten years, having difficulty talking about it.

"Ears on."

Cody's little quips always made her smile and lightened her mood. "My son, Oakley, was born with a genetic condition."

The cowboy stopped what he was doing and actually gave her his full attention. "Is that right?"

She nodded. "And in a world that puts such a high value on beauty, his condition has made it, at times, unbearably painful."

He was leaning over the top board of the stall, waiting on her to continue, and she truly appreciated him caring enough about her, about her son, to let her get it out on her own timeline.

Instead of spending a whole lot of time explaining it to Cody, Journey scrolled through her pictures of Oakley and selected her favorite one.

"This is Oakley."

She had learned to watch the faces of people who first see a picture of her sweet boy.

"Nice-lookin' boy," Cody said, and she couldn't believe it but she heard the ring of truth in the cowboy's voice. Truth, she believed, had a resonating tone.

"Thank you," she said.

"Now, what's goin' on with him? What's it called?"

"Treacher-Collins," she told him, still looking at her son, who was now, and had always been, her handsome angel.

"And what's that mean?"

"Um, there's varying degrees of facial deformities, from cleft palate, receded chin, ears malformed or missing. Oakley doesn't have a left ear, and is deaf on that side, but we are working to get a prosthetic. Poor kid, he's had so many surgeries already." When she realized he wasn't recoiling like some did, she felt encouraged to tell Cody, "Some do think that he might be challenged intellectually, but that's not the case with most people with TC. He's such a smart boy."

"Well," Cody said, "I'll look forward to meeting him."

Journey had to turn away and press her fingers into the side of her eyes to stop tears of relief at Cody's reaction. His kindness was such a testament to who he was as a man, and it occurred to her that this was the reason he still had so many fans years after his career as a world-renowned rodeo cowboy had ended. Beneath that surly, rough-hewn exterior was a man among men: kind, hardworking, dedicated, with more emotional intelligence than she had ever seen.

She turned back to him. "Thank you."

"What for?"

"For being decent."

"Ain't no reason *not* to be," he said. "And yes, I'm aware of the double negative. But that's how my kinfolk talked and that's how I talk every now and again."

"You allow them to live through you."

He looked at her with what she could only describe as admiration. "You certainly do know how to turn a phrase, Journey."

She smiled, her emotional meter starting at ugly crying to incredibly flattered.

"Now," Cody said in his abrupt manner, "just because your son has some challenges that life's given him, that does not mean you can hover and mother hen while I'm working with him."

"I will watch from an appropriate distance, I promise."

"We'll see about that," Cody said. "You've proven your-self to be a big ol' thorn under the fingernail."

Even though he was basically calling her a pain in the hind parts, when he was coming out of the stall, she met him there and flung herself at him. And instead of rebuff-ing her, he, as he always seemed to do, accepted the hug, and hugged her real tight, too.

She hadn't been in a man's arms for so long, it felt scary and wonderful and every other emotion in between. He was strong, burly, and the miles he had clocked on the odometer didn't matter. He was handsome—undeniably—but what she had grown to love was his honesty, his character and the heart he brought to every single thing that he did, no matter how big or how small.

"Well—" Cody cleared his throat several times "—work's still got to be done."

And she knew Cody Ty well enough to know that this was his way of saying the hug needed to be over.

"Finish cleaning up this mare," Cody said before he walked with his familiar limp out of the barn.

"Can I confide in you, Rose?"

The mare opened her eyes and used her lips to play with the cuff on her jacket. "I've got a crush on Cody Ty Hawkins. And maybe, just maybe, Cody Ty has a crush on me. Sounds like an epic Harlequin romance in the making."

Matteo tied the straps of the little black salsa dress he had purchased for Danica. He ran his finger down her back to the deep vee right above her compact derriere.

"You were made for this dress." He kissed her bare shoulders. "Turn around and look at yourself in the mirror."

Danica turned around and looked at her reflection. She had never seen herself in this type of dress; she had worn thousands of demure cocktail dresses designed by the top designers in the world. Up-and-coming designers had lobbied to have her wear their designs when she went to New York Fashion Week or to the governor's mansion. As a part of her persona, she was always elegantly dressed and put together to perfection.

She moved her hips one way to make the tulip skirt dance; this was a very clingy material that showed every possible bulge, and she couldn't wear her regular underwear. A thong or nude were her two choices.

Her entire arms were exposed, her neck, most of her legs, the majority of her back. The only thing that she had in her closet that was a close comparison was lingerie.

"Dare I?" she asked herself, not Matteo.

Matteo took her hand, twirled her under his arm, caught her, dipped her and then kissed her passionately before bringing her back up.

"Well?" he asked her. "What does your heart tell you?"

"My heart is telling me to—call my sisters."

Matteo was kissing her neck up to her chin and down to her bare shoulder.

"If you keep doing that, Matteo, we won't be going to any club."

He smiled and stopped his amorous moves. "That is for dessert."

She video-called her sisters. Ray and Charlie were together and when they saw her, they both yelled, "Jennifer Grey, Patrick Swayze, *Dirty Dancing*!"

Then Ray added, "No one puts Danny in a corner!"

"So this is a yes?"

"That's a hell yes!" Charlie said loudly.

"You look frickin' amazing, Danny," Ray said. "Wear it, own it, and have the best darn time you've had in years. You deserve it!"

She hung up and looked at Matteo, who was leaning against the back of a chair, sexy himself in black slacks, a bright blue shirt unbuttoned enough to show off his fabulous pecs, looking at her like she was a snack, jacket thrown casually over his shoulder.

"I believe that's a yes," he said.

"I think so, too."

Matteo crossed to her, took her in his arms and kissed her in a way that really made her waffle between salsa or the bed.

"Let's go." He helped her into her coat. "I want to show you off."

Going to the salsa club was one of the best decisions she had made in her life. There, she was anonymous, out of the public eye but out in public. She had danced for hours, learning new steps, following Matteo's lead. He was not only a doctor, a lawyer, an excellent cook, animal lover; she could add incredible dancer. And again, it only confirmed why he was the most eligible bachelor in the land of movie stars and multimillionaires crammed into a very small radius.

They closed the bar, caught an Uber, and then made love in the shower. Being with Matteo couldn't take away the pain she felt over her unraveling life in LA, but it certainly stopped her from winding down into a pit of despair.

Naked in Matteo's arms, she felt at home, but she couldn't make any decisions about this new relationship when she was still so mired down with the old.

"You're leaving today," she said, running her hand over his chest.

"Yes."

"Thank you for coming."

He kissed her hand and then placed it back over his chest. "I'll miss this."

She nodded and then said, "But I bet you will be happy to see Lu Lu again."

"Well, yes." He smiled. "Of course. I will look forward to a time when both of my girls are under one roof again."

They made love one last time before she helped Matteo pack up his few belongings and then saw him to the lobby.

There, they hugged tightly. "Come home to me soon, my flower."

She truly didn't know what to say, because her life was in free fall. The thought of closing up shop in LA to make a move to Montana wasn't even on her list of possibilities. She could imagine a relationship with Matteo in which they spent time in both places. And the idea of him shuttering his thriving medical practice? She would never want that for him, knowing how much time, sweat and sacrifice he had made to build that practice.

They kissed and then she waited for him to be out of sight before she went back into the hotel and rode the elevator to the penthouse. And, as if on cue, one of her attorneys called.

"There's an offer and I, we, are recommending that you take it."

"Okay." She sat down, put on her reading glasses and opened her email to quickly read over the main content.

"This isn't serious, is it?"

"It is."

"He wants to buy *me* out? And buy the house?"

"He thinks it will be a wonderful place to raise a child."

That knife was stabbed into her gut and twisted. "Yes, I am aware. We were going to raise our children there!"

She was yelling at the man she was paying to give her good, unemotional advice, and she didn't want to hear it. She didn't want to take it. She wanted to turn back the clock all the way to the point when she had met Grant at an entrepreneurs' conference where he charmed everyone with his California looks, his pearly white smile and his sense of fashion. He talked a good game, but when push came to shove, he had ridden on her coattails all the way to the present. And the kicker was, she knew it for years and she was too busy, too complacent, to do anything about it.

"I need to think about this."

"We understand," her attorney said, "but this could wipe the slate clean, you will have enough money to do anything you want in your life."

After she hung up the phone and spent time thoroughly reviewing the offer for her business and her home, Danica sat at the desk, head in hands, her heart in her throat, crying uncontrollably for what seemed like hours. She was mourning her business, her house, her life, and it all seemed like a bad dream. What would her act two be? What would she do?

She finally sat up, dried off her face and then sat on the terrace to find some clarity. If she signed the agreement,

Grant would win. He would have her business, her home that she designed with an architect, every lovingly selected stick of wood, tile and window treatment. It had been home for such a long time, and she had imagined raising her children, taking pictures of their sons or daughters on the winding, sweeping staircase, and growing old there. How could this be? How could it be that those moments would be for Grant and Fallon?

"Hi, Matteo."

"Hi, sweetheart," he said. "I just got home. Are you okay?"

"No. I'm not," she said. "Would you please look over a settlement document? My attorneys think I should take it."

"I'm only an attorney on paper," he reminded her. "I haven't actually practiced law in years."

"I know. I trust you."

There was a pause and then he said, "Thank you. I'll look them over right now."

They hung up and between phone calls, Danica paced around the large suite, her stomach in knots, gurgling, and she felt nauseous. If she agreed, this would sever all ties with Grant, but it would also be severing the life she had built for over a decade.

When Matteo called back, she fumbled with the phone, dropping it on the ground, and she was unable to hit the green button in time. Annoyed, she hit Redial.

"So? What do you think?"

"I think your attorneys have a point," he said seriously. "If you don't, you have to contend with Grant because he doesn't seem like he's leaving anytime soon."

Danica knew it already, but the confirmation was difficult. She slumped down into a pillowy oversize chair, unable to think, much less find words.

"As a fellow Trekkie…" Matteo said after the moment of silence.

"Live long and prosper." When she finally found words, these were the ones that came out.

"If all the variables were the same," Matteo asked, "What advice would Spock give to Captain James T. Kirk?"

Chapter Thirteen

The day that Oakley and her mom arrived at the farm was a happy day for Journey. There was magic on this land; she felt it, and she knew it, and she could see Oakley thriving on this ranch. He would relish the freedom he could never have in the city. When Oakley sent a text saying that they were turning onto the long drive to the main house, Journey put on her winter layers and raced down the steps, grateful she didn't slip and land on her tailbone. She wanted to be there the moment Oakley and her mother arrived.

Waving her arms in greeting, Journey cried happy tears for being reunited with her son. The SUV parked, and then Oakley opened the door and rushed over to her and hugged her. She could pick him up just a little and swing him around, but these days were ending.

"Are you taller?" she asked. "You're taller!"

Oakley's eyes looked like they were being pulled down and to the side, his chin was very recessed, and he had some scarring from when they fixed his severe cleft palate. And as his mother, none of that mattered. All she saw was her perfect son.

"Is Cody Ty here?" Oakley asked.

The driver had put the luggage on the front porch while she greeted her mother.

"How was the flight?"

"Good," her mother said. "This is more beautiful in person."

"Isn't it?"

Then Oakley asked again, "Is Cody Ty here?"

And this time, as if on cue, Cody Ty walked out of the barn and headed straight for them.

"There he is, right there," she said, pointing.

That was all she needed to say for her son to run at record speed toward Cody. Inwardly, she cringed, always nervous when someone new met her son, especially when he was about to hurl himself into the cowboy's arms.

Cody, as she had witnessed firsthand in Bozeman, let Oakley hug him and returned that hug. Over Oakley's head, Cody caught her eye and winked. That was when all of her anxiety and fear went away. And it was that very moment, with Cody walking toward her, arm around Oakley's back like they were pals from way back, that Journey realized that she had fallen in love with Cody Ty Hawkins.

"Cody says that he'll autograph my hat!" Oakley said in a voice fused with excitement and disbelief. How many times did people actually get to meet their idols?

"This is my mother, Lucy," she said.

"Ma'am—" Cody lifted up his hat for a second, accompanied with a nod "—my pleasure."

"Thank you. Likewise," Lucy said. "I've heard wonderful things."

Cody helped them get the bags into the house and then he headed back out to the barn. He heard Oakley ask his mom if he could follow along and that made him turn around and stop. Cody and Oakley were both waiting on her answer, and she could see her mother in her periphery nod her head.

"Are you sure you don't mind?"

Cody said, "I can always use a set of strong arms. Flex those biceps for me, son."

Oakley laughed, raised his arms like he was a body-builder in a competition, and Cody said, "Come on and bring those guns with you."

Journey hugged her son, made sure he made eye contact and then said, "Mr. Hawkins…"

"Cody."

"Mr. Cody is a very busy man, and you need to listen to him very carefully."

"Okay. I will." And then the reunion was over, and Journey couldn't stop from feeling let down because Oakley was enamored with Cody, and she said as much to her mother.

"Oh, let him be, Journey," Lucy said, unpacking her toiletries. "I haven't seen him this excited *ever*. If working with Cody can give him confidence, what's the harm in that?"

"You're right." She sat down at the end of the bed. "I just don't want him to get hurt. He's got so much against him."

Lucy sat down next to her. "You can't protect him from everything, Journey."

"I know."

"And I like this Cody Ty fellow. He's got a nice way about him. Humble. I didn't expect that from someone as famous as he is or has been."

"He is a very nice man," Journey said. "I have grown very fond of him."

"I could see that," Lucy said, "and I believe he's grown very fond of you."

Then Lucy yawned and Journey wanted her to rest after taking on the full-time job of watching Oakley for the past two weeks. Journey got her mother settled into the main bedroom, but her mind was on her son, and she just felt like she needed to see him working with Cody.

"I do think I will take a nap," her mom said.

"Yes, please do. It's so peaceful here." She hugged her mom. "After one week, you'll never want to leave."

Cody took an immediate liking to Oakley; yes, he could see that he had a different look about him, but he had no difficulty looking past that. The horses gravitated to Oakley and that was a sign of a good soul. Oakley was kind, gentle, soft-spoken, and the horses responded to that.

"Bring that wheelbarrow over here, son," Cody said to Journey's boy.

Oakley did as he was asked. "Do you think I'll be able to ride while I'm here?"

"Well—" Cody gave a shake of his head "—I'm not sure we'll be able to get your mom on board with that idea."

Oakley's shoulders dropped. "Just because she's afraid of horses doesn't mean that I have to be."

"That's right," he agreed, "but she's the boss applesauce and she gets veto power. But I'll put in a good word or two with her."

"Thank you," the boy said. "Maybe coming from you, she'll agree to it."

Cody didn't want to ruin it for him, but he didn't think he had much sway with Journey. She had taken major steps forward in her relationship with Rose. But he didn't imagine he'd ever see her in the saddle and that was okay.

When Cody was done mucking, he showed Oakley where to dump the manure and then they went back inside the barn. When they returned, Journey was in the barn scratching Rose's ears. And just as usual, the moment he laid eyes on her for the first time and every day since, his knees got week, he felt dizzy, with his throat closing in. If that wasn't a sign of love, he surely didn't know what else would be. A big barrier here was the matter of age; he wasn't sure of her age, but they weren't from the same generation. So as much as he had grown to care about Journey, and the waters did run deep, he had worked overtime to stop any feelings he had for her from getting in the way of teaching her about the majestic animals he had loved for his entire lifetime.

"How's it going?" Journey asked.

"Mom! Cody taught me how to muck stalls!" Oakley was overjoyed, as if Cody had bestowed a great honor upon him.

Journey gave him a playful raise of the brow. "You do know that there are still child labor laws in place."

"This isn't labor, Palomino," he said without stopping to choose his words carefully. "This is character-building."

The minute his private nickname for her was spoken aloud, all he could do was hope that she hadn't noticed. If she had noticed, she was playing it cool.

"We need to let Mr. Cody get his work done," she told her boy.

Oakley appeared crestfallen but didn't argue the point.

"I'll be working some young horses in the round pen for the next couple of hours. You're welcome to watch."

Oakley's eyes turned hopeful as he sought out his mother's gaze.

"Okay," Journey said, "but only if you promise to watch quietly."

Oakley made a cross over his heart, hugged his mother tightly and then turned his attention back to Cody.

"You're sure?" Journey asked him.

"I like the company," he told her, and it was true.

Oakley did have a unique face that he was certain drew unwanted attention from strangers. Behind those facial features was a golden heart. And perhaps it was because of his unusual features that Oakley seemed to have an old soul. A gentle soul that the horses gravitated to. A boy like that deserved to be taught how to work with horses, and once his mother saw that Oakley was building self-esteem, he was darn sure that Journey would approve. He could see how dedicated she was to her son, and he admired it.

"Thank you." Journey had some unshed tears in her eyes. She hugged her son one last time, and when he began to wiggle out, his mother let him go.

"I'm going to be okay," Oakley said. "Mr. Cody will watch out for me."

"That's right." Cody nodded. "Now, we've got work to do. Come on over here, Oakley, and I'll teach you how to put a halter on."

He did take a moment to watch Journey walk away, a sassy swing in her hips, her thick wheat-blond hair in a braid, and her long legs that reminded him so much of a gangly filly not even a month old. She was a beauty. And he knew that when it was time for Journey to leave the ranch, he'd miss her like he'd miss a limb. There would be phantom pain for years, of that he was certain.

It took all of Journey's willpower not to spy on Oakley and Cody. She did satisfy her curiosity by peeking out the window, but she realized that she didn't feel overly anxious when it came to Cody working with her son. This feeling of calm confidence she had with Cody had only happened with her mother. And this security, unexpected but welcome, only validated her growing romantic feelings for Cody.

"What are you doing?" her friend Riggs asked on video chat.

"Looking up a palomino."

"What's that?"

"I don't know," she said. "That's why I'm looking it up."

"Okay, while you do that, you'll be happy to know that I sold my boat."

"That does take a load off," Journey said with playful sarcasm. "Is that why've you been MIA?"

"Have I though?"

"Yes. You have." She looked at the pictures of the most beautiful golden horses with light blond manes and tails. "He does have feelings for me!"

"Rewind," Riggs said. "When the cat is away, Journey will play."

"Cody Ty Hawkins," Journey said. "I sent you links to videos."

"And I watched one or two before I had to turn the attention to me again," Riggs said. "I will say this, he's good-looking. Kind of old, but still doable."

"He's not old," Journey said defensively. "He's more productive than most of our friends."

"Whatevs." Her friend frowned and was beginning to look very bored. "Why do you think this very *youthful* cowboy has a crush?"

"He called me *Palomino*."

"Not ringing a bell on my end."

"I just sent you a link."

Riggs opened the link and then he said, "He has a crush. Big-time."

"Wow." Journey sat back in her chair, looking at the wall, stunned. "I would never have known except for his slip of the tongue."

Riggs's keen eyes were on her now and this is why he asked, "Do you want him to have a crush on you?"

Journey was silent for a second and then she said, "I'm in love with him."

Riggs's eyes widened, his jaw went slack, and he appeared to be completely shocked. "I leave for a couple of days—"

"Seven."

"...and you go off the rails! I have to go buy a boat."

"You just sold your boat."

"But I'll work you into my *schedge*," Riggs said with a dramatic sigh. "You need me more than I need sushi today."

"Was it a close call?" she asked with a laugh. "Me or the sushi?"

"A *very* close call."

After touching base with Riggs and tiptoeing past her mother's room, she sat down at the desk in her room, opened her laptop, pulled up the Word document, and typed the words *Chapter Two*. And then she sat there for what seemed like an eternity, but it was only ten minutes when a knock at the front door gave her the excuse she needed to avoid writing. When she wrote her first book, it had come easily. Now she could barely get through a sentence without putting her head into her hands and trying to think of the next bit of dialogue or a scene in general.

Journey opened the door and found Ray and Charlie on the threshold.

"Our sister needs us in California," Ray said.

Charlie added, "We are catching a plane today. If you need anything, please get in touch with Wayne."

"I hope everything is okay," she said. She really liked each Brand triplet.

"It will be," Ray said. "Once we get there, it will be."

She was shutting the door and the sisters had taken the porch stairs down when Ray stopped and called her back.

"Totally off subject. But I bought your book, and I loved it! When I get back, I would love for you to sign it for me."

"And my copy, too," Charlie called over her shoulder.

And then the sisters were gone, leaving her standing just inside the cabin, feeling shocked with her spirits raised. Perhaps those one-star reviews had gotten into her head and decided to build a permanent residence there. But Ray and Charlie were cowgirls at the core, native Montanans and fifth-generation ranchers.

"Well," she said, "what do you know?"

She walked back to her computer with her head lifted, shoulders back. One five-star review from Charlie and Ray meant more to her than one hundred one-star reviews.

Fingers on the keyboard, with a new resolve, and the feeling that the block was a thing of the past, Journey drew from the ranch, the Brand sisters, her newfound horse sense, and of course, her time with Cody Ty, while her fingers began to fly and all of the words she had pent up inside her came pouring out.

"Are you sure you don't need me to come back?" Matteo asked, looking dapper in his white coat and a stethoscope around his neck.

"No, thank you," Danica said, her nose stuffy from all of the crying she had done over the last couple of days. She hadn't cried this much as an adult and couldn't remember crying much in her childhood, either. But then again, she had never had to sign away everything she had built just to get Grant and Fallon out of her life.

"Okay." He sounded unconvinced. "If you need me, I'll hop on the next flight."

"I know you would," and as she said it, she knew it was true. Matteo had proved his feelings for her and his willingness to come to her when times were tough. "Thank you for giving me access to Lu Lu's cameras. I can't be sad when I watch her and it's certainly better than raiding the hotel bar."

"I'm glad it's helped," he said. "She misses you. When she hears your voice, she runs around oinking and her little curly tail just wagging a mile a minute."

That made her laugh through her fresh tears. "I know! That's why I don't talk to her through the camera because she tries very hard to figure out where I am!"

There was a knock on the hotel door, and that's when she saw that her sisters had texted that they had arrived. "Ray and Charlie are here."

"Okay, keep me posted."

"I will."

"I love you," he said.

And with an automaticity that caught her off guard, she said, "I love you, too. Goodbye."

Danica didn't have time to dwell on that slip of the tongue. She needed to pull it together and go to the house that she had named *La Dulce Vida*, the sweet life, and pack up her personal belongings and other items that were agreed upon during arbitration.

"Hi," Danica greeted them, so relieved to see her sisters. For many years, they had each focused on their own lives taking them in opposite directions. Now she couldn't imagine going through anything without them. As were their parents' wishes, the ranch had brought them back together and cemented their bond as triplets.

They got into their triplet hug, touching foreheads, before they broke apart, knowing that they needed to get to *La Dulce Vida* to meet the movers.

"Oh, my." Danica looked at her reflection in the mirror. Her nose was red as Rudolph's and her skin was blotchy. Her eyes were puffy and resembled an inner tube.

"Don't worry your pretty little head over it," Ray said. "We are going to fix you right up and you'll face this next challenge looking like *the* Danica Brand."

Danica let her sisters fuss over her; she lay down on the bed and let Charlie put a damp cloth with ice in it over her eyes. After they depuffed some, Ray put some caffeine cream around her eyes.

Feeling more like herself, she fixed her hair and then put

on her makeup. She put on one of her "boss" tailored suits in deep red. She turned in a circle for her sisters' approval.

"Two thumbs up," said Ray.

"*Four* thumbs up," Charlie said.

Hiding her still-puffy eyes behind stylish sunglasses, Danica walked out of that hotel with a carefree attitude on display that she did not feel inside. She was well-known in prominent social circles in LA and, not completely surprising, there was a photographer she recognized from a news rag, and she looked at him, smiled, chin up, confident, and then she disappeared inside an awaiting SUV with her long-standing driver.

Her driver took them to her estate in Beverly Hills.

"We're so sorry, Danny," Ray said.

"Thank you for coming." Danica took off her sunglasses. "I couldn't face this alone. And I don't know who is a friend anymore."

"We wouldn't want to be anywhere else," Charlie said, her jaw set. "This is a raw deal."

Danica shook her head, still in disbelief. "It seems like a dream."

"Nightmare," Charlie said.

"Everything I fought so hard to build, gone."

"You'll rebuild. Bigger and better." Ray reached out to take her hand.

"I don't even know what I want to do."

"You don't have to know right now," her identical triplet said. "You'll come home, regroup, and then you'll know."

"And whatever it is that you want, we will be here to support you."

"I love you both very much."

"And we love you," Ray and Charlie said in unison.

The rest of the ride was quiet. What could they say that hadn't already been said? When the car pulled up to her gate and the number was punched in, the wonderful world she had created unfolded before them. She heard both of her sisters gasp and it struck her now that her sisters hadn't seen it before.

Along a winding drive, up the hill, the Mediterranean-style home was revealed. The house sat on one acre and was built to maximize the views of the LA cityscape.

"How big is this place?" Charlie asked.

"Thirteen thousand square feet, nine bedrooms, twelve bathrooms."

"That's a lot of toilets to clean," her tomboy sister added.

"It is, but I didn't." She smiled at the thought. "We run a full staff here. I hope Grant keeps them on. Most of them have been with me since I built this house."

They stepped out of the SUV into her private sanctuary. Behind those gates, she had felt free to leave the stress of her job at the curb and enjoy the fruits of her success. As they walked through the front door, a grand staircase was the star of the show, leading up to a second story. Imported marble was on the floor of an entertainer's kitchen where various chefs would cook for her parties. An imported chandelier twinkled in the sunlight flooding in from a massive picture window.

"Why did you need all of this?" Charlie asked.

Danica looked around at her beautiful house filled with everything she had loved and cherished and couldn't give her sister an answer. Now, having stepped back from her fast-paced life, where keeping up the Joneses wasn't good enough, where she needed to overtake the Joneses and leave them in the dust—second place was for losers—she couldn't really remember needing all this.

"It's impressive." Ray always tried to sugarcoat things and put a positive spin on it. "Look what you achieved, Danny! It's amazing. *You* are amazing."

The movers arrived and her sisters followed her around the house, starting with her closet and her home office, and then they headed downstairs to the kitchen. The walls of the house were filled with an art collection that she had started with a small Picasso. The collection had grown as she and Grant picked out paintings together. The only painting she wanted was that Picasso. The rest of the collection would be appraised, and she would be reimbursed. She didn't find anything in the kitchen of use to her but there were several items that her sisters spotted that had come from their childhood home in the library.

"I've never seen this many books in one place other than the public library." Charlie looked around, hands on her hips.

"I love it," Ray said. "Will you be taking anything from here?"

Like every room that she had entered, she didn't want much out of the library either. It was odd, this detachment that she felt for her own home, her own belongings. But that was how she felt. She just didn't want it anymore.

Danica walked over to one of the shelves, slid a book out of its space, closed the protective glass door and then opened the book in her hand to the title page. She looked at her father's inscription, ran her finger across it, and then carried it with her as she left the library, knowing that this would be the last day she would see it.

"I think that's it," Danica said quietly.

"Mom and Dad would be so proud of you," Ray said.

"Yes," she said with a waver of emotion in her voice, "they would. But do you know what I regret now?"

Her sisters waited for her to continue.

"I regret that Mom and Dad never came here for a visit. I regret that neither of you came here—" she shook her head "—because I didn't invite you."

"It's okay, Danny." Her sisters were at her side.

"The things in life that I had placed so much value on seem like bottom-shelf items now," she told them. "Thank you for helping me on the next chapter in my life story."

Then, they joined together for their triplet hug and Danica could feel that she was on the right path, doing the right thing, at the right moment. This newly found bond with Ray and Charlie was her home. For now, and forever.

Chapter Fourteen

"You're really that certain?" Estrella asked him.

Matteo had put on his best cowboy duds, with dark-wash Wrangler jeans and a blue-and-white Western-style shirt with pearl snaps, and felt ready to meet Danica at the private airport where she and her sisters would be arriving.

"I'm sure."

Estrella sighed but said, "If you're sure, then I'm sure."

"Thank you, *hermanita*." He called her "little sister" in Spanish, which always garnered a smile from Estrella.

"So," he asked, "how do I look?"

"Like a real cowboy."

"Well," he said, smiling broadly, "that's what I was going for."

He ended the call, grabbed his heavy coat, and then braced himself against the cold and the freshly falling snow. Once inside his truck, he backed out of his drive, and slowly, cautiously made his way toward the place where he would see his true love again. Yes, they spoke on the phone and video-chatted, but nothing could take the place of feeling her body next to his, holding her in his arms, and smelling the clean scent of her skin and her hair. He had missed hugging her, kissing her, and this "missing" her felt like an ache he'd never experienced in his life. And it confirmed to him that Danica was his person in this vast world. No matter how long it took for Danica to heal from this breakup with her life in California, he was ready to wait.

From behind the wheel of his truck, he saw the jet land and his heart began to pound like he had just run ten miles in a minute. He watched impatiently for the door to open and for the stairs to descend. And then, finally, Charlie appeared at the top of the steps, followed by Ray, and then his beloved appeared. She looked for him, and when she saw him, her smile was as big as his. He jumped out of his truck and walked quickly toward the jet.

Charlie and Ray also smiled at him; he had to believe that his care and concern for their sister had earned him a treasure trove of "attaboy" tokens.

The ground crew appeared and opened up the baggage compartment. Charlie and Ray hugged him tightly and then he had Danica in his arms again. Still with that broad smile of happiness to see him again, Danica stepped into his arms, and he picked her up and swung her around.

Laughing, Danica said, "I'm happy to see you, too!"

The three women, followed by their baggage, and with him holding Danica's gloved hand, made their way to his truck. Baggage had to rough it in the bed, while they piled in, and he cranked the heater.

"Thank you for picking us up," Ray said. "Cows love to have babies in a snowstorm."

"And horses," Charlie added, "and goats."

Danica had her body turned toward him, her face alight with joy, and he would bet that this joy was also reflected in his expression. He took his hand off the steering wheel for a moment, reached over, took her hand, and said, "I've missed you."

"Me, too," she said.

"Oh, Lord almighty," Charlie said, "get a room."

"Leave them be," Ray said. "I think it's magical. I love the two of you together."

"I guess Journey isn't the only hopeless romantic at Hideaway Ranch."

"Guilty as charged," Ray said. "Lightning struck me twice."

Charlie slumped down in her seat, crossed her arms, pulled the knit cap she had on her head over her eyes and then began to lightly snore a minute later.

"Charlie can literally sleep through a blizzard." Danica turned around so she could meet Ray's eye.

"Especially when uncomfortable subjects are broached."

The remainder of the ride was quiet. There were so many things that he wanted to say to Danica, but those words were for her ears only. He turned off the highway onto Hideaway Ranch land. Soon he reached the common area that included the barn, main house and a large structure that once was Butch Brand's workshop.

Ray tapped Charlie on her thigh, and she pushed up the cap, opened her eyes a crack, and then, realizing that she was back home, she quickly unhooked the seat belt, mumbled thanks to him and then hauled her travel bag out of the back of the truck.

"Hideaway Ranch meeting tomorrow!" Danica called after her sister.

Not turning around, Charlie lifted her hand and made the thumbs-up sign.

"Broke the mold," Ray said about her sister with an affectionate smile.

"Agreed."

Next was the Legend family ranch, where Ray had been living with her fiancé Dean.

Ray had texted Dean that they had arrived, and he came out to help her with her bags.

"I'm so glad to see you." Ray hugged Dean tightly and then hugged Dean's youngest daughter, Luna, who had launched herself into Ray's arms. With her arm around Luna's shoulders, and with Dean carrying her bags up the brick steps to the enormous, custom-carved, double front door, Ray smiled over her shoulder at them, just before she disappeared inside the sprawling house.

Now back in the truck, Matteo leaned over to kiss his beloved. Danica returned the kiss and then made a face. "Your nose is so *cold*!"

"Sleeping on the job," he teased her. "You need to warm it up."

She kissed him three times while his nose warmed up, and then he said, "We've got to get someplace private. I don't think Dean would appreciate us making out in front of his house."

Danica laughed and it was a sound that he loved. "No. I suspect not."

Matteo asked, "Your place or mine?"

"Yours," she said. "Definitely yours."

He backed out, and then put the truck in drive while he asked, "Lu Lu?"

"Of course," Danica said, nodding. "Lu Lu."

* * *

Danica had been overwhelmed with emotion when she stood at the top of the jet's stairs and saw Matteo waiting nearby. He had welcomed her home and for the first time in over two decades, she did feel that Big Sky was her home. She certainly couldn't have foreseen the events that had led her back to Big Sky; it certainly was a twist of fate that had put her on an unexpected path. And on this unexpected path, she had found Matteo and Lu Lu. The timing of it all—the naysayers, and she supposed ex-friends, told her that it was too soon to get into a relationship. Or that Matteo was a rebound. Danica discovered, and was very pleased with this development, that the only voice in her head that mattered was her own.

"I love when you cook for me." Danica sank down onto the comfy couch where Matteo joined her after he built a fire.

"I love to cook for you," he said, inviting her to lean back on him while he held her in his strong, comforting arms.

Leaning on anyone, physically or emotionally, was not her way of being in the world. She strove for independence, full control, and did, at times, think poorly of women in her universe who leaned on others. Now she understood that to trust others enough to lean on them was a strength.

"I missed you," she said, resting her hands on top of his.

He kissed her on the side of the neck. "I missed you. Very much."

In silence, they enjoyed the warmth of the fire and then she got up, held out her hand to him, and led him to a soft rug in front of the fire. One garment after another, she removed his clothing as he removed hers. Lying in front of the fire, their bodies skin to skin, their arms and legs intertwined, and his lips kissing her neck, her shoulders as if she were the only dessert he needed.

He rose up on his arm, admired her face with his eyes, and he said, "I love you, Danica."

She put her hand on his face, loving every part from his soulful eyes to his strong chin and nose, and those capable lips.

"*Te amo*, Matteo," she said—*I love you* in Spanish.

She did love him. Did she know what that meant for the future? No, and perhaps that was part of the enjoyment with this handsome doctor. Her plan was to not have a plan. She wanted to live her life without a rigid schedule or the hunt for that record-breaking price per square foot for her high-end clients. She had been a tigress to be reckoned with in California; deadly claws, razor sharp teeth, and never one to back down from a fight.

Was she still all of those things? Yes, of course. They would always be a part of her. But now she didn't need that armor anymore.

Now, she lay next to Matteo, covered in a soft blanket, her nails lightly running through his chest hair, her leg over his and her head on his strong heart.

"This was worth the wait," Matteo murmured, drifting off to sleep.

"Agreed."

Something in her voice made Matteo's eyes open up. He looked down at her and when he caught her eye, he gave a small shake of the head and asked, "Lu Lu?"

Danica pushed herself upright quickly. "Is it okay?"

"Do you mean leaving me, leaving this fire, leaving this blanket, so you can go see Lu Lu out in the freezing cold?"

"If you don't mind," she said, starting to hunt for her jeans, socks and shirt.

"If I did, would it matter?"

She found her underwear on a nearby lamp. "No."

He laughed as he threw off the blanket and got up. "Then I don't mind."

The man was truly a work of art, chiseled and gorgeous, but even that recognition couldn't stop her mission to see the most amazing, fashion-forward pig in the world. Once dressed, she rushed over to her largest suitcase, unzipped a pocket, and then pulled out something she had had made for Lu Lu.

"Look!" she said, showing the matching crocheted winter hat with flaps and an under-the-chin strap that held it in place along with a matching sweater. "Do you think they'll fit? I sent the request to one of my childhood friends who makes just about anything that can be crocheted."

"Well." Matteo had his jeans on but still unbuttoned in a way that made the nerve endings in her body abuzz. "She loves you and she loves pink."

Danica smiled joyfully. "I can't wait to put them on."

Matteo grabbed his shirt, but before he could pull it on, Danica traced the outline of his six-pack and that brought a glint into his eyes when he asked, "Do you approve?"

"Please," she said in a teasing, disbelieving voice, "any woman would approve."

Matteo reached for her, brought her close and kissed her deeply. "You're the only woman in this world whose approval matters to me."

She rose up on her tiptoes and kissed him. "I'm glad."

"And now can you see Lu Lu?"

"Now can I see Lu Lu?"

Matteo pulled on his shirt. "I have to tell you, this is the first time I've been put in second place behind my pig."

Danica raced outside as if she had been living in the North Pole. She loved her roly-poly friend. She crossed the yard, slipping on a couple of steps that made her move more cautiously until she reached the front porch of Lu Lu's playhouse.

When she opened the door, the house was cozy and warm, and Lu Lu was sleeping in a fluffy bed with layers of blankets around her. When Lu Lu saw her, the pig got up, oinked and chattered on her way over, her curlicue tail wagging, and when the pig reached her, she flopped over, put her head in her lap and begged for some belly scratches.

"We haven't lost a beat, have we?"

Soon after their reunion, Matteo banged the snow off his boots and opened the door.

"I see the love affair continues?"

She smiled, in part because Lu Lu was smiling bliss-fully. "I know all the best places to scratch."

"Well, when you're done, I have a container of goodies that Lu Lu can find if you want to do the honors."

Danica leaned over and whispered to Lu Lu, "Do you hear that? Goodies!"

"Are you going to try her new sweater?"

"No." Danica went over to Lu Lu's closet, put the sweater and hat together on a shelf, and then selected Lu Lu's warm, "hanging in the backyard" clothes. Once she had dressed Lu Lu, she opened the door and picked up the basket of the pig's favorite veggies. Danica stood in the center of the snowy yard, bent her knees to get an extra oomph when she stood up quickly and tossed all of the veggies up into the air, letting them fan out around her.

Beside herself, Lu Lu's sounds were loud and grating to the ear, but Danica didn't care. She could learn to wear earplugs. But what she couldn't, wouldn't, do was to let her life, a mystery at the present time, get too busy to share these moments with Lu Lu and Matteo. All of the excitement of being back with Matteo and her most favorite pig made her feel carefree and grateful. These were not the feelings she had anticipated back in California when she was putting her electronic name and initials to the documents that transferred the home she had designed and the business she had built with hard work and gumption.

Danica bent down, made a snowball, and threw it with rather good aim, and the snowball found its target—the side of Matteo's handsome face.

"Did you just hit me with a snowball?"

She was busy making her second snowball. "Maybe."

"You've crossed a line, woman!"

While Lu Lu was on a vegetable hunt, Matteo defended himself against her snowball onslaught. He managed to land some snowballs as well, but she clearly dominated. So much so that Matteo crossed the designated boundaries, picked her up and fell back into a embankment that offered a soft place for them to land.

Laughing and winded, Danica said, "You had to resort to cheating! I won!"

"No." Matteo leaned down to look at her directly in the eye. "I won. I won because I have you."

"Where have you been all my life, Dr. Katz-Cortez?"

"Waiting for you."

The writing block was over, and Journey was well on her way to finishing Chapter Four. It had taken her some time to trust Cody, but she did. She trusted Cody with her precious son. A blast of frigid air smacked her in the face when she opened the front door to the main house and stepped outside.

"Hey." Her mother was wrapped up in a thick, quilted blanket, sitting in a rocking chair that she had staked out as her own territory. "How's writing?"

She sat down in a rocking chair next to her mother. "I've finally broken the block."

"Good. Good."

"How's it going with Cody?"

Her mother nodded toward the barn. "I've cried."

"Cried?"

"Twice."

"Why? What's wrong?" Journey stood up, ready to rush to Oakley's side.

"Sit." Her mother gestured. "Sit, sit. Nothing's wrong. Everything's right."

As if on cue, Oakley came out of the barn leading a large horse to the round pen with Cody a couple of paces behind them.

In that moment, Journey was rendered speechless. Oakley had his head held high, and she could plainly see that his self-confidence, in record time, had skyrocketed.

"Do you see?" her mother asked her.

Journey's hand was over her mouth, ecstatic tears in her eyes, and she nodded as she sat back down.

"This is the third horse he's led to that area."

"The round pen," she offered.

"Well," her mother laughed, "that makes sense, doesn't it? It's round and it's a pen."

Her mother's jubilation caught Journey off guard; her mother wasn't one for overusing happy emotions. So Lucy's joy only added to her own joy.

"Cody's been teaching him how to lead a horse, stop a horse, have a horse back up from him."

"He looks so little."

"He's a natural, Journey," her mother said. "This is what our boy was made for."

Journey couldn't deny it. Oakley looked happier than she had ever seen him. "And Cody? Would you give him five stars?"

"Hell," Lucy said, "I'd give him ten stars if I could. That is a man among men, just like my dad."

"High praise."

"Well-deserved praise."

Then there was a small lull in the conversation when she saw Cody hand Oakley a long crop with a woven cord; Oakley and Cody stood in the middle of the round pen, and with Cody standing behind her son, with his arms on top of Oakley's, Cody used the crop to move the horse to the outer edge of the round pen.

"What's he doing?" Journey stood back up. "That's too much."

"Sit down, Journey," her mother said. "Cody's got him."

She sat back down, hands in lap, her eyes focused on Oakley. First, he showed her son how to make a horse walk near the edge of the round pen and then had him move the horse into a trot, using clucks and body position to increase the horse's speed.

"I can't believe this," she said. "I've never seen him this happy."

Her mother nodded and she could see more tears of joy; Journey reached over and grabbed her mom's mittened hand and squeezed it.

"You know," Lucy said, "I owe you an apology."

"No," she said. "What in the world for?"

"Because I thought all of this was a fool's errand. You wanting to write romance for a living—and yes, I was very proud when you published your first book."

Her mother looked at her with such sorrow in her eyes that she hurt for her as Lucy continued, "I didn't believe that it could be a career. I was wrong for thinking that. I was just worried that you were going to use up your savings and then what? I should've been more supportive."

"But you *have been* supportive! You took care of Oakley so I could get some research done and some chapters under my belt before you arrived."

"Well, if I've been helpful then I'm glad," her mother said. "When we drove up to this place, I lost my breath. And I could feel that there was something special about this place. I got goose bumps up and down my arms. Oakley felt it, too. He said that this is magical, and I agree. I see it so clearly now—you will write this book. And then the next and the next."

"Thank you, Mom," Journey said, still holding her hand. "Thank you."

Journey returned to writing with a renewed sense of energy. She had just finished the last page of Chapter Four when she heard the front door open and then slam shut. Her son appeared in the doorway, his face flushed and wind-burned, his eyes shining like blue diamonds. His face was smudged with dirt; he had dirt under his fingernails and dirt on his clothes.

"Mom! Guess what?"

"What?" She turned and gave her son all of her attention.

"I learned how to put a halter on a horse and lead it to where you wanted him, or her, to go. I learned how to make a horse stop, walk, trot and canter by clucking my tongue and walking closer or farther away! This is the best day of my life!"

Oakley ran toward her, hugged her tightly and said, "And everything's okay, Mom. Cody watches out for me."

"I know he does," she said, still hugging him, not wanting to let him go. "You smell like horse."

Oakley stood up and smiled at her broadly. "I know. Isn't it great?"

A couple of days back in Montana and Danica was working on finding a new routine now that the move was a permanent one. She was paying a pretty penny for her rental but was rather lucky to find a place at all. Real estate in Big Sky was extremely limited, and drew the very rich and oftentimes famous. She was, now that the sale of the business and *La Dulce Vida* were done, a wealthy woman, but she would not pay the inflated prices for a home. And this was one of the things that she wanted to discuss with her sisters at their weekly meetings about the ranch.

"How are you, Danny?" Ray hugged her tightly when she arrived at Charlie's home.

"I'm good," she said, and it was the truth. Once the fight was over, and the decisions were made, she was able to let it go, for the most part, and focus on the future that she could make of her own design.

"Coffee?" Charlie brought a pot over to the table.

"Absolutely!" she said.

Once they were sitting together at the table, Ray asked, "So how has it been with Dr. Make Me Feel Good?"

That made her laugh. Wherever they went together, women, and some men, would stop and stare at Matteo. And that was because he was undeniably handsome. The cheekbones, the jawline, the broad shoulders and the height. Matteo was a walking, talking, living, breathing example of male perfection, and of course women wanted those genes for their children. No different than lions: the one with the best mane has the pick of the pride.

"He's living proof that sometimes you *can* judge a book by its cover," she said, petting Hitch, the orange tabby that ruled the roost. "He's as beautiful on the inside as he is on the outside."

"I'm so happy for you, Danny. You deserve it." Ray had tears in her eyes when she hugged her tightly. "Is it serious?"

"No. Not yet," she said. "But it has potential. I have strong feelings for him and he for me. But for now, I just want to have fun with Matteo. Enjoy his company, date, without the stress of living together."

Her twin agreed. "There's something about dishes and laundry that sucks all of the romance out of the relationship."

After a minute, Charlie chimed in, "If you're in love,

that means you'll be on hand to take Hideaway Ranch to the next level."

Ray sat back down with a disapproving look on her face. "It's not all about the ranch, Charlie. Why are you always so focused on the ranch? There is a world beyond our property lines."

Charlie was using her pocketknife to clean the dirt out from under her jagged fingernails; she put it away and said, "Because this ranch is our past, our present and our future."

"I can't believe that I'm saying this," Danica said, "but I agree with Charlie. We're here for the ranch, so let's get down to business."

The meeting was fruitful, and Danica understood now that her place was in Montana. And yes, she often clashed with Charlie because of how different they were and how they didn't have much in common other than sharing a womb and growing up in the same house with the same parents. But now she could see clearly that Hideaway Ranch was the business that needed her attention, and she respected Charlie's singular focus on the ranch.

"Are we done?" Charlie asked. "I've got a couple of irons in the fire."

"Almost," Danica said, sending a text.

A few minutes later, Charlie's fiancé carried a large box into the kitchen.

"What's this?" Charlie stood up to kiss her cowboy.

"That's a question for Danny," Wayne said. "I just carry the boxes around here."

And then Wayne, a man of few words, left.

"Ray," Danica said, feeling excited, "open it."

Charlie cut open the box with her knife and then Ray

tugged the box open and took out one of the T-shirts she found inside.

She held it up so Charlie could see it. It read, *Goat Yoga, Hideaway Ranch.*

"Look at the back," Danica said.

Ray read the back aloud. "'Yes, I do need this many goats.'"

"Thank you, Danny." Ray hugged her again. "I love them."

Charlie had taken a shirt out of the box, checked the size, and tugged the T-shirt she was wearing over her head and off her body before putting on the new Hideaway Ranch goat yoga T-shirt.

"I like it," Charlie said. "Fits good."

And then Charlie left the meeting and headed back outside.

"Do you love them?" she asked Ray.

"I do," her twin said. "You *do* love goat yoga."

"I can't deny it. I love it." Danica laughed. "I have no idea what's happening to me. I am quite perplexed. How did I manage to live without goat yoga and a pet pig?"

Chapter Fifteen

The next day, early in the morning, Matteo joined her for a hike on one of Hideaway Ranch's two small mountain peaks. Sadly, Lu Lu had to sit this hike out—the terrain would be too challenging for her. But Danica told her that she would join her on a fun forage when they returned. She had been spending some nights with Matteo, but she also valued her alone time, something that she rarely had in California.

"I like the color," Matteo said, while they were sitting on a bench placed there by her father, who enjoyed sitting in the woods to enjoy nature and to think.

"Thank you," she said, reaching for his hand. "I like you."

She had gone to a stylist that Ray had recommended, and she had changed the color of her hair from an ice-queen blond to a honey wheat. When she looked in the mirror, she didn't really see herself, so the hair color would take some getting used to.

"Are you ready?" he asked after they had shared a protein bar and some water.

"Ready."

Some areas were iced over and could be treacherous but

with Matteo's support, they both reached one of the sights she had wanted to show him.

"Here it is." Danica touched a large tree growing precariously at the edge of a rocky cliff.

"See here." She pointed to a heart carved into the tree by her father. Inside the heart were their initials. "My dad asked my mom to marry him here."

Matteo seemed to be fascinated with the tree. "It's beautiful. Your father was a romantic."

That made Danica laugh. "Every now and then. He was gruff most of the time. But a good man, a hard worker and a wonderful father. He loved all of his girls deeply. My family calls this tree our Love Tree."

Matteo put his arm around her and kissed her beneath the bows of the tree.

"My nose is all runny!" She laughed again. She could probably count on one hand how many times she *genuinely* laughed in the last ten years. Now in Big Sky, she seemed to be laughing without reservation. It was a revelation to her. Had she been unhappy in California but just didn't realize it?

"I'm a doctor. It doesn't bother me," he said.

"Well, that makes one of us!"

Matteo ran his finger along the carved heart. "This is beautiful."

"My parents were engaged here. We spread my parents' ashes here. And this is where Wayne asked Charlie to marry him."

"Thank you for sharing this with me."

She smiled as they headed upward to the pinnacle—a small area of quartz and rock faces. Some trees had been fighting to break through the rock and that always made Danica feel a kinship with these intrepid trees. She too had a desire to fight to break down barriers in her life. From the pinnacle, there was a bird's-eye view of a glorious valley that, during summer and spring, was filled with a carpet of wildflowers.

Matteo had packed some waterproof tarps upon which to sit but she was too busy using his binoculars to look at the wildlife below.

"It's a moose!" Danica exclaimed. "But it's all alone."

Matteo smiled at her. "They don't travel in herds."

"Oh," she said with a smile of her own, "shows you how much I remember about moose."

She continued to watch the lone moose, with its enormous antlers and its thick dark brown and black coat.

"We have Shiras moose here," Matteo told her. "They're actually the smallest breed of moose. They also have these weird snouts that help them not get water up their noses when they eat plants they find in water."

"Now it's ringing a bell." Danica joined him on the tarp. "My dad gave all of us girls nature lessons about the wildlife on our land, but I haven't exactly needed moose knowledge or bear spray on Hideaway land."

"Oh yeah?"

She nodded. "Plenty of people wanted permission to hunt on our land but dad wouldn't allow it. That's why we don't offer hunting. The only hunting would be to reduce numbers if they couldn't sustain themselves due to lack of resources."

"I never knew your dad, but I think I would have really liked him."

"You would have," she agreed. "Everyone loved Butch Brand."

Matteo offered her coffee and she accepted.

"Mmm," she said after her first sip. "What's in it?"

"Cinnamon. This is how my *abuelita* taught me."

"Well, your grandmother was a genius."

"My grandmother on my mother's side."

She kept her hands wrapped around the cup, feeling its warmth through her gloves. "You were a very good learner."

"Thank you," he said, leaning over to steal a kiss. "Sometime soon I will fix you some Jewish cuisine."

"If you want to win my heart, homemade matzo ball soup and latkes with applesauce and sour cream will be required."

"Well, I am trying to win your heart," Matteo said sincerely. "Next cheat-day meal."

Together, they sat, absorbing the peace and the quiet at the top of the mountain. Danica felt completely at home on that peak, which was unexpected considering her desire, when she was eighteen, to leave Big Sky as quickly as possible and never look back.

"Penny for your thoughts."

"Latkes, mainly," she said with a smile. "Nothing profound."

"I must disagree. Mulling over the awesomeness of the latke *is* profound. All of the great thinkers like Socrates and, more recently, Stephen Hawking, often opined about the latke."

Danica bumped her shoulder playfully against his. "Socrates? Stephen Hawking?"

"Just to name a few."

When the cold became too much of a barrier, they packed up their few items, put them in Matteo's backpack, and then began the slow and methodical descent. Matteo wanted to take a selfie of them in front of the Love Tree to post on social media. He wasn't shy about documenting their relationship, which meant that he was absolutely serious about her and their relationship that was still in its infancy. It was both exciting and nerve-racking at the same time. Exciting because she was in a new relationship with a wonderful man and nerve-racking because he seemed to be further down the road to commitment than she was. The last thing she would ever want to do was hurt Matteo.

Instead of continuing down the path, Matteo stayed rooted in his spot next to the Love Tree.

"Are you okay?" she asked, confused.

Matteo held out his hands to her and she naturally took them into hers and looked at him.

"I didn't know about this tree or what it meant to you and your family," Matteo said, and her heart plummeted into her stomach. "But I can't let this moment pass me, pass *us*, by."

"The tree has been here for seventy years, give or take, and unless something catastrophic happens like a lightning strike, it will be here another seventy years. No rush."

"No," Matteo said quietly, "this is the place, and this is the moment."

"I don't know that it is."

"Danica," the doctor continued undeterred, "I love you. I want us to be together. Build a life. Have children."

She was now in fight-or-flight mode, and it took all of her willpower not to find an escape route.

"I know it's early."

"Very early."

"And I know you have gone through a challenging breakup."

"It has been," she said. "Still is."

"But, having said all that—" Matteo sought out her eyes and held them captive with the mesmerizing brown-black eyes "—are you ready to say that we are committed to each other?"

She wanted to yank her hands away and scream "no" as loudly as she could, but that didn't happen. She *did* slip her hands from his, gently but noticeably.

"That's a *no*," Matteo said, frowning.

"No, it's not," she said. "It's an *I don't know*."

Matteo took a step back away from her, and that made her feel like a world-class jerk.

"Do you see yourself with me, Danica? Down the road?"

She couldn't seem to speak. Every thought that came into her shocked brain seemed like a horrible choice. Matteo was pouring his heart out to her and she wished that she could reciprocate, but she couldn't. She just couldn't. Not yet. And maybe not ever. The last long-term relationship she was in cost her everything. And no matter that she could see that this was a great change, a chance to work more closely with her sisters, it didn't change the real trauma she had gone through, and it wouldn't be easily forgotten. Did this make her skittish when it came to a committed relationship? Yes. Absolutely yes.

Matteo had his hands in his jacket pockets, pain was present in his eyes, and she hated it.

"What about children, Danica? Do you still want children?"

"Well—" she looked over his shoulder and not in his eyes "—I think I do, but everything in my life has been turned upside down. I'm starting over, really, and it's difficult to know, right in this moment, what my future looks like."

He stared at her, and she stared at him, and she wished she had a rewind button that would take her all the way back to when she suggested a hike on one of her family's favorite trails.

And then, feeling anxious in the quiet moment, she said one of the horrible ideas aloud. "If you need to have a child, Matteo, and it's a nonnegotiable, I may not be right or you. I care too much about you to hold you up. There are women in a fifty-mile radius ready to line up to give you a child."

"So let me get this straight. You want me to find another woman to give me a child?"

"Well, yes, but it sounded worse when I said it than when I thought it."

Matteo's face was drawn and tense; his lips, the very ones she had kissed in the selfie, were unsmiling. "It looks like this tree doesn't hold the same magic for us, Danica."

And with that said, he started off to a nearby trail. Neither of them spoke on the path back. Matteo, always a gentleman, helped her across some slippery ice patches, but that was the extent of their interactions. And this pattern continued until they reached the edge of the woods, close to Charlie and Wayne's restored farmhouse.

"I've got to get back," Matteo said.

"Matteo, wait."

He stopped, looked at her with shuttered eyes and waited.

"None of that came out the way I wanted it to," she said.

"I think it was the truth whether it came out right or not."

She couldn't deny it, so she didn't try.

"Danica, I love you enough to let you go," the handsome doctor said before he headed back to the main house where he had parked his truck.

Stunned speechless again, it took her a moment to think to say, "But I promised Lu I would go on a forage hunt with her."

Matteo kept on walking with long determined strides to his truck. Danica stopped walking, feeling too many emotions to unpack in this moment.

Ray came out of Charlie's house and asked, "Was that Matteo leaving?"

"Yes."

Ray put her hands on her hips. "Well, I was going to invite him to lunch. Vegetable soup and sourdough bread."

Danica stood in her spot and watched Matteo walk away from her until she could no longer see him. Ray came out of the screened-in porch, looked at where Matteo had gone and then looked at her.

"What's wrong?" her twin asked. "What happened?"

Danica put her face in her hands, shaking it and trying to make sense of the terrible turn their hike had taken. Concerned, Ray put her arm around her and led her to the porch and then inside Charlie's house. Danica sat down on one of the kitchen table chairs and was immediately joined by Hitch. The rotund red tabby curled up on her lap and began to purr.

"Thank you, sweet boy," she said, feeling comforted.

"Here's a cup of coffee," Ray said, joining her. "Now what happened?"

Danica did her best to recount the disagreement, but her

memory was spotty even for a conversation that happened moments ago.

"So he wanted a commitment?"

Danica nodded. "A promise of a commitment, I suppose, looking back."

"You have said that you have strong feelings for him."

She finished her coffee. "I do. I love him. But that doesn't mean I can commit right now or even anytime soon! I need to figure out who *I* am."

"And he couldn't accept that?" Ray asked. "I know we don't really know people when they are behind closed doors. But it's hard for me to believe he's so rigid."

"Well…"

"Oh no," Ray said, and then asked, "What did you say, Danny? When your mouth is a mile in front of your brain, you can say some really…"

"Stupid?"

"…things."

"I can't deny it."

Ray leaned forward, resting her head on her hand. "What did you say?"

She shrugged, not even wanting to repeat what she had said to him. She did already regret it.

"I told him that I don't know if I want to have children anymore."

"Oh, this is bad."

"And because of that truth, that I didn't want to hold him back."

Ray groaned.

"And I can't remember every word."

Her twin groaned louder.

"But it was something in the neighborhood of choosing

a mother for his child from the long line of women wanting to have his baby."

Ray shook her head, rolled her eyes heavenward, with
an expression of complete bewilderment.

"And then he left."

"Yeah, I saw him leave," Ray said. "I can't imagine why.
You only told him to go find another woman to have his
baby. No biggie."

Danica had a clearer mind farther down the mountain
than she had at the Love Tree. Could there be plausible de-
niability because of difficulty with the altitude?

"Not my best turn of phrase."

"No."

"In my defense, I didn't know he was going to ask me
for a commitment and nail me down about bearing his children on our hike, which happened to have the Love Tree
as part of the scenery."

"Danny!" Ray exclaimed. "Not the Love Tree."

"Again—" she pointed to herself "—caught off guard."

Ray sat quietly and that only made things worse, so she
asked her twin, "Is it as bad as I think it is?"

"Yes. It is," her sister said honestly without a moment's
hesitation. "And if you don't want to lose Matteo for good,
you'd better figure out how to clean up your mess."

"G-Ma!" Oakley rushed up the porch steps to where his
grandmother often sat, bundled up in a thick blanket and
drinking hot cider. "Guess what?"

"What?"

"Cody says that since I'm a real cowboy now, I need
cowboy clothes!"

His grandmother reached out her arms to him; G-Ma, as he liked to call her, had been one of his best people. She always encouraged him, had a kind word for him, and was willing to watch every single documentary about cowboys, horses and the Wild West. He was pretty sure that she didn't like those shows so much and that only made him love her more.

"Well, then," she said to him, "I think you'd better go ask your mom."

He gave one more hug to G-Ma, raced to the front door of the main cabin and pushed the door harder than he had intended. The door hit inside wall and the bell clanged loudly.

"Oakley?"

"Yes, Mom!"

"Are you okay?"

He ran down the hallway to the room where his mother was writing and crashed into her in his excitement.

"What is going on with you?" his mother asked, smoothing his hair off his face and back under his *signed* Cody Ty hat. "Is a bear chasing you?"

He shook his head, feeling out of breath. He loved Cody Ty and had dreamed about one day meeting him. Even in his wildest dreams, he couldn't imagine spending whole days with him.

"Cody says that since I'm a cowboy, I need cowboy clothes."

"He said that?"

"More than once," Oakley said, feeling like ants were in his pants that were making him sway back and forth, waiting for his mother to say yes.

"What kind of clothes?"

"Cowboy hat, button-down shirt, silver belt buckle *and* steel-toed boots."

His mother had always been thoughtful and, often from his view of the world, too slow in her deliberations.

"Well," his mother said, "I'm just finishing up a chapter."

His heart was beating so fast, like a hummingbird's wings, because she was using her "possible" face. "Let me finish and I'll think on it. Okay?"

Oakley's shoulders slumped forward and his face crumpled with disappointment. He wanted cowboy clothes now, not later! Being a cowboy was his calling and the sooner he began to look like a cowboy, the quicker his mother and his G-Ma would know this wasn't a fad. This was who he had always been and now he knew it for certain.

"He's coming over now, Mom!"

His mother's eyebrows drew together. "Now? Why?"

"Because he's going into Bozeman already, so I could go to the store with cowboy clothes then."

His mother didn't speak for really long minutes, which made him follow up with, "*Please*, Mom. *Please!*"

After another excruciating second or two, his mother smiled, and she closed the laptop and stood up. "Well, let's go get you some duds, cowboy."

Oakley grabbed her hand and led her to the front door. "Mom, could you please never say the word *duds* again? It's embarrassing."

"Okay," his mother said while she donned her winter clothing. "For you, I will try."

Good as his word, Cody was waiting at the bottom of the porch steps and had just tipped his cowboy hat to his

G-Ma. He could tell his grandmother, who wasn't always the social kind, liked Cody. And he could also see that when Cody looked at his mom, his eyes got all soft and today wasn't any different. In his mind, if Cody and his mom got married, he'd be able to keep on being a cowboy.

"Hi, Journey," Cody said to his mom. "How's the writing?"

He looked from Cody to his mom; his mom kind of acted weird around Cody, kind of shy and flirty, and he hoped that was a good thing in light of his plan to get Cody Ty to marry her.

"Slow and steady."

"Good," Cody said. "Glad to hear it."

"Cowboy clothes," he said, wanting everyone to stay on track.

"Oakley said that you said that he needs new clothes?" his mother said.

Cody gave a quick nod. "He needs the boots right now. If a horse steps on his foot, it will keep him safe."

Oakley added, "But Cody also said that it wouldn't hurt for me to have a cowboy hat, a silver buckle and a button-down shirt right now either."

"It wouldn't hurt?" his mother asked Cody.

"It wouldn't," Cody said.

"Looks like we're going into town. Mom, do you want to come?"

"No," his G-Ma said. "I'm happy where I sit."

Chapter Sixteen

Journey's afternoon had certainly taken an interesting turn. She had been on a good writing roll, and she hated to break before she had finished the chapter. But she also had picked up so many authentic ways a real cowboy moved in the world from Cody, and Wayne Westbrook, that moments like these enriched her writing.

"I told Cody that sometimes people stare at me kind of rudely, but that we do our best to ignore it."

Journey turned around, smiled at her eager son with a deep sense of appreciation and gratitude. *This* Oakley? This was her first time meeting him. Yes, he had built a thicker skin because of his facial differences and yes, he had to endure the pain of multiple surgeries as well as understanding that there were many more to come, and this had made him strong and mature, light-years past his same-aged peers.

"But Cody says that horses don't care about what we look like," Oakley said. "That's because Cody says that horses read our souls."

"Is that right?" She smiled at her son, and then to Cody, she said, "*Cody says* is a very big thing in our household now."

"I hope it's not a bother," Cody said from behind the

wheel of his truck. Billy Dean, her hero in her second book, had a similar truck.

"It's not," she said. "And you will tell me if Oakley tagging along becomes a bother to you."

"It's no bother," he said. "He's a great kid with a heart of gold. That's why the horses take to him so quick-like."

"Then I guess neither one of us is bothered."

"Looks that a'way."

"And thank you," she said with a waver of emotion in her voice, "for seeing my son as he truly is."

"Nothing easier from my way of thinking."

Again, she said, "Thank you."

The drive into Bozeman was picturesque and it felt good to see new scenery. Cody focused on the road, and she did her best not to stare at him like a bug under a microscope. Even after their earlier trip to Bozeman, it was still odd to see Cody off ranch property, his habitat, like a real person.

And that thought made her chuckle, which drew a brief look from Cody, but she shook her head and didn't voice that thought. Her son was a talker and if anyone gave him a chance to take center stage, he was going to take it! Oakley told her, in great detail, everything he had learned from Cody. She was impressed by how much Cody had already taught her son, but she was also impressed with how much Oakley had absorbed. Her son was smart with a higher-than-average IQ, and this was a challenge for them during homeschooling because he raced through the content so quickly that he was closing in on finishing middle school. She had heard of many homeschooled communities in her area whose children had attended college four or five years before what was typical. Her son was likely to be no exception. And because of his high IQ, Oakley tended to get bored after the first couple of days of new content, but this wasn't the case with what Cody was teaching him. This cowboy life, Journey believed, was meant for her son.

"You've taught him so much," she said, after Oakley stopped explaining what he had learned for over thirty minutes.

"You boy's like a giant sponge," Cody said with a pleased, rare smile. "If I say it, if I show it, he'll learn it."

She looked at Cody's profile—he had a strong profile that had aged well; his day-old stubble was mostly coming in silver-white. Yes, he had lines around his eyes and beneath his cheeks, there were some folds of skin on his neck, but it didn't take away from his appeal. He had been a handsome man in his youth when she googled images of him; he was still handsome. She had already felt drawn to Cody, from the first moment she saw him. She hadn't known who he was or what he was about, so it wasn't his career or fame that had piqued her interest. Like what Cody said about her son's soul, Cody's golden soul had resonated with her.

"I'll just be a minute." Cody parked his truck in front of a post office.

Journey watched him take a large box out of the bed of his truck and continued to watch him as he walked up the steps with a stiff limp. He opened the door for two women coming out of the post office before he went inside.

"Cody got that limp 'cuz a bucking bronco landed on his knee, and busted it up but good," Oakley told her using some of Cody's phraseology. "The doctors said that he might never walk again without a cane and that he'd never rodeo for the rest of his life."

Oakley paused and then continued, "He won two more championships just to prove them wrong."

"He's tough like you."

Oakley nodded. "I'm tough like him."

"Now, don't bother Cody, okay? He's got a lot of work to do."

"Aw Mom, I'm not!" her son said, exasperated. "You just heard him say it himself."

"He's polite, Oakley."

"Not about this, though. Horses are everything to him and he sees that I'm interested and that I have talent with horses, so he says that he's proud to pass on his knowledge to young cowboys just starting out like me."

She turned her body to look at her son over her shoulder. "Oakley, I want you to remember that we leave in less than two weeks."

"I know." Her son frowned. "But I'll just find my way back when I'm done with school. I'll find Cody. I know I will."

She turned back facing forward, feeling sick in her gut. She had never seen her son so passionate about anything other than video games that allowed him to have online friends without them actually seeing his face. In those worlds, he had avatars of his choosing.

"We'll figure something out," she said, putting it on her to-do list to find stables and horses near their home.

"Cody's mailing that package to his mom. Her name is May Bell and she lives with her sister, Regina. His mom likes to do crossword puzzles and crochet. Cody sends money home to Regina every month so she can take care of their mother full time."

Journey was surprised at how much Cody talked to her son. When she was with the cowboy, he barely managed to get a couple of sentences out!

"When he was my age, he saw a palomino horse on a farmer's land about a mile from where he grew up. He fell in love with that horse, and he vowed that one day he would own a palomino." Her son leaned forward and asked, "Do you know what a palomino horse is, Mom?"

"As a matter of fact, I do."

"Are you trying to make me have a nervous breakdown, Matteo?" Estrella asked him with an exasperated look on her face.

"No. Not intentionally."

"Well, you are!" her sister said, annoyed. "Why did you accept Mom's request to be friends on Facebook?"

"Why wouldn't I?"

"Because, *hermano*," she retorted, drawing out the first word, "when you post nothing but pig pictures and pictures of your poker team or hiking pics, and then you start posting selfies with a mysterious blonde? Mom noticed and she's been grilling me because you are out of range, playing doctor."

"I'm not playing a doctor; I am a doctor."

"Big whoop." She frowned. "I'm really tired of running interference for you. Seriously."

Estrella and he had always been very close and he could plainly see that this was taking a toll on her.

"I'll talk to her tonight."

"Tonight, tonight?"

"What other tonight could there be?"

"When you're involved, who knows."

"Te amo, hermanita."

"Besos." His sister blew kisses to him.

When he hung up with his sister, Lu Lu brought something to him and dropped it on the ground at his feet.

He bent down and picked it up. "Is this the custom beret Danica had made for you?

"Is every single woman in my life—my sister, my mom, my girlfriend, my pig—*all* mad at me?"

He asked Lu Lu, "How can I make this better?"

Lu Lu oinked at him twice and then started walking in a circle making that horrible, mind-numbing squeal that could wake the dead.

"That's not helpful, Lu Lu," he said, "not helpful at all!"

Ever since her conversation with Matteo, Danica was filled with regret, especially because he had been radio silent with her. She had slid into his DMs and nothing! She had texted, emailed, left a card in his mailbox, and all of her efforts to reconnect failed. She was never one to quit when it mattered and she realized, very clearly during their time apart, that Matteo meant something to her. Yes, she was still raw from Grant and everything that entailed, but that didn't mean that she couldn't forge a new path, at a snail's pace, with this incredible man she loved and who loved her.

"Did Matteo get back to you?" Ray asked.

"As a matter of fact, he did!" She said, "Finally! He made me work for it, I'll say that."

"And?"

"And he's coming for the campfire!"

Ray stopped peeling potatoes and hugged her. "I'm so happy. I know you've tried to hide it but you're my twin. I feel your pain and sadness as if it were in my own body."

"Me too."

About once a month, they tried to have a campfire cookout with stew wrapped in tinfoil, cooked on an open fire, cowboy coffee, and of course, toasted marshmallows and s'mores.

"I love him, Ray," she said, "really and truly. The timing isn't right, I know that. But the love is real."

"It's no different than Dean and me." Ray went back to peeling potatoes. "I thought I would be back here for maybe six months while I tried to figure out who I was after the divorce. And then I reconnected with Dean."

Dean had been Ray's first love, her first *everything*, and everyone had thought that they would get married after college. But that wasn't what happened. They both married different people, had wonderful children with those partners, and then found themselves back in love around Christmas time.

"And you're certain?"

"About Dean?" Ray asked.

She nodded.

"One hundred million percent," her twin said. "Like you, I didn't think the timing worked but it happened, and Buck was the person who really reminded me of how short life is. I didn't want to look back on my chance to rekindle our relationship. That would have been real regret."

Danica asked, "And how is Dean doing? I rarely see him."

"He rarely wants to be seen," Ray said, and then asked

her to get another roll of tinfoil out of the cabinet. "But he will be at the campfire tonight."

"Good, I'm glad."

Ray nodded, focused on her work.

"Question."

"Shoot."

"Do you have a good recipe for black-and-white cookies?"

Matteo pulled up to the main house on Hideaway Ranch, eager to see Danica again. His heart ached for her heart, her lovely face, her laugh and the softness of her skin when he held her in his arms. He looked back at the moment, and he wished that he'd never allowed himself to be inspired by the Love Tree. It was too soon to try to ask Danica to enter into yet another serious relationship after what she had endured and all that she had lost. He had another chance— she had given him another chance—he needed to practice patience and give Danica time. That's what she needed and as enthusiastic as he felt, finally finding that woman he had dreamed of—a woman who was intelligent, kind, strong, self-possessed and loved Lu Lu as he did—if he pushed her away, he would live in regret for the rest of his life.

"Dr. Dangerously Handsome, is that you?" Danica asked as she walked toward him with an open posture.

"At your service."

"Is that any service of my choice?"

Matteo smiled at her. "Your wish is my command."

Danica stepped into his arms and hugged him tightly, her head resting on his chest above his heart.

"I have missed you," he said quietly.

"I have missed you," she said.

She took his hand into hers and said, "Let's not do this again."

"Agreed," he said readily, "never again."

When they reached the campfire, he was greeted like a hero returning home. He had struggled sometimes to find his people in Montana, but Danica's ranch felt right to him. And he said as much to her.

"Have you thought about building here, at the ranch?" he asked, taking his stew to a nearby chair.

"Yes," she said, "I am gloriously wealthy. And I plan on putting a large chunk of it into building more cabins, brand expansion, *and* a forever home for me. But first, I have to figure out who I am and what I want."

"I love it here," he said. "I have peace here."

"So—" she touched his arm and met his gaze "—you would consider living here one day?"

"Are you asking me to move into your fictitious house?"

She laughed. "Yes, I suppose I am."

"Well, you'd have to put a ring on it first, Ms. Brand." He winked at her. "But if you *did* put a ring on it, yes. I would."

The trip to Bozeman had been one of the most important trips of Journey's life, only second to the trip to Montana as a whole. If she had any doubts about the integrity and decency of the man who had been her muse since the first day at Hideaway Ranch, those were gone. Wiped away, like dirt on a glass window. She already knew that, like the last trip to Bozeman, Cody Ty would be surrounded by fans. She also knew, from ten years of experience, that Oakley would draw rude stares wherever they went. And as always, she had to do her best to not return the rudeness by telling them to mind their own darn business.

"Do you know what Cody says about that?"

"No, tell me."

"Cody says that in his day, if people were rude and stared, back in his time, he'd say, *take a picture, it'll last longer.*"

She laughed and looked at Cody who appeared to be rather sheepish. "Maybe that wasn't the best thing I taught your boy. Apologies."

"No need," she said. "It gets the point across."

Cody took a lot of pictures for the fans, and plenty of pictures were taken with Cody Ty with his arm protectively over Oakley's shoulder. And it struck Journey that this was the first time she'd seen someone other than her mother or herself protecting Oakley. It made her feel so grateful that she had to excuse herself to the bathroom to stop tears from coming. This was a happy day for Oakley, and she couldn't do anything to detract from that.

By the time they left the store, Oakley had three big bags full of his cowboy garb. The first salesperson to greet them appeared horrified by Oakley's appearance and Cody acted immediately and went to the store manager. Apologetic, the store manager helped Oakley's transformation and he turned into a cowboy, right in front of her eyes. Cody helped him find a cowboy hat that fit perfectly, Wrangler jeans like the ones he wore, a tooled leather belt with a nice-size silver belt buckle, and of course, steel-toed boots.

"Mom—" Oakley spun around for her to see "—do I look like a cowboy now?"

"You do." She got up, hugged him and kissed him. "You certainly do."

On instinct, she hugged Cody and kissed him on the cheek. "Thank you."

"I didn't do hardly nothing," the cowboy said, his cheeks a bit flushed as he looked at the toe of his boot. "But if you need to thank me, then thank you and you're welcome."

That night, Oakley got to show off his new cowboy clothes and he was so proud, so happy and so handsome as a cowboy, that Journey knew that one way or the other, she had to find a way to keep Oakley in this cowboy life.

With a big dinner, good company around a roaring fire on a cold, clear Montana night, Journey sipped on a hot buttered rum while Wayne played his guitar and led the group in campfire songs. When Cody joined them, and she was worried that like the hermit crab he would disappear into his shell, she saw a man who had stolen her heart. Who he was, the way he moved in the world with integrity, honesty and honor, that alone would have attracted her. How he treated Oakley with love and acceptance, that only confirmed for her the reason behind that deep, abiding love she had developed for him.

Cody pulled out a harmonica from his jacket pocket and began to play along with Wayne, and Oakley jumped up, clapping his hands and stomping his foot to songs.

"Where has our shy, introverted boy gone?" his mother asked.

"I'm not sure. But what I am sure of is that this is what Oakley needs to have to live his best life."

"I can't disagree," Lucy said. "Let's discuss it tomorrow."

"Take Oakley in with you?"

Her mother tapped Oakley on the shoulder, and of

course, he was upset to be going to bed while his new friends, Paisley and Luna, were allowed to stay longer.

"Mom, *please*, Paisley and Luna are still here," Oakley begged her, and how could she argue with his logic. Not only had he discovered his inner cowboy, but he had made friends.

"Okay, son," she said. "You can stay up with your friends."

Thrilled, Oakley ran over to the other side of the fire where Paisley and Luna were sitting on a log, toasting marshmallows. He joined then on the log and, for the first time in such a long time that she couldn't even pinpoint the memory, Oakley was just doing what all girls and boys do at a campfire. Dean's daughters were angels as far as she was concerned. Made of great stuff.

"That is a sight," her mom said.

Journey stood up and hugged her mom tightly. "This place is magical."

"It is, baby girl," Lucy said, "truly magical. And is truly a match made in heaven for our wonderful, magical boy."

Her mother had a keen mind and an otherworldly connection to Oakley. If she saw what she was seeing, a move to a place that suited Oakley better would be on the table. But proximity to health care and his large team of specialists was crucial. One day, those specialists would be able to make Oakley's face look closer to the norm and that would make his life easier for sure. Now, this place, this life, would make Oakley's life more fulfilling and that could not be ignored.

As the fire died down, Cody knew it was time for him to head back to the bunkhouse on the property, the place he had been hanging his hat ever since he had come to lend a hand with the horses at Hideaway Ranch. Earlier in the day, he had spent time in Bozeman with Journey and her boy. Oakley was a good egg; gentle, calm and steady, that boy had all the makings of a world-class cowboy. And he was proud for whatever he was able to teach Oakley of the ways of the cowboy. Dean Legend and Ray took their girls home and Wayne and Charlie headed back to their house. Soon after, Danica and Matteo left the firepit and then the count was down to Journey, Oakley and him.

"I'll take care of this fire," Cody said, always having difficulty not to stare at Journey. She was always beautiful to him, but, tonight, in the firelight, she was more than beautiful, she was like an angel from heaven. He'd thought that he knew his own heart and he had certainly thought he had been in love a couple of times along the highway of his life. But he hadn't been. He couldn't have been. The love he had for Journey, for her boy, was selfless, gentle, and rocked him at his core. And because this love he felt was selfless, he knew that he could never let Journey know that he loved her. It would be unfair. She was still young, and vibrant, and had a lifetime to find love. He had it rough most of his life. Even at the pinnacle of his career, he'd played it fast and loose, drinking, womanizing, gambling. He'd lost more than he saved, and he wasn't a good risk for someone as levelheaded and exceptional as Journey.

No. He would love her from afar and help her son as if he were his own flesh and blood. And he was proud of Oakley and didn't give a damn what other people thought of him. The boy had a special heart, and he wouldn't hesitate to claim him as his own.

Journey stood up, stretched, yawned and said to her boy, "Say good-night to Cody."

Oakley had milked the staying up after bedtime for all it was worth; he'd managed to be one of three people left at the firepit.

"Thank you, Cody." Oakley hugged him so tightly, he felt touched by it. "This was the best day of my life."

"Good night, cowboy."

Oakley looked up at him with admiration that he wasn't all that certain he deserved. "Good night, cowboy."

Oakley then hugged his mother and asked her, "Hey Mom, can I get a harmonica?"

Journey laughed and met his gaze over the soft flames of a dying fire. "We'll discuss it in the morning. Run off to bed, sweet boy."

And then there were two.

Journey walked around the fire and so did he. They met halfway and he kissed her. Plain, simple and full of love. The truth was all of the conversations he had in his head about letting her go so she could find a love more suitable for her and for her son meant nothing. Because when his heart started beating like a drum, pounding so hard that his thoughts were drowned out—any thoughts other than the one that demanded he take his palomino into his arms and kiss her like a man who had everything to lose if he let her slip away.

"I'm old, Journey," he confessed. "Broke down, bad knees, bad back."

Journey put her hand over his heart. "Kind heart, kind soul and more of a man than I've ever met in my life."

"I've got bad habits."

"I'm obsessed with clipping coupons. I have a bookcase full of them. They take up a lot of room and I always forget to take them with me when I shop."

He took his rough hands and put them on the soft skin of her face and once she looked up at him, he let her see his soul. "I have to tell you that I love you. I don't think it's a smart idea for a woman like you to be shackled to a man like me."

Journey held out her wrists, palms facing upward. "Put those shackles on me, Cody Ty Hawkins. Oakley and I, we love you, and want to go wherever *you* go."

Chapter Seventeen

Matteo was at Danica's condo helping her organize her boxes. Even though this was a rental, she wanted to put her personal touch on the space to make her feel more at home.

"If I had any doubt of your affections, this has dispelled them completely," she told him, handing him a hot tea.

"How so?"

"Moving? Unpacking boxes? Hanging things on the wall with materials that won't harm the paint? Loathsome business. Only the truly devoted would sign on."

Sitting down on the couch, Matteo smiled at her with his ridiculously handsome face. "Why are you looking me like that?"

"Like what?"

"Like I'm a science project."

Then she laughed, because she was trying to put two and two together. "I was actually trying to imagine what our child would look like."

Matteo put his tea down and gave her his full attention. "And?"

"Well, it would have to be a boy if he got that bone structure. Tough for a girl, I think," she said, then asked, "How do you feel about a surrogate?"

His eyebrows knit together. "I don't feel one way or the other. Why? Is that what you want?"

"I don't know, really," she said thoughtfully. "I want to be a mother. I always have. And I love Diane Keaton and she first became a mother in her fifties like a boss. But she adopted and I want to use my eggs. Those suckers weren't easy to extract, let me tell you that."

"But not fertilized?"

"No," she said quickly. "Lord, I can only imagine the fight I could've had on my hands if we had."

She continued, "Now I'm almost forty-one, and I know that's not old in brain years, but the body doesn't bounce back so easily now. I mean, look at Serena Williams! She's a superstar and it was nearly impossible for her to get back into competition shape to get back onto the court to compete. I'm certainly not in the same league as her. How would I fare?"

"I'm not opposed to it, but just like moving in together…"

She smiled at him. "I've got to put a ring on it."

He lifted up his left hand and pointed to his ring finger. "Right here, baby."

They made some more progress on the boxes and then headed out for a well-deserved lunch at a local bar and grill that was healthy and fresh food–focused. Matteo ordered New Zealand green shell mussels while she selected a salad made with fresh fruit, vegetables and a blackberry vinaigrette, all handmade on-site.

"Hmm." Danica nodded her head while she chewed. "This is excellent."

Matteo agreed, digging into his mussels.

"You know what?"

He raised his eyebrows.

She leaned forward and whispered, "Why can't we open a farm-to-table restaurant at the ranch? Ray is able to make down-home, stick-to-your-ribs winter dishes and then lighter foods such as salads with veggies grown at the ranch."

"I love that idea."

"We can tap into some of that wedding destination money," she added. "I've got the money now to build a barn for a ranch-chic wedding venue. My mind is spinning with ideas!"

"I think it's a great idea."

They both finished their meals and then ordered coffee. A man came out from the back of the house, weaved his way to their table and then greeted Matteo. "Dr. Katz, it's such a pleasure to see you again!"

Matteo stood up out of courtesy, shook the man's hand and then introduced him to Danica.

"It's a pleasure to meet you, Ms. Danica." Oscar, the owner of the restaurant bowed his head. "I hope you enjoyed your food?"

"It was delicious."

"Thank you, thank you." Oscar bowed his head again. "But I would be remiss if I didn't mention that my daughters are very upset that you are off the market, is that what young people say now?"

"I am sorry to hear about your daughters' dashed hopes," Danica said, "because I am afraid that I am the woman who has taken Dr. Katz off the market."

"Well, it was such a pleasure to meet you, Ms. Danica." He shook Matteo's hand one last time, and then went on with his business.

"Taken me off the market?" Matteo smiled at her with a wink. "That sounds official."

She waited for the waiter to fill their coffee cups before she said, "That's because it is official. You are mine and I am yours."

"I am yours and you are mine."

They touched coffee cups lightly and then fell into an easy conversation while they enjoyed their coffee.

"I did want to mention something to you," Matteo said.

"Uh-oh." She put her coffee cup down.

"It's nothing bad. Don't look so worried."

"Okay."

"So, you may have noticed that you are a regular person on my social media."

"I noticed."

"As did my sister, my parents, all of their extended family and on and on," he said.

"Okay," she repeated, impatiently waiting for the other shoe to drop.

"I'm not one to really post pictures of women on any of my feeds."

"Go on."

"I only post pictures of my friends, or nature pics, Lu Lu of course."

"Of course," she agreed. "That goes without saying."

In truth, she wasn't one to spend time on social media for personal reasons, only professional. What Matteo posted was more a passing curiosity versus something she honed in on all the time, every day, all day long.

"And when I say that I rarely post pictures of women, I meant that I *never* post pictures of women."

"Never?"

"No," he said, "not since my last relationship."

Danica sat back, her mind now fully involved. "But you've posted my pictures."

"Yes."

"And your family is wondering who the heck is this woman all over Matteo's feed?"

"Yep."

"And?"

"And they want to meet you."

Danica thought for a minute or two, and then said, "Well, it was bound to happen."

"Yes."

"So, why not?" she asked. "I asked Ray for a black-and-white cookie recipe because I wanted to make some for your folks, when the time was right, and send them as a greeting."

"God, I love you." He reached for her hand.

She reached for his. "Did you tell me in a public place so I couldn't flee?"

"Probably, yes.

"Since we're asking questions, answer this one for me. Did you make up with me just so you could see Lu Lu?"

She smiled broadly at him. "Probably, yes."

They were scheduled to leave the next morning and Journey knew that she wasn't ready to leave, and she knew that Oakley felt the same way. This morning, she had found Oakley in his bed, crying softly because he would be losing the horses, Cody, and his two new friends, Paisley and Luna Legend.

"I promise you, Oakley, we will be coming back."

"Do you promise?"

She wiped away his tears with a tissue. "I promise."

"How do you know?"

"Because I do," she said. "Do you trust me?"

He nodded and then used the tissue to blow his nose.

"Okay, cowboy, you'd better hop to it and get dressed. Isn't Cody getting you up on a horse?"

"Yes!"

Journey left her son's room wondering how she had managed to go from being terrified of horses to agreeing to put her most beloved person, her son, on the back of a horse.

She walked out to the barn where she found Cody tacking up Atlas, the biggest horse in the barn.

"Good morning," she said to him with a smile.

He left Atlas's stall to hug her and to kiss her. "I keep on thinking that this was all a dream."

"Me, too."

"You leave tomorrow."

"Yes."

"I want to show you something before you go," Cody said, "and your boy."

After one more secretive kiss, Cody swung a saddle onto the draft horse's back.

"Did you have to pick the biggest darn horse in the barn?"

Cody chuckled. "My dad was mean when he was sober, worse when he was drunk, beaten down by life, and he died angry and bitter. But the man did give some advice that served me well over the years."

"And your father's advice is the reason for putting my ten-year-old son on a massive animal that bolts first and asks questions later?"

"Yep," he said. "Pop always told me that if I was ever to get into a bar fight, go after the biggest one in the bunch. Even if you lose, it will build your confidence."

"I see the parallel, I really do. Let's just keep that story between adults."

He laughed, one of those rare moments. "Yes, ma'am, mama bear."

She stopped by to give Rose some love; this little mare had taught her so much about herself—that she was kind and gentle and Rose always walked forward toward her and had helped her move past some of the trauma from her past.

"I love you, sweet Rose." She kissed the mare on the nose. "I will miss you. But this isn't goodbye. It's see you later."

When she left the barn, she saw Oakley in the round pen with Cody and Atlas; her mother was videotaping from the porch, so she decided to take pictures to stop herself from screaming "no" at the top of her lungs and racing to her son's side to stop this madness! Oakley had traded his cowboy hat for a riding helmet for safety.

Oakley, of course, looked more excited than she had ever seen him and as difficult as it was to watch, she had to let him live his life without overlaying her issues on him.

"Mom! G-Ma! Watch me!" Oakley waved at her before he climbed up the mounting block steps, stepped into the stirrup while Cody kept the horse standing in its spot, and then it happened. Oakley swung his right leg over the horse's back and sat down gently in the saddle.

"I did it!" she heard Oakley exclaim, and sat steady in the saddle as Cody told him to click his tongue to let the enormous draft horse know he wanted him to walk forward.

Journey rushed over to where her mom was standing. "He's doing it, Mom. He's really doing it!"

And then it happened. Cody took his hands off the reins and stepped back, coaching Oakley from the center of the ring.

"Look at him, Mom," she said, in awe of her son's bravery and tenacity. "He's a cowboy."

"Yes, he is," her mother said, tears on her cheeks. "He surely is."

Danica had not met anyone's parents for nearly two decades and it made her feel jittery with nervous butterflies in her stomach at the thought of meeting Matteo's family. She would be attending video Shabbat dinner with his family. Shabbat was the Jewish day of rest and began at sunset Friday until sunset on Saturday. Matteo's father, mother and sister shared Shabbat dinner Friday night on video chat.

"I hope the cookies arrived and are in good condition," she said nervously, feeling sweat form on her upper lip. She went into the bathroom, dabbed the sweat off her lip, reapplied her lipstick and checked her hair.

"How do I look?" She spun around in her navy blue dress with a simple strand of pearls around her neck.

"Perfect," Matteo said. "You look like my future."

"Oh, I just love you, Dr. Katz-Cortez!"

He went in for a kiss but she dodged it. "*After* dinner. And then you can mess up my hair and makeup as much as you like."

Matteo smiled at her with a sexual glint in his eyes. "I'll look forward to it."

Seated at Matteo's marble bar top, Danica felt horrible.

Still sweating, her stomach now hurting, it only confirmed the fact that she loved Matteo. She couldn't put herself through this if she didn't. Matteo had donned a black yarmulke with a silver Star of David in the center; it was the first time seeing him wearing this traditional cap to keep his head covered.

"Hi, Mom and Dad!" Matteo's parents joined the meeting. "Shabbat shalom."

"Good Shabbas, son," Dr. Katz said, "and Good Shabbas, Danica."

"Thank you, sir, Good Shabbas."

"And this is my wife, Mariposa."

"So nice to meet you," Danica said, taking an immediate liking to Matteo's parents. "Shabbat shalom, Mrs. Katz."

"Oh! You are so pretty, Danica! So pretty," Mariposa exclaimed, raising her hands to the heavens. "Finally, I see a woman in my son's life. I've been praying and praying and look, Ezra, what beautiful babies they will have."

"Let's take this one day at a time, my dear."

"I only want to say that I approve," his mother said. "*Gracias a Dios!* Thanks be to God. So many prayers have been answered."

After his sister Estrella logged on, Shabbat candles were lit and "Shalom Aleichem," a song that welcomed angels to the table, was sung. Matteo's father blessed the wine and the bread, and then they were able to eat the wonderful-smelling challah bread that Matteo had baked. And then, finally, Matteo's family opened the boxes of cookies she had sent to them.

"These are your first black-and-white cookies?" Estrella asked.

BIG SKY BACHELOR

"Yes," Danica said. "The kitchen is not usually my friend."

"For this cookie, it was!" Dr. Katz said, holding the cookie for her to see.

After an hour together, Estrella logged off and then it was time for his parents to leave as well.

"This was wonderful," Danica said. "Thank you for letting me join."

"I hope you will join us every Friday," Ezra said. "And maybe you can get him to attend Saturday services at the temple."

"No, no." His mother shook her head. "Don't listen to him, Danica. Please make sure my son makes it to Sunday services. There must be a Catholic church close by."

"Good night, Mom, Shabbat shalom, Dad." Matteo moved the mouse to the red "leave call" button.

"And those were my parents and my baby sister," Matteo said, with a curious look on his handsome face.

"I love them."

"They loved you—even Estrella, who can be tough on the women I've dated."

"And they loved my cookies!"

"Yes, they did." He pulled her into his arms, held her tight and kissed her. "And I love you."

"I love you, Matteo," she said, wanting more sweet kisses. "More than words can say."

"Where are we going?" Oakley asked from the back seat of Cody's truck.

"Cody says it's a surprise," his mom said, and then added, "Now *I'm* saying 'Cody says'!"

"It's catchy, I reckon." Cody had a small smile on his face.

Oakley felt sad, really sad, and he couldn't understand how anyone could feel happy when he had to leave Montana, the one place on earth he wanted to be, and leave the one man he wanted to be like and be with.

"Do you know that I'm leaving tomorrow, Cody?"

The older cowboy looked at him in the rearview mirror. "Yes, I do, son, and I'm real sad about it."

"Yeah, me, too."

His mother turned around so she could look at him. "We will be coming back."

"When?"

"As soon as we can."

Oakley crossed his arms over his chest and scowled at the scenery outside the truck window. He didn't want to leave but he was just a kid. He didn't get a say. If he did, he'd never leave. Not ever!

Cody asked his mom about the book.

"I don't know what happened," his mom said. "I was on a roll and then something just—held me back and I don't really know what it is."

"Tell me more about it."

"Well, the hero is based on you, so that part's good."

"Happy to help."

"And it's not even the characters, really," she said. "I think all of the bad reviews of my first book still get to me, as much as I try to forget them. I'm actually surprised my editor wants to see a second book from me after those horrible one-star reviews."

"You know what my old man used to say?"

"What did he say?"

"Don't let people rent space in your head. And I've taken that advice in my own career. People want to build you up and then knock you down. So I don't let nobody rent space in my head and neither should you."

Oakley listened to them talking and couldn't understand how they could talk about trivial stuff when his life was unraveling! How could they? How could Cody?!

Cody turned off the highway onto an overgrown drive that didn't hold any interest to him.

"We're here," Cody said, putting the truck into Park and shutting off the engine. "We'll have to hoof it. No way to get the truck back there."

"Come on, Oakley," his mom said.

"No." He crossed his arms over his chest. "I'll wait here."

Cody Ty opened his door and unbuckled his seat belt. "Come on, cowboy, I promise you, you won't want to miss it."

"Okay," he grumbled, getting out of the truck.

Together, the three of them picked their way through winter brush that seemed to match his depressed mood, with brown and black foliage and the crooked branches of trees that had died years ago.

"What is this place?" he asked Cody, doing his best to keep pace with his idol.

"This is my place," Cody said, stopping at a bluff that overlooked a small valley with a hill on the other side.

"There's a building site over there." Cody pointed. "I reckon we could build us a two-story house. Enough room for all of us and a spot for your mother when she visits."

Oakley was aware that adults had conversations without him knowing about it and he was very confused. "Wait a minute. Did you say that you are going to build a house for us here?"

"If your mama will have me."

His eyes darted from his mother's face to Cody's face like a pendulum on a clock, back and forth, back and forth.

"Well," his mother said with an odd flush on her cheeks, "I suppose you should ask me."

Cody turned to his mother, and he asked, "Journey Lamar, would you do me the great honor of being my wife and building a home right here, on this land?"

And to his total amazement, his mother said yes and then, still in shock and confused about what he had just witnessed, Oakley saw Cody and his mother lean toward each other to seal the deal with a kiss, nearly directly above his head, so he had to cover his eyes.

"How do you feel about this, Oakley?" his mother asked him.

"Are we really going to live here with Cody?"

"Yes," his mother said, "if you're okay with it."

"I'm okay with it!" Oakley shouted, sending some birds up into the sky.

"Then it's a done deal," Cody said to him. "Let's shake on it."

After they shook hands, man to man, cowboy to cowboy, Oakley waggled his head, his eyes wide open, trying to burn as much of this future home into his brain as possible.

"It's beautiful," his mother said, brushing tears from her cheeks.

"I'm glad you like it."

"I do," she said. "It's perfect."

"Is this my life?" Oakley asked loudly.

"Yes," his mother said, "this is your life."

Cody knelt down beside him and pulled the harmonica out of his pocket and handed it to him.

"Are you giving this to me?" He turned the instrument over in his hands.

"Nope, I'm not. That there is a loan. Just so you know that this here land is your home, and you can return it to me when you come back."

Oakley put the harmonica in his shirt pocket and hugged Cody like he never wanted to let him go. "I love you, Cody."

"I love you, son."

"For keeps?"

"For keeps."

And on that cold afternoon, as the sun slowly disappeared on the horizon, Oakley held Cody's hand while the cowboy held his mother close, the three of them quietly daydreaming about a life they would forge together, as a family, on this pristine Montana wilderness that stretched out before them.

Epilogue

Matteo awakened on Valentine's Day to the smell of challah French toast cooking. He threw off the covers, stood up, stretched and then pulled on his pajama bottoms after he retrieved them from on top of the lampshade.

"Hmm." He walked up behind his woman, wrapped her up in his arms and kissed her on the neck. "Good morning."

"Good morning," Danica said, looking sexy in his pajama top. "Happy Valentine's Day."

"Did you feed Lu Lu?"

"Yep," she said, "already done."

"I should have known." He sat down at the kitchen island and looked at Lu Lu, who was upside down in her bed with a smile on her face. "She never looks this content if she's hungry."

"True." Danica emphasized her point with the spatula.

"So you've raided the challah for Shabbat tonight."

"I won't tell your dad if you don't."

Matteo twisted his fingers over his lips like he was locking them. "It will go to my grave."

They ate together at the island, cleaning their plates and

drinking orange juice. After Danica cleared the dishes and loaded them into the dishwasher, Matteo watched her, loving this ritual of her making breakfast for him with the challah bread he always made. He usually cooked for her, and it was special that she wanted to cook for him as well.

He took a shower and shaved, and then waited for Danica to shower as well. She emerged from the bedroom with her hair worn loose to her shoulders, a more carefree look for her that he loved. She was so beautiful and sweet and talented that he counted himself fortunate to have found her and to have won her heart.

With a playful expression on her face, she pulled her arms from behind her back and presented him with a small box. "Happy Valentine's Day."

"Ah! We are of the same mindset," he said, accepting the small present. "Check Lu Lu's collar."

"You didn't!" Danica exclaimed, kneeling down by the happy pig and unhooking a small box from her crystal-encrusted collar.

Danica brought her small box over and put it next to the small box she had given to him. "Who goes first?"

"Ladies first."

Danica slowly untied the ribbon, set it to the side neatly, and then one piece of tape at a time, she methodically unwrapped the paper.

"It's almost time for Shabbat dinner," he said.

"Oh hush," she said. "You open your present your way and I'll unwrap mine my way."

With the paper finally off, Danica opened the lid and took the small black ring box out and placed it on the island.

"It's not a ring," he said, hoping to waylay any anxiety she may have.

"It's not?"

"No."

Danica cracked open the velvet box and stared at the present he had gotten her for their first-ever Valentine's Day.

"It's..." She shook her head, and then continued. "It's so lovely, Matteo. Thank you."

"You're welcome, *mi amor*," he said, and then asked, "Would you like for me to put it on?"

She nodded as he took the large heart-shaped locket, made of platinum on a heavy platinum chain. There was a heart-shaped diamond in the center of the platinum.

"Is there a picture inside?"

"Open it and see."

Danica opened it and then she laughed. Inside the locket was a picture of Lu Lu in the crocheted outfit Danica had made for her.

"God, I love you, Matteo."

"Lucky for me," he said, putting it on for her.

She touched the locket. "It's perfect, Matteo. I love it."

After he received his kiss, he said, "My turn."

He ripped off the paper and ribbon in one fell swoop, then shook the outer box to get the small ring box out. Then he opened the box and his smile faltered and his heart started racing.

"Is this what I think it is?"

"What do you think it is?"

Matteo looked at the platinum ring, with a large bezel-set diamond glimmering in the early morning light. "An engagement ring?"

"I'm putting a ring on that," she said, smiling that loving smile he would never get tired of seeing.

Matteo put on the ring and looked at it. It looked foreign to him even though it was the perfect fit.

"Thank you." He stood up and drew her to him. "Happy Valentine's Day."

"Happy Valentine's Day to you, my love," she said.

After they shared a kiss, Danica asked, "You do know what this means, don't you?"

"What's that, *mi corazon*?"

"The Big Sky bachelor is officially *off* the market."

* * * * *

HARLEQUIN
Reader Service

Enjoyed your book?

Try the perfect subscription for Romance readers and get more great books like this delivered right to your door.

See why over 10+ million readers have tried Harlequin Reader Service.

Start with a Free Welcome Collection with free books and a gift—valued over $20.

Choose any series in print or ebook. See website for details and order today:

TryReaderService.com/subscriptions

RSBPA24R